CRIMINAL MINDS: KILLER PROFILE

This Large Print Book carries the
Seal of Approval of N.A.V.H.

CRIMINAL MINDS: KILLER PROFILE

MAX ALLAN COLLINS

Based on the CBS Television Series created by Jeff Davis

THORNDIKE PRESS
A part of Gale, Cengage Learning

GALE
CENGAGE Learning

Detroit • New York • San Francisco • New Haven, Conn • Waterville, Maine • London

GALE
CENGAGE Learning™

Copyright © 2008 ABC Studios and CBS Studios Inc.
Thorndike Press, a part of Gale, Cengage Learning.

Thorndike Press® Large Print Crime Scene.
The text of this Large Print edition is unabridged.
Other aspects of the book may vary from the original edition.
Set in 16 pt. Plantin.
Printed on permanent paper.

LIBRARY OF CONGRESS CATALOGING-IN-PUBLICATION DATA

Collins, Max Allan.
   Criminal minds : killer profile / by Max Allan Collins.
     p. cm. — (Thorndike Press large print crime scene)
   "Based on the CBS television series created by Jeff Davis"
—T.p. verso.
   ISBN-13: 978-1-4104-0927-0 (alk. paper)
   ISBN-10: 1-4104-0927-9 (alk. paper)
   1. United States. Federal Bureau of Investigation—Fiction.
2. Criminal profilers—Fiction. 3. Criminal investigation—Fiction.
4. Chicago (Ill.)—Fiction. 5. Large type books. I. Davis, Jeff.
II. Criminal minds (Television program) III. Title. IV. Title: Killer profile.
PS3553.O4753C754 2008
813'.54—dc22   2008021099

Published in 2008 by arrangement with NAL Signet, a member of Penguin Group (USA) Inc.

I would like to acknowledge my assistant on this work, coplotter/researcher Matthew V. Clemens.

Further acknowledgments appear at the conclusion of this novel.

M.A.C.

*In memory of criminalist
Frank Louis Tarasi III,
who helped put the puzzle
pieces together.*

PROLOGUE:
APRIL 17
OAK PARK, ILLINOIS

April showers bring May flowers, Connie told herself as she studied the red smear that (courtesy of The Weather Channel) seemed centered not just over Illinois or Chicago or even Oak Park, but their very house.

Her reassurance rang hollow because she also knew April showers, here in the Midwest, could bring lightning, hail, and high winds. Much as she loved the two towering oaks in the front yard, they concerned her in thunderstorms (like the one going on just beyond the bedroom windows): the trees' sheltering presence could be cleaved by lightning into crashing timber.

And tornado season wasn't that far away either.

Connie, watching the wall-mounted TV from her bed, would have been shocked to learn that many of her friends and family considered her an inveterate worrywart. She had tried hard not to be one, but her parents had been worriers, never able to enjoy anything, always waiting for the other shoe to drop, and never in a good way.

To her parents, children of the Depression that they'd been, God had it in for them and would watch for any sign of happiness so He could pounce and deliver a good old-fashioned dose of misfortune.

She had vowed not to live her life that way and, at first, she hadn't; but now, with kids of her own, the trait seemed to come bubbling to the surface out of her DNA.

And what was there to worry about, really, in the comfortable brick house that offered, as Bob Dylan put it, shelter from the storm? Smack in the middle of the Frank Lloyd Wright historic district, their ranch-style home may not have not been designed by the great architect, but it fit right in with those that Wright and his Prairie Style cohorts had created.

Set sideways on its Linden Avenue lot, the house had a picture window in the family room that faced out toward the street on the west end. The rest of the house stretched toward the back of the lot, with a dining room, kitchen, three bedrooms and two baths. Off the north side, stood a tall, detached two-car garage more like a carriage house, with her husband's locked work space upstairs.

Connie — a tall, slender, lovely brunette, forty, with high, sharp cheekbones, an aquiline nose, and full lips — lay on top of the covers wearing a pair of her husband's gym shorts and a blue Cubs T-shirt. Her brown eyes were wide set and bright and her short hair didn't look like she had been sleeping on it, though she had been until the call that came fifteen minutes ago, ordering her husband in to work in the middle of the night. And the middle of the storm.

The crawl on the TV and the superimposed map said the area was under a severe thunderstorm alert and she wondered if she should wake the boys and take them to the basement for safety's sake. No sirens had sent her scurrying, but the threat was there.

Kevin and Kyle were thirteen and eleven respectively, and tomorrow was a school day, and of course she wanted them to get their sleep. She had sent them to bed at their normal time — ten — and now, glancing at the clock in the corner of the TV screen, she noted that not quite two hours had passed.

Outside, a lightning flash startled her, the nearly instantaneous thunderclap making her jump a little. Goose bumps crawled up

11

her arms as she looked toward the curtained windows and the darkness beyond. She got under the covers. The TV and a dim light from the master bathroom, where her husband had the door ajar, provided the only illumination.

"It's not like you're with the power company," she said, trying not to sound like a raving bitch. "The world doesn't *need* you to go out. . . ."

"But my boss does," he said from the bathroom. "This is that dirty job that somebody's got to do that you hear so much about."

"I suppose," she said. "But does it always have to be you?"

"If they want it done right, it does."

He strode out into the bedroom now, in black Reeboks, black jeans, and a black T-shirt, still every bit as boyishly handsome as when she'd met him twenty years ago. His curly brown hair seemed to beg for her fingers to run through it and those green eyes seemed to be able to look right into her soul and read her every thought.

Always a sexual being, Connie resisted the urge to pull him down onto the bed with her right now; images flickered through her mind of making love as lightning strobed through the bedroom windows. But her husband had been distant lately, and their lovemaking had become a regimented thing, not at all spontaneous, scheduled around times when the two boys were not at home.

Not that she thought, even for a moment, that things were bad between them. Despite his odd hours away, he was not having an affair; she was convinced of that — the only "other woman" was his job. Things were good now, they were comfortable with work and home, but when they had first met, things had been . . . well, they'd been perfect.

She'd been a model with the top agency in Chicago and he a photographer on the rise straddling the fashion and art worlds, already having had one successful gallery show and several big fashion magazine covers. When they met, the sparks had been instantaneous, two young attractive people making the kind of magic, both personally and professionally, that others could only dream about. They had fallen in bed, in love, and into a sort of muse/artist relationship that seemed to take his work to a new level. For two years, the work, the creativity, the money, the electricity of their sexual relationship, had flowed.

Then they got married, had their first child (Kevin), and, as in so many marriages

13

she guessed, things had changed. Or, anyway, shifted.

Her husband was a good father, attentive and caring, but something had come unraveled in his professional life when Connie moved from muse to mother and stopped modeling to stay home with their son. Her husband began working with other models, but nothing really clicked. He seemed to lose the magic and the galleries lost interest and the big ticket clients in the fashion world (always a limited market in Chicago) moved on to the next hot prospect.

To his credit, he never seemed bitter and did not hold her responsible for him having to get what he called a "real" job, one that paid respectably and brought him genuine satisfaction as a photographer, with the only significant drawback that it sometimes caused him to have to leave in the middle of the night. They'd had their second son, Kyle, whom her husband adored; and theirs was, measured by any reasonable yardstick, a happy family life.

Even so, true to her nature, and like her parents, Connie spent a lot of time waiting for the other shoe to drop. . . .

Her husband crossed the room, bent down and hugged her to him and gave her a quick kiss.

"Get some sleep," he said into her ear.

She held him an extra moment. "I sleep better with you next to me."

He gave her another kiss. "That'll be me, snuggling in next to you, before you know it."

He drew away and moved toward the door.

Pulling the blankets up to her throat, Connie said, "Don't forget your raincoat."

"Not likely," he said with a grin, "in this."

"And don't forget I love you."

He said something that might have been, "I love you," but she didn't quite make it out. Then she heard the door close and he was gone.

Thunder rumbled and rain lashed the windows. She snapped off the TV and lay trembling. She began to cry. Not heaving sobs, just tiny self-pitying tears.

She'd been doing that a lot lately, and had no idea why.

April 17
Chicago Heights, Illinois
Adrienne Andrews (Addie to her friends), with only one more month until prom, was determined not to be a virgin when that magical night arrived. A lanky, pale-skinned, light-blue-eyed girl who wore her blonde

15

hair short and shaggy, thin Addie was sure she would look better if she could only, please, Jesus, lose another five pounds off her hips. Tonight, she had hidden the offenders under loose-fitting jeans. Her black T-shirt had been tucked in when she left the house, but once out of sight of her folks, she had pulled it out and knotted it so that her tummy (and pierced belly button) showed.

Addie had a straight nose and a nice mouth despite rather thin lips, and her crooked smile could turn the heads of a lot of the boys, especially, thankfully, Benny Mendoza's.

Like Addie, Benny was a senior at St. Vincent's Catholic High School on Ashland, and he was a babe, a stone fox. Tonight, the Hispanic boy wore a White Sox home jersey with his jeans, white with black pinstripes, the name of his favorite player, THOME, stenciled on the back above the number twenty-five.

With his close-cropped black hair and slenderly muscular frame, Benny was everything Addie wanted in a guy — long, narrow, handsome face, with deep brown eyes and lips so full that Addie had to hold herself back from kissing them every time she saw them.

Now, for instance.

They sat next to each other in the bucket seats of his navy blue Hyundai Tiburon. The car was actually Benny's mom's, but Mrs. Mendoza rarely drove it, and the vehicle had become, in a de facto kind of way, his. Either that, Addie thought with a laugh, or his mom had left behind the Ozomatli CD they were listening to!

Turning to her in darkness cut only by the dashboard glow, Benny smiled and asked, "What is it, *querida?*"

She loved him calling her that. "Nothing," she said, reaching across the console and touching his knee. Squeezing his knee . . .

After their third date, he had started calling her *"querida."* When she had asked him what it meant, he'd said, " 'Darling.' Or it can also mean, you know, 'lover.' "

His eyes had lowered then, his embarrassment obvious. But she had kissed his cheek and told him she liked it. Since then, she had been *"querida"* whenever they were together.

Now, his eyes went back to watching the traffic on the rain-slicked Dixie Highway as they headed south, toward home. Traffic wasn't heavy, but they weren't the only ones out late on this windy, rainy night.

Normally, their parents would have

pitched fits about them being out past midnight on a school night, but tonight was special. Benny had been invited by his baseball coach to a White Sox game at U.S. Cellular Field. And Benny had convinced the coach to let him bring Addie along as his guest. (And convinced her parents, too.)

They had met the coach outside the park and gotten the tickets. They had even enjoyed the first few innings as the Sox got an early lead on the visiting Detroit Tigers, but then the rains came. The trio had waited bravely with the other diehards for the storm to blow over, but the game had finally been called just before eleven and they had been trying to get home since.

"Tell me what you were laughing at," he pressed.

She shook her head, her hand covering her mouth in embarrassment. "I can't tell you."

"Come on, *querida*," he said, all honey-voiced. "You know you want to." His fingertip touched her arm and she felt a surge of heat rush through her.

"No!" she squealed. "I'm not telling you."

His hand moved, finding a rib and tickling.

She slapped it away. "Will you please *drive?*"

He grinned. "Yeah, drive you *crazy* till you

tell me what was so damn funny."

He tickled her ribs again, this time his hand brushing a breast and, even as she giggled, warmth surged through her. If they hadn't been so late, tonight would have been the night — *the* night.

But she wanted it perfect for them both, and this evening — which was supposed to be Benny's big night at the ballpark — should have been just the thing. The coach seemed sure Benny would be taken early in the June amateur draft and that there would probably be some nice bonus money. Benny had worked hard for this, Addie knew, and he deserved it.

She'd been planning to top off his big night by finally giving in to him, but they were so late now, there was just no way. Another night would have to do.

Still, Addie knew one thing above all: she didn't want to wait until prom night.

Some of the other girls, who had already done the deed, told her it would hurt a little (*at least* a little) and it could be messy (*would* be messy). That wasn't the experience she had in mind for prom night, not to mention her prom dress. That night needed to be extra special perfect. Better to get the thing out of the way before, and hope it was fun, at least.

There would be other nights, no doubt, but she was so primed this night. . . .

"Tell me," he said, tickling her once more.

"All right!" She pushed his hand away. "It's just . . . embarrassing."

He shrugged. "So what? Tell me."

"I was just . . . thinking about the CD being in your mom's car? Like how funny it would be if it was *her* music or something."

"It is her music," he said.

"You're kidding!"

"No," he said, his voice as calm as the sky wasn't. "She really digs Ozomatli."

"*Your* mom is into multiculti hip-hop rock?"

Benny nodded. "She's not a hundred years old, you know."

Part of the reason she loved Benny was she never knew for sure when he was serious and when he was just kidding her. Like now, for instance.

"Which song's her fave, then?" she challenged.

"This one," he said, skipping to song number eight on the live album — "Love and Hope."

She listened carefully. The chorus was about how love and hope never die and, no matter what, your heart and soul will survive — a positive message sung over an almost

20

traditional Mexican song with horns and hip-hop drop-ins.

Addie liked it immediately and wondered if she really *was* listening to one of Mrs. Mendoza's CDs.

Benny gave her a sideways look. "You'd believe anything I told you, wouldn't you?"

She realized he had been pulling her leg the entire time. She smacked him in the shoulder. "You!"

"Ay, *querida,* you're way too gullible."

Mildly annoyed he'd fooled her yet again, she turned the tables. "Does that mean I should never believe anything you tell me?"

"Like what?"

"Like if you said you'd be careful not to get me pregnant, if we ever . . . you know."

"*Querida,* I don't joke about serious things."

"Oh? Then tell me something I *can* believe."

Benny, casual as could be, said, "You can believe I love you."

Addie sat there for the longest moment, not knowing what to say. She adored hearing him finally say those words, but even the throwaway way he'd spoken them seemed to have sucked all the air out of the car.

When the Dixie Highway veered at One-

21

hundred-eighty-third Street, Benny turned left. They stayed off the expressways — one of the rules Benny's mom had laid down for him being able to use the car.

Finally finding her voice, Addie said, "You love me? Really love me?"

Benny didn't hesitate. "Sure I do."

"You better not be fooling."

"No way, *querida*," he said, his voice softer now. "I told you before I don't joke about serious things. I love you."

Once Benny graduated in June, he would almost certainly be drafted by a major league team, meaning he would spend the rest of the summer playing minor league ball. Addie wasn't sure how or where she fit into that plan, but she knew two things for certain: they were going to prom together, and she was in love with Benny Mendoza.

"I love you, too," she said.

He grinned at her and she smiled back.

Leaning over, Benny gave her a quick kiss.

"Drive," she said, pushing him away. She wanted to pull him to her, but waiting until they weren't driving in a rainstorm with cars all around them might be a safer plan.

He took the right that jogged back to the Dixie Highway and once again headed south. Addie had learned a long time ago that few things ran straight in the Chicago area. Streets veering off in odd directions all over the place was an accepted part of living in the city. She still remembered, as a child, commenting about nothing being straight in the city, and her father replying, "You think the streets are something? Wait until you're old enough to understand politics."

The answer had stuck with her because it made no sense when she was six, but now, as her government class studied how things in the city worked, Addie realized what her father had meant. The streets weren't the only things in the city that were crooked.

They wove southeast until Benny took the short right onto Ashland that carried them south to Joe Orr Road, then right again and back west to Travers Avenue, and a left south until the right onto her street, Hutchinson Avenue.

Technically, Addie lived on Two-hundred-seventh Street, but since she lived on the corner, Benny liked to park next to her house on the Hutchinson side. That kept her father from spying on them through the front door while they kissed good night. And kissing good night sometimes lasted a while with Addie and Benny.

Most people, especially those from anywhere other than Chicago Heights, immediately thought "slum" when they were told of the suburb's location on the south side of the city. That wasn't true at all.

The neighborhood where Addie lived was a multiracial middle-class neighborhood with blacktop streets, no sidewalks, and houses varying from ranches to split foyers to the new brick castles coming up when the old houses were razed.

One of those brick monstrosities sat across the street to the east from her parents' modest ranch with its one-car garage and flowers planted everywhere. Houses lined the south side of Two-hundred-seventh right up to where Hutchinson teed into it, then east of the intersection, on the south side, Swanson Park spread before them, an oasis of green with its soccer fields and softball diamonds.

Benny pulled the Tiburon in alongside Addie's house and killed the lights. They were pointed south on Hutchinson, the park visible through the pounding rain, the parking lot on its far side obscured by the downpour.

She caught a glimpse of the clock as Benny turned off the car: 1:15. Her parents were going to be mightily pissed. Addie had wanted tonight to be *the* night, but there was just no way. . . .

Benny undid his seat belt, slipped it off,

leaned over and kissed her.

The rush she felt as his tongue snaked its way into her mouth was like nothing she had ever felt before. Heat rushed from her lips to her tongue, down her throat, extending out through every fiber of her being, to burn somewhere just south of her waist.

His arms were around her, then they were unfastening her seat belt. Next his hands were roving all over her T-shirt, leaving a wildfire trail in their wake.

Benny's hands were at her back now, sliding up under her shirt, soothingly cool as they met hot flesh. She wanted him to touch her everywhere at once. She felt the clasp release on her flimsy bra and then his hands were under the shirt in front, inching up, cupping, squeezing, all the time his tongue like a wild animal in her mouth.

Control was slipping away and even though it was nearly 1:30 in the morning on a school night, her parents less than a hundred feet away (certainly not asleep and almost certainly waiting up for her), Addie was about to let Benny Mendoza get her ready for the prom. . . .

Not like this, she told herself as she wrestled for control. Not a quickie in a Hyundai, even if it was with Benny, the man she loved. *Make it perfect,* her voice said in her brain, *make it perfect.*

With more strength than she knew she had, Addie broke away.

Benny's concern was instant and sincere. "What is it, *querida?* What's wrong?"

"I can . . . *can't,*" she said.

"I thought this was something you wanted."

"It is," she said, and, despite her best efforts, she found herself crying.

His arms engulfed her as she wept full tilt now, sobbing into his shoulder. It felt good there, in his arms, and slowly her tears subsided.

"Querida," he soothed. "There's plenty of time for that. I love you. We'll wait for the right moment. No rush. I'm not going anywhere."

She pulled back from him a little to look into his eyes. "You will go away . . . this summer. . . ."

"Addie," he said, gazing at her, "that's just one summer. We're going to be together *forever.*"

She kissed him again, with a painful urgency. When their kiss broke, she thought she saw someone standing next to the driver's door, outside in the rain. *Oh shit,* she thought. Was it her dad?

Instinctively, she pulled away a little from

Benny, who looked confused.

The form outside the car was definitely a person. Addie saw something come up between the figure and the car, then there was a flash that caused Addie to blink. When her eyes opened, the window shattered and Benny's left eye exploded in a pink cloud, splashing her face like rain from within the car.

Finally, she heard the roar of the gunshot and something else, someone screaming — *herself*.

As Benny's body slumped into her, his head a broken melon, only one eye and a corner of his mouth looking like something that had been a face, Addie realized he had been right.

They *were* going to be together forever.

She saw the pistol rising again, the small black hole pointed at her face, Benny's voice in her mind: *Together forever, querida.* That thought gave her a moment of peace as Adrienne Andrews saw the last thing she ever saw: a muzzle flash.

April 17
Oak Park, Illinois
Connie had not slept particularly well. She never did when her husband worked odd hours, and now she rolled over and looked

at the alarm clock for the zillionth time since he'd left last night.

Just after five, she fought the urge to just say, "Screw it," and get out of bed. She could read or watch TV or something. The kids wouldn't be up for another hour and a half.

But she decided to give it one more chance and rolled over. Squeezing her eyes shut, Connie thought back to those early days when she and her husband had been so happy. Though she loved her kids and knew they were easily the greatest thing she'd done in her life, she still reflected on those earlier days as the happiest of her marriage.

Whenever she needed to calm herself, Connie went back to a day before they were married, before they were dating even.

They were doing a photo shoot, their first together.

She had been the ingenue, the new girl on the Michigan Avenue block, while her photographer was the hot young shooter who was already a star and in from New York to do the fashion magazine layout. Another model had gotten the cover but Connie had garnered the spot for a well-known fashion line the photographer was also shooting.

She wore a bikini for the summer issue, though the temperature outside the old Chicago Water Tower in early March hovered just above freezing. Her photographer wore a wool turtleneck and down vest over his jeans. He looked toasty warm while she was freezing her ass off.

Still, he was doing everything he could to keep her comfortable and happy until the rain came. After the sudden cloudburst, the two ran for his rental car parked just across Michigan Avenue on a side street while the rest of the crew tried to keep the set from getting ruined.

He held the door for her, closed it after her, got soaked running around the car and, when he finally got in and they were out of the rain, they started laughing. He got the engine running, turned on the heater and they sat there talking for a while, then the talk turned to kissing and the kissing to serious necking, and she and the photographer moved to the back and her bikini came off and she couldn't believe what they were doing right there off the Magnificent Mile. Steam had covered the windows, though, and they couldn't see out. She hoped no one could see in.

Her eyes still shut, Connie felt more relaxed than she had in days. They were about to make love in the backseat of his rental car when she went to sleep.

She felt him climb into the bed next to her, the mattress creaking slightly as he settled in. She stirred.

"Shhh," he said, his voice soothing. "It's not time to get up yet."

He touched her shoulder and she felt herself sliding back into the backseat dream.

She was almost completely in the dream moment when a harsh voice said, *"WLS News talk 890 time is six oh five, let's get the first on-demand traffic report from our traffic reporter Marin Ashe."*

Connie hit the snooze and rolled toward her husband. "How did it go?"

His face was pale and he was wet either from the rain or a shower she had not heard him take when he got home. She didn't know which.

He looked at her for a long moment, his eyes blank.

Finally, he managed a thin smile. "Think I got some good shots."

"That's nice, dear. That's nice."

"Imitation,"
Oscar Levant said,
"is the sincerest form of plagiarism."

Chapter One:
July 28
Quantico, Virginia

For local detectives, one or more of four murder motives figure in ninety-nine percent of the homicides they encounter. These motives are, in no particular order, love, money, sex, and drugs.

No matter the circumstance, no matter how far afield the killers' motives seem to be, the four basics almost always pertain: love, money, sex, or drugs. Love and sex, of course, have considerable overlap, but then so do money and drugs.

And when a crime comes up where the motive doesn't clearly fall into those categories, that special one percent of murders that the local police cannot solve on their own, the best option remaining, in the minds of many in local law enforcement, is to bring such cases to the attention of the Behavioral Analysis Unit of the Federal Bureau of Investigation.

Just south of Washington, D.C., across the

Potomac River from Maryland, the U.S. Marine Corps base at Quantico, Virginia, serves as home to dozens of Marine Corps schools, the DEA training academy, and the FBI Training and Development Division. Also nestled within the nearly four hundred acres of woods, surrounding what its inhabitants sometimes call the Facility, is the Behavioral Analysis Unit.

Within the walls of the blandly modern, anonymous concrete buildings, the BAU consists of several multiperson, close-knit teams, the nature of whose duty often creates a strong sense of family. Supervisory Special Agent Aaron Hotchner's team was no exception; and his profilers were due back today from a weekend off — no duty, no on-call, no anything, just some much deserved R and R.

Rest and recreation meant, for Hotchner, reading through fitness results, budget analyses, and police reports for one day of his time off, rather than two. Other agents, both on and off his team, considered Hotchner a driven, somewhat humorless taskmaster. He considered himself only a professional with a job that required both concentration and detachment. Without the latter, burnout or even madness could be the consequence, as Aaron Hotchner was a modern-day Van Helsing tracking down real-life monsters who made the likes of Dracula or the Wolf Man seem quaint.

This took its toll. He and Haley, his wife of eleven years, had separated last fall. Now, they were facing divorce, their marriage another victim of the monsters Hotchner pursued. The severe tension of the initial breakup had eased some, however, and he had been welcomed to her sister's house where he spent Saturday afternoon with Haley and their son, Jack. Three now, Jack was harder to chase down than most of the UnSubs Hotchner had been after during his FBI career. They had gone to a kid-oriented pizza place for supper, as a family, if a broken one, and while Jack played, the soon to be ex-husband and -wife had talked in a guarded but not unfriendly way about where things were, currently, with how they'd gotten there undiscussed.

After half a day with the two people on the planet he loved most, Hotchner had gotten the best night's sleep he'd had in months. After sleeping in yesterday, he had read the Sunday paper in the kitchen, where the emptiness of the house almost overwhelmed him. He spent most of the day in his home office, going over reports, coming out only to microwave his meals and catch up on cable news.

For many years Haley had exhibited saint-like patience with his workaholic ways, but these last several years had included an array of horrific cases that had made Hotchner only more withdrawn and had taken him away from home for days and even weeks at a time. When he'd turned down a nine-to-five job on the white-collar task force, Hotchner had finally pushed Haley too far.

"You can't stop *all* the monsters," she'd said.

"I have to try. I've seen what these creatures do to families. Think of our son."

"No, Aaron. *You* think of our son. You need to put our family first, and everybody else's family needs to go into second place."

"Try to understand. Stopping these people *is* my way of protecting my family."

"Oh, fine, wonderful. On some spiritual, metaphysical level, I'm sure that makes perfect sense. But how do you protect our family, *this* family, if you're away all the time?"

"This is who I am, Haley. Please try to understand that."

"I do understand that, Aaron. And I do love you. I do still love you. But I have to leave."

And she had.

He awoke early Monday morning, after not nearly enough sleep, eased out of bed, showered, dressed in his best navy blue suit, and came into the office.

A tall, broad-shouldered yet slender man with dark hair and burning brown eyes, Hotchner bore the pale complexion of an indoor animal, although spending half a day outside with Jack and Haley had added a little pink to high, sharp cheekbones. His look, his demeanor, were fitting for the CEO of a Fortune 500 company, but he made considerably less, even if his responsibilities were similarly demanding.

Seated behind a desk neatly piled with files, Hotchner sipped his coffee and checked his watch. The rest of the team would be rolling in over the next half hour.

That Hotchner was in charge of the team went beyond his assigned role to his nature, and it was in his nature to lead by example. Part of that meant being first in (and last out) of the office, with the exception of media maven Jennifer Jareau. Consequently, he had unlocked his door a full hour before the start of shift.

The first agent to get off the elevator and stride into the bullpen area below Hotchner's office was Emily Prentiss. A willowy, quietly stylish brunette whose hair touched her shoulders, the thirtyish Prentiss had been a member of the BAU for over a year now. The well-connected daughter of a diplomat, with the looks of a fashion model and the intellect of a physicist, she'd served FBI tours in both St. Louis and Chicago before the FBI foisted her on Hotchner; but he had come to respect and value her — Prentiss worked hard, maintained a cool professional attitude on site, and never complained about an assignment. Further, she'd been embraced by the rest of team over time — no small thing, as she'd replaced a popular agent who'd gone over the line. As she sat at her desk, Prentiss glanced up at him through the window separating Hotchner's office from the bullpen. When she saw him through the open venetian blinds, she nodded and smiled, just a little.

Hotchner nodded back, did not return the smile, then looked down at the file in front of him. He worked a while.

Next in was the team's youngest member, Dr. Spencer Reid. Twenty-six and a five-year veteran of the BAU, the gangly Reid wore gray slacks and a blue blazer with a white shirt and a red-and-gold-striped tie, though the collar button remained unbuttoned and the knot loosened. The strap to his briefcase rode his left shoulder, the case tucked under his right arm. The overall effect of the outfit was that Reid looked like a scholarship student who was late for a chemistry class at some private prep school.

Reid was doing better now. A sensitive young man who hid behind statistics on every subject, he had not so long ago suffered through a traumatic stretch; one of their UnSubs (unknown subjects) had taken Reid captive and subjected him to mental and physical abuse and, briefly drug dependence. The ordeal had made Reid question whether he belonged in the BAU, but Hotch and their former teammate Jason Gideon had counseled Reid and convinced him to stay — ironic, now that Gideon had suffered his own burnout and had gone off on his soul-searching way.

Every agent on his team was talented, even gifted, but Hotchner knew that Reid — with his triple PhDs in Chemistry, Mathematics, and Engineering from Cal Tech — was a special case, and very likely the most brilliant of them all. The young man had an eidetic memory, and a 187 IQ with a capacity to read twenty thousand words per minute. More important, the wealth of data at the agent's mental fingertips had over time interwoven with his ever-growing profiling skills. No question, Reid was a key asset to Hotchner's team.

Coming into the bullpen from her office was Supervisory Special Agent Jennifer Jareau, a quietly stunning blue-eyed blonde who served as the BAU's Media and Local Law Enforcement Liaison. JJ looked typically crisp and professional in black slacks and black pumps with a white blouse under a black waistcoat. A Georgetown journalism graduate, she wasn't much older than Reid and, hence, the second youngest member of the team. Over the last several years, Hotchner had watched with considerable satisfaction as Jareau's maturity leapt beyond her youth.

The newest member of their team was nothing less than a legend in the FBI, and a bestselling author to boot, as well as a top lecturer both within the profession and without. The fiftyish David Rossi had the look of a professor at a small college — black hair, well-trimmed goatee, and casual business attire (blue work shirt with a striped tie under a gray sports jacket and, of course, jeans). When he strolled out of the elevator, as if he owned the joint, his confidence managed to stop just this side of arrogance.

Maybe he didn't own the joint, but Rossi

had certainly helped build it. Back in the day, along with Max Ryan and Jason Gideon (a Ryan protégé), Rossi had pioneered criminal profiling, which led to the creation of the Behavioral Analysis Unit. Of this three-man profiler Hall of Fame, Ryan had retired to a quiet life away from the violence and heartache that accompanied their job, Rossi to the bestseller list, the talk show stage and lecture circuit, and now Gideon was gone, too.

With Gideon's sudden and unexpected resignation, Rossi had volunteered to come back, for reasons of his own, and Hotchner had hoped this venerable hero of their field might fill the void left by Gideon. But Gideon had been the heart of the team, its conscience, its spiritual center, whereas Rossi was a loner who — while his value could not be underestimated — as yet showed limited signs of wanting to play father confessor or lead them in a round of "Kum Ba Yah" around the campfire.

And there had been some friction when Rossi returned — he had his way, the old way, the team had theirs, the new way. The transition had been difficult for Hotchner who had, after all, been recruited to the BAU by Rossi. Now as his mentor's boss, Hotchner occasionally had to redefine their roles in this new circumstance.

As he came up the few stairs to the elevated level and passed the window of Hotchner's office, Rossi gave Hotchner a scampish little grin and a nod, then moved on. There was something both friendly and hostile about it — Rossi reminding the stoic Hotchner that a profiler could actually have a sense of humor.

The last to show was Derek Morgan, an African-American with short hair and a killer smile, who had the build of the ex-athlete he was. Originally from Chicago, Morgan graduated from Northwestern Law, was an ex-cop (his father had been a cop, too) and had spent some time with ATF before joining the BAU almost ten years ago.

Morgan had no shortage of brains, but if there was muscle on Hotchner's team, Morgan was it — in addition to his BAU duties, he also taught hand-to-hand combat at Quantico. Morgan wore a light blue pullover sweater, dark dress slacks, black rubber-soled shoes, his service pistol riding his hip. He strode through the bullpen with a confidence considerably less surreptitious than Rossi's, headed up the few stairs, and came straight to the door of Hotchner's office.

Morgan knocked.

"Come in," Hotchner told the closed door.

Morgan did, leaving the door open.

"Morning," Hotchner said.

Dropping into one of the visitor's chairs opposite Hotchner's desk, Morgan smiled easily at him. "Have a good weekend?"

Hotchner nodded. "I spent Saturday afternoon with Jack at Haley's sister's."

"Nice. That's one afternoon."

"Right. Saturday."

"Hotch, we had *two* days off."

"Right."

"Tell me you didn't just hole up in your office at home and work the rest of it."

"How did you spend your weekend?"

Morgan lifted a hand. "I went away with a woman. We danced. Drank some beer. Generally chilled. Now I am refreshed and ready to work."

"Fine."

Morgan tilted his head. "Hotch, you're working too hard."

Hotchner shrugged. "Lot to do."

"You can't work 24-7. Don't tell me it's not my place, because I am counting on you to be bright-eyed and bushy-tailed as our fearless leader."

Hotchner actually smiled at that.

Morgan smiled, too, bigger.

"Point taken," Hotchner said. "Did you stop by my office just to play guidance counselor?"

"No. I came in to tell you I got a call this weekend. Remember Tate Lorenzon?"

Hotchner shook his head, but then said, "Wait — he's a friend of yours, isn't he? From back home?"

"Sweet home Chicago. Grew up on the same block. He's a detective in the city now. His father worked with mine."

"I see." Hotchner was wondering where this was going. That Morgan's cop father had been shot before his young son's eyes was not lost on the team leader.

"Listen, he's got a case he wants us to look at."

Hotchner worked at not frowning, without success. They had a protocol for these things, and calling in favors from old friends was not part of it. "All right. And what did you tell him?"

Shrugging, Morgan said, "I told him to go through channels."

"Good."

"So he called JJ," Morgan said.

Hotchner sighed. "Well, that skips a channel or two, but —"

As if she'd been summoned, Jennifer Jareau appeared at the door and knocked on the jamb.

His eyes still on Morgan, Hotchner said, "Yes?"

Jareau came over to the desk, flashed Hotchner a businesslike smile; usually she'd be bearing a sheaf of papers from an impending case, but now she held only a small stack of photos. "I think I've found our next case."

"Wild guess?" Hotchner said, watching Morgan who was looking around the office as if it were a crime scene and he couldn't be bothered right now. "Chicago?"

"Good guess," Jareau said, "but not exactly."

"Where, then?"

"The Chicago suburbs."

Hotchner nodded to the other chair opposite his desk. "Explain."

Jareau sat and said, "Over the weekend, I got a call from a Chicago detective named Tate Lorenzon."

Morgan seemed interested in something on the front of his shirt.

"He e-mailed me these three photos." She reached forward and spread them out on the desk like a grisly hand of cards.

Hotchner took in the crime scene photos, one at a time. "What am I looking at?"

"All three of these were sent to the jurisdictions the crimes were committed in," she said. "The first one, the car . . ."

"Wait a minute — these aren't police crime scene photos?"

"No. They are photos taken *at* the scene of crimes, before the police got there. And then sent to the police."

Interested, Hotchner gave Morgan a wide-eyed look and Morgan lifted an eyebrow and nodded, which was as close to saying "I told you so" to Aaron Hotchner as Derek Morgan ever got.

Jareau picked back up: "The first one? The car . . ."

She waited until Hotchner shuffled the photos around and looked at the one of a young couple shot to death in a car parked on a rain-soaked blacktop, a crumpled piece of paper on the road near the driver's door.

Jareau said, "Adrienne Andrews and her boyfriend Benjamin Mendoza were gunned down in a car outside her house around one in the morning on April eighteenth, at the corner of Two-Hundred-and-Seventh Street and Hutchinson Avenue. This photo, almost assuredly taken by the killer, showed up at Chicago Heights PD on the nineteenth."

"Via the Internet?"

She shook her head. "Snail mail. No prints, no DNA, no nothing. The second crime is the two decomposed bodies."

Hotchner flipped to a photo of two skulls and several large bones on the ground in a wooded area.

"The bones belong to two women who went missing on June fourteenth from Bangs Lake in Wauconda, a northern suburb in the lake counties. The photos showed up at the Wauconda PD on June sixteenth. Again, snail mail. The bones were found a week later, a few miles away in Lakewood Forest Preserve."

The third photo showed a fifty-five-gallon blue plastic barrel sitting in the hallway of what appeared to be a vacant apartment.

"This is the only crime that took place in Chicago proper," Jareau said. "This barrel with a body in it was found in a vacant apartment on Twenty-fifth Street in China-town on July twenty-second."

Hotchner stared up from the photo at Morgan, who finally met his eyes. They both knew what these photos represented, and it was more than just three disparate crime scenes.

"Let's get Lorenzon on the phone," Hotchner said.

With an embarrassed smile, Morgan said, "That won't be necessary. He'll be here in about ten minutes."

"Here?"

Morgan nodded. "He and an associate flew out. His chief was eager that he do so. And I think we're past talking about protocol and proper channels, Hotch."

Hotchner could only agree. He said, "As soon as Detective Lorenzon gets here" — his eyes on Jareau — "I want the team in the conference room."

Jareau appeared slightly puzzled at the rush, but her nod said she would make it happen and she left the office.

Turning his gaze back to Morgan, Hotchner said, "Why didn't you call me at home with this?"

"Lorenzon told me about it over the phone on Saturday," Morgan said. "He and another detective flew in on Sunday — strictly his idea, Hotch — and we didn't sit down until I got back to the city . . . since some of us actually know the meaning of R and R . . . and we had dinner last night. Tate didn't know what he had."

"Not at all?"

"Well, he figured they may have a serial killer on their hands. But he didn't understand these MOs being all over the map. But of course, we have a rough idea."

Hotchner nodded. "Did you explain it to him?"

Morgan shook his head. "Hell, Hotch, I *knew* we'd end up taking the case, and it would wait till then. I mean, could anything be more up our alley?"

"No," Hotchner admitted.

"I figured Tate could find out today and have one last good night's sleep before we turned his world upside down."

Hotchner, with no sarcasm whatsoever, said, "Considerate."

Morgan shrugged.

"How did *you* sleep?"

Rising from his chair, Morgan said, "You really don't want to know. You'd send my ass home for an all-day nap."

By the time the pair marched through the bullpen, two men were exiting the elevator. One was older and Hispanic, maybe Rossi's age, the other younger and African-American. The Hispanic was shorter, balding, with full cheeks and sleepy brown eyes, dark hair showing signs of gray at the temples. He wore a tan sport coat, blue jeans, a brown button-down shirt open at the collar and brown loafers with no socks.

The African-American had an easy smile, sharp brown eyes, a wispy black mustache and goatee, and close-cropped hair. He wore a black T-shirt under a black suit and had the build of a former athlete, maybe one who still took time out for hoops.

Morgan said, "This is Chicago Detective Tate Lorenzon."

Hotchner shook hands with the black detective, who had a firm grip and eyes that met Hotchner's.

"Thanks for seeing us, Agent Hotchner," Lorenzon said. "I know we're kind of barging in."

"Not a problem," Hotchner said. "My friends call me Hotch."

"And I'm Tate." Then, turning to his companion, Lorenzon added, "Supervisory Special Agent Aaron Hotchner, meet Detective Hilario Tovar, Chicago Heights PD."

Grinning and extending his hand, Tovar said, "It's Hilly, and we really do appreciate your time. I mean, we know all about the BAU — you're the first team, and you don't waste time on the small stuff."

"Hilly," Hotchner said with a nod, shaking the man's hand. "We're happy to help, if we can."

"That's good to hear," Lorenzon said. "There are plenty of cops back our way who think Hilly and me are off the rails on this one. You say 'serial killer' to a cop and he thinks you've seen too many movies."

A needle of apprehension jabbed Hotchner. "You both know we can only enter cases where we've been invited."

"You and vampires," Lorenzon said.

The remark was one, in seemingly endless variations, that Hotchner had often heard before; he hid any irritation and said, "Be that as it may . . ."

Tovar held up a hand. "Listen, both our departments may think we're gonzo, but Tate and me have pretty good track records, so to shut us up, if nothing else? They've agreed to extend you an invitation . . . *if* you think the two of us are on the right track. On the other hand, maybe they just wanted to get us out of town where you could talk some sense into us."

"So you know what you have," Hotchner said flatly — a statement, not a question.

"We think so," Lorenzon said, and sighed. "But like I say, nobody else wants to believe it."

Morgan said, "Who'd want to?"

Jareau came up to them. "Everyone's ready."

Introductions were made and she shook hands with both men.

"We appreciate your time," Tovar said to her.

"It's our job," she said. "If this develops into anything, I'll be working media."

"From D.C.?"

"No, if we come to Chicago, I'll be part of the team."

Hotch saw Morgan smile, just a little. The two out-of-town detectives could hardly have failed to notice just how striking a young woman Jareau was, and having her around wouldn't be the worst fate in the world.

Jareau led them into the conference room, giving Tovar and Lorenzon seats on Hotchner's left, Rossi on his right, the rest of the team fanned out around the large mahogany table that was the room's centerpiece. Morgan and Reid sat to Rossi's right, Prentiss to the left of Lorenzon, Jareau remaining on her feet as she made the introductions.

A picture window with venetian blinds occupied the wall immediately to the right of the door, a twin to the window in Hotchner's office. To the left was a cupboard and counter with a copier, a fax machine in the corner beyond. The wall to the left had three narrow bulletproof windows that served only to let in light, a brown sofa under them, a potted tree beside it. A wall-mounted whiteboard had been cleaned.

The sections of corkboard on either side of the whiteboard still held tacked-up notes, photos, reports, and other detritus from their previous case. The wall opposite the door contained a HDTV flat screen on which could be displayed PowerPoint presentations and videos from cases.

"The reason these detectives came to us," Hotchner said, "is these photos you are about to see. JJ?"

Jareau pushed a button on the remote and the first crime scene photo popped up on the HD screen. They all took a good look: a young couple in a car on a blacktop road next to a house, wadded piece of paper on the rain-soaked street under the driver's door.

No one said a word.

Then Jareau spoke. "This photo was sent by snail mail to the Chicago Heights Police Department and turned over to Detective Tovar. Does it remind you of anything?"

Morgan, who Hotchner knew already had the answer, said nothing. The others also stayed mute, but Reid seemed focused on something in the photo and Hotchner knew the young man was close to seeing what he and Morgan had long since picked up on.

Hotchner gave Reid a hint. "Detective Tovar, could you tell us the date of the crime and intersection where it took place?"

"April seventeenth," Tovar said, "or actually early April eighteenth, one a.m. Corner of Two-Hundred-and-Seventh Street and

Hutchinson Avenue."

Almost before the words were out of the detective's mouth, Reid quietly said, "Berkowitz."

"*David* Berkowitz?" Prentiss asked, eyes and nostrils flaring.

Nodding rapidly now, Reid said, "Son of Sam. On April seventeenth, nineteen seventy-seven, two lovers — an eighteen-year-old actress, Valentina Suriani and her tow-truck driver boyfriend, twenty-year-old Alexander Esau — were necking in a parked car near the Hutchinson River Parkway in the Bronx when they were shot to death by Berkowitz. Though they were the ninth and tenth victims he shot, they were only the fifth and sixth to die. One of the police officers at the scene found a letter addressed to the lead detective on the so-called case of the .44 Caliber Killer — Captain Joseph Borelli. It was the letter where Berkowitz gave himself the name 'Son Of Sam.' "

Lorenzon spoke up. "You're talking about the guy who got his marching orders from a damn dog?"

"A Labrador retriever named Harvey," Reid said in his lilting, matter-of-fact way. He might have been answering a question in a round of Trivial Pursuit. "Was there anything on the crumpled piece of paper?"

"No," Tovar said.

"We'll get it to our lab," Hotchner said. "They might be able to find something."

"The murder weapon," Morgan said. "What do we know about it?"

Tovar said, "It's a —"

"Would it be a Charter Arms Bulldog," Reid interrupted, ".44 caliber special?"

Hotchner watched the detective sitting there open-mouthed, staring at Reid as if a two-year-old had suddenly spouted the Gettysburg Address.

"It, uh, *was* a .44," Tovar said. "What are you, kid, a witch?"

"That would be 'warlock,' " Reid said.

Morgan cut in. "But he is a doctor and a supervisory special agent, so 'kid' may not really be appropriate."

"Sorry, Dr. Reid," Tovar said, flustered.

Reid waved that off, while Hotchner said, "You just want to make sure you take Dr. Reid seriously. Because he doesn't just pull these things out of the air."

Morgan said, "Or the other place you might assume he's pulling it out of."

"Point is," Reid said, "it's the same gun Berkowitz used."

Jareau touched a button on the remote and the second photo came up on the screen: bones found in the Lakewood Forest Preserve.

Jareau said, "Detective Tovar got this photo from a friend on the job in Wauconda, one of the far northern suburbs in the lake counties."

"Jake Denson," Tovar said. "He sent me the photo when I asked him if he'd received any in the mail; but Jake thinks, because of the difference in MO? His nut and our nut are different guys."

Reid said, " 'Nut' is probably not a good way to describe this individual, and it *is* one individual. You're dealing with someone intelligent and even sophisticated. Don't underestimate him."

The two detectives exchanged awkward glances. They had the look of minor leaguers thrust into the big time.

Rossi, whose face assumed a deceptive blankness when he concentrated, nodded toward the image of bones and asked, "What's the story here?"

Jareau said, "Hikers found the remains of two young women in Lakewood Forest Preserve on Saturday, June twenty-first. There were two skulls, four femurs, and a jawbone. The remains were identified as Donna Cooper and Casey Goddard, two young women who disappeared from Bangs Lake in Wauconda on June fourteenth."

Prentiss said, "Like two young women last seen with a handsome young man, with a cast on one arm, claiming he needed help getting a boat off his car."

"Oh hell," Morgan said.

"Ted Bundy," Rossi said.

Reid said, "The date is off by exactly one month, but it matches the disappearance of Janice Ott and Denise Naslund in Washington state. Their bones were found later in Lake Sammamish State Park."

"Damnit," Tovar said, and pounded a fist into a palm. "I never put that together . . . but yeah, that fits what Denson told me. He just included so much extra crap I never saw the pieces for what they were."

Lorenzon said, "Then mine's a copycat too."

Taking the hint, Jareau switched to the third photo, the plastic barrel in the vacant apartment. "On July twenty-second, this was found by policemen following up on an anonymous tip about a domestic dispute in an apartment building in Chinatown."

Eyes narrowed, Reid said, "The address? Is it in the nine hundred block of Twenty-fifth Street?"

Lorenzon stared at him for a long moment, probably about the way Moses looked at the burning bush, Hotchner thought.

Then the Chicago cop slowly shook his head. "You got the street right, but there is no nine hundred block, Dr. Reid — the street's too short. It was in the two hundred block . . ."

"Two thirteen," Reid said, unfazed.

"Now, man, that's freaky," Lorenzon said. "How did you know? Goddamn, is Dr. Reid here psychic?"

Hotchner said tightly, "No. He's a profiler."

Reid, trying not to look pleased about Hotchner's remark, said, "The apartment house where the original blue barrel was found was nine twenty-four North Twenty-fifth Street in Milwaukee, Wisconsin — the apartment number was two-thirteen. The occupant was a thirty-one year old man who had recently lost his job at a chocolate factory . . ."

"Oh Christ," Lorenzon said. He swallowed thickly. "Goddamned Jeffrey Dahmer."

His expression grave, Morgan asked, "What about the victim?"

"Male, young Caucasian, twenty, maybe — probably a runaway — haven't identified him yet. The ME thinks he had been in the barrel for the better part of a month before he was found."

"Did the medical examiner give you a cause of death?"

Lorenzon shook his head. "The body was nearly too decomposed . . . broken hyoid bone, though. Probably manual strangulation."

Reid asked, "What about the sexual aspects of these crimes?"

"I don't know about the Wauconda case," Tovar said. "I haven't seen the entire file and the photo just shows bones. I can tell you there was *no* sexual evidence with the shooting in the Heights."

Reid nodded thoughtfully. "There was no direct sexual evidence in the Berkowitz killings either, though. What about the barrel?"

"Again," Lorenzon said, "he was just too decomposed."

Rossi said, "Berkowitz hated women, as did Bundy, while Dahmer killed gay men — a sexual aspect in each case, but this Un-Sub is taking two from column A and one from column B in an unusual way."

"What does that tell us about the killer's sexuality?" Prentiss asked. "He's copying both straight and gay killers."

Hotchner said, "The killer could be straight, gay, or judging by the complete lack of sexual evidence at the scenes, asexual. In fact, by avoiding the sexual aspects of the case, the UnSub might even be trying to remove his own sexuality from the equation."

"I think that's it," Reid said, nodding. "He's trying to compartmentalize his own sexuality from these crimes, which is not easy considering the extreme degree of sexual dysfunction in the crimes he's copying."

Rossi lifted an eyebrow and added, "That may be because he views himself as a performance artist, for whom the ultimate expression is not the murder itself, but the photographic record of that murder."

Shaking his head, Tovar said, "So, where does that leave us — back at square one?"

"Not completely," Reid said. "We know his signature."

"Yeah," Lorenzon said, "his signature is he kills people."

"Signature?" Tovar asked. "He's used a gun on two, cut up two, and God only knows what he did to the other."

Rossi said, "Don't confuse signature with MO."

"There's a difference?" Tovar asked.

With a nod, Rossi said, " 'Modus Operandi' is how he does the crime. 'Signature' is what he has to do for the crime to get him where he's going. What gets him off."

"And what's that?"

Rossi pointed at the picture on the flat screen. "The photos."

Morgan twitched a frown. "Someone is re-creating murders by some of the most infamous serial killers of all time — why?"

"Simple," Prentiss said. "This guy wants to be infamous, too."

They all turned toward her, Hotchner noticing that Rossi gave her an encouraging nod.

"Is there any other way this pathology makes any sense?" she asked. "An UnSub who wants to make a place for himself in the Hall of Infamy?"

Nobody seemed to have an answer for that.

Raising his voice just a little, bringing the focus of the room to the oldest old pro among them, Rossi said, "He's killed five people in three different jurisdictions — which means he's working hard at not getting caught, even though his desire for recognition has him sending photos on ahead. He's got to have some knowledge of police work, and even police politics — he knows these jurisdictions won't cooperate with each other without someone like

Detectives Lorenzon and Tovar pushing them."

Hotchner nodded, adding, "The UnSub probably also knows the more places he hits, the longer it will take for people to identify his MO and ID him as a serial. Despite the photos he's sending, he likely expected to go longer without us being brought in."

Lorenzon looked toward Morgan. "Then you *are* going to help us?"

"Not my call," Morgan said, and turned to Hotchner.

"Yes, Tate," Hotchner said, "we're going to help."

Lorenzon nodded. "Thank you. We're going to need it."

No one disagreed.

"JJ," Hotchner said, "let's start by you telling Wauconda PD we're coming in at the invitation of both Chicago and Chicago Heights. Tell them we'd like to oversee a joint task force among the jurisdictions involved in the case. My guess is, before this is over, it won't be just three."

"On it," Jareau said.

Turning to Reid, Hotchner said, "Background history on the cases he's copying."

"Pleasure," Reid said.

"Prentiss, read the police reports and start

working on victimology."

"Right."

Hotchner sighed heavily. "All right, people, let's get packed up. We're wheels up at Andrews in an hour."

Tovar said, "Thank you for coming on this."

Hotchner said, "We'll do everything we can, Hilly."

"Does that mean . . . ?"

"It means we'll catch him."

They all rose except Rossi, who lingered. He sat staring at the last photo.

"Damn," he said, and then he laughed, once, harshly.

They all turned to him, with Morgan halfway out the door.

"It's a serial killer greatest hits album," Rossi said. "By a goddamn cover band."

CHAPTER TWO:
JULY 28
CHICAGO, ILLINOIS

Derek Morgan kept his eyes closed, not letting anyone know he was awake yet. They were still in the air, somewhere over the Midwest. Around him, the others were chatting quietly or working on their laptops. Always a hundred-and-ten-percent effort kind of guy, Morgan had not outslept his fellow teammates due to exhaustion or indolence. He just knew that this would be the last chance to really rest until they brought this killer to ground.

Morgan had spent part of the hour before they left calling his mother to tell her that he would be coming home on a case, promising he'd find time to see her — he just didn't know when. His mother had just been happy to hear his voice. "Whenever you have time, son," she had said. "I know how demanding your work is. I'm proud of you!"

Anyone who encountered the BAU team

would soon identify Morgan as the resident tough guy. Nonetheless, Morgan still phoned his mother every Sunday. Family remained important to him, and that was no axiom: his had been a close, tightly knit family. That the BAU was going to Chicago to help families that weren't that much different from his own was not lost on him. The two young women found in Lakewood Forest Preserve could have been his own sisters but for the age difference.

Someone plopped onto the seat next to him, but Morgan forced himself to not move or open his eyes.

"You really think," Prentiss said, "pretending to be asleep is going to fool a profiler."

Smiling, Morgan said, "Maybe you're not that good."

She ignored that. "Hotchner asked me to brief you about what we're doing when we hit the ground."

"Don't say, 'hit the ground' in midair. It's bad luck."

"After we *land*," she corrected herself. "I never would have pegged you as the fear-of-flying type."

"More fear of dying."

"That, either, frankly. You might as well open your eyes. We're having a conversation, you know."

65

His eyes came reluctantly open. "Is that what this is?"

"Seems to be. When we land, Hotch says he wants the two of us to take the Chinatown crime scene. He thinks you're the only one who knows the city well enough to find it without help."

"Not a problem," Morgan said with a yawn, then rubbed his face with one hand and sat up a little straighter. "How long?"

"Till we hit the ground?"

He grinned at her. "You're evil."

"I like to think of it as 'wicked.' We land in about half an hour."

Morgan glanced around the plane. "What are everybody else's assignments?"

"Rossi and Reid will go to the first scene — Chicago Heights — using Tovar as a guide, though Rossi's a Chicago boy himself. Meanwhile, Lorenzon will accompany Hotchner and JJ to talk to the Wauconda PD, and then they will visit *that* crime scene."

He grunted. "Something, isn't it?"

"What is?"

"A killer hiding inside the MOs of other killers."

"It's a variation on an old theme, Morgan."

Morgan nodded. "Hiding in plain sight."

Nearly an hour later, the team was loading up three black Chevy Tahoes provided by the Chicago FBI field office. The heat was even more oppressive than usual, the humidity so high it couldn't have been much harder to breathe if they'd been under Lake Michigan.

Having walked out with two carry-ons and loaded them into the Tahoe, Morgan found himself dripping sweat. Once their gear was stored and their weapons ready, the vehicles took off in three different directions, Hotchner and Jareau, accompanied by Lorenzon, to the north, Rossi and Reid, along with Tovar, to the south, while Morgan with Prentiss in the rider's seat drove east.

He followed I-90, then turned south after it merged with I-94. Outside, the afternoon sun blazed down, reflecting off their vehicle's hood; but inside the air-conditioning hummed quietly. Morgan left the car radio off — he was in work mode.

They had been on the road the better part of ninety minutes when Prentiss asked, "How much longer?"

He gave her a sideways, arched-eyebrow look. "Didn't you work in Chicago before you joined the BAU?"

Prentiss smiled but didn't look at him. "Yeah."

"For how long?"

"A while."

"Then you *know* how much longer, don't you?"

She nodded. "Just making conversation."

"You don't have to go out of your way to be friendly with me, Emily. I like you."

"Gee, thanks."

"By which I mean, I respect you. You've done well." He returned his eyes to the swarming traffic. "But you figure Hotch is still testing you."

"Why would he be testing me?" Her voice sounded a little defensive. "It's been over a year, and I wasn't exactly a novice when I joined the BAU."

Morgan grinned. "Hell, Emily, he's still testing *me.* I'd say he's still testing himself. He's the team leader. That's part of his job. And just maybe you've noticed he's wrapped tighter than a new spool of thread."

"He lacks confidence in me."

"Why do you say that?"

She shrugged. "Hotch knows I know Chicago. But he had *you* drive."

"Maybe he thinks it's a man's job."

"Are you kidding?"

"Yes." Morgan laughed. "Is there a possibility you're overthinking this?"

She smiled again and looked away as they

crossed the Chicago River. He had to pass the street they wanted and exit the expressway at Thirty-first Street, then work his way back to Twenty-fifth. He went west on Thirty-first for a block, turned north on Wentworth and followed that through the light at Twenty-sixth, taking a left onto Twenty-fifth, only to find that the street was blocked by fireplug-sized columns of cement after about a car-length, turning the street into a cul-de-sac, leaving Morgan on the wrong side. Still, an alley ran back south and that would keep him from having to make a U-turn to get out.

"Of course," Prentiss said, "*I* would have known not to do that."

"Are you kidding?"

"Yes," she said.

The first building on the south side of the street faced Wentworth, the alley running behind it. Across the alley to the west, the first thing Morgan saw was a set of four concrete stairs with wrought-iron railings, the stairs leading to thin air, the building they rose to long since demolished, going nowhere except to overlook a stretch of grass and weeds, surrounded by a four-foot cyclone fence.

Prentiss gave him a look. "Stairway to heaven?"

"If it is," Morgan said, "next door you'll find the stairway to hell." He looked down the block at the next residence from the building-less stairs.

The house with 213 stenciled on the mailbox next to the front door was a dirty beige two-story. From his angle parked at the northeast corner, Morgan could see that something drastic, probably a fire, had happened to the huge structure once upon time.

The front half of the building was the dirty beige siding; the back half was old, bronze-colored brick. A door on the east side split the border of the two halves, which would be the entrance to the middle apartment, and where the alley curved around behind the building would be the entrance to the rear apartment. The length of two normal houses, the ungainly structure might have been constructed half from LEGOs and half from Lincoln Logs.

"Weird damn building," Morgan muttered.

He drove down the alley, then turned west on Twenty-sixth and then right again on Wells, taking one last right, coming around on Twenty-fifth, then pulling up to the building in question.

He parked in front.

They were in the heart of Chinatown, the

part tourists never ventured into. Chinese-American pedestrians strolled up and down the street and through the alley; several others sat on back porches of the three-story building that faced Wentworth, many smoking as they watched the strangers in the fancy SUV climb out into the late afternoon swelter.

More sat on stoops along Twenty-fifth, all with their eyes on Morgan and Prentiss. The old cliché about Asians being inscrutable was contradicted by the faces whose eyes were trained on the two FBI agents — reading the distrust and suspicion there didn't take much in the way of profiling skills.

Prentiss, trying out a smile on several of the neighbors, asked, "How did a killer get that barrel into the apartment with this many witnesses?"

"My guess is it's a little different at night," Morgan said. "Chinatown's always been a closed community to the Bureau. What happens in Chinatown stays in Chinatown."

"You mean, 'Forget it, Emily. It's Chinatown?' "

"Something like that."

"Well, according to the report, the police thoroughly canvassed the neighborhood."

Morgan glanced at her. "What did they find?"

"They got exactly as much information as you would expect."

"Meaning nothing."

"Meaning nothing."

Using a pocketknife, Morgan cut the crime scene tape. Then from the pocket of his slacks, he withdrew a key Lorenzon had given him and unlocked the door.

"After you," he said.

Prentiss smirked; she was a good-looking woman and even her smirk wasn't hard to look at. "I don't care what anybody says, Derek Morgan — you're a gentleman."

They entered the dark building, each using Mini Maglites to help find their way through the shadows. Even though the windows lacked curtains, the glass was so grimy that little light made it through.

Using her Maglite, Prentiss searched and finally found a light switch. She flipped it, but nothing happened.

"Not a surprise," she said.

"No wonder no one saw anything," Morgan said. "If we can't see out, it's a good bet nobody can see in."

"Where was the barrel situated?"

Morgan glanced around in the gloom, getting his bearings.

"Over there," he said, pointing to a hallway that led to a bedroom.

The layout was fairly simple: a living room led into a small kitchen with an eating area and a tiny bedroom down the hall, which led to the second floor and two more bedrooms and a bathroom. Morgan walked the whole thing and got the feeling no one had lived here for a long, long time — nobody but an occasional homeless inhabitant, anyway.

Once he was back downstairs, he found Prentiss shining her light around the edges of the windows.

"You read the report," Morgan said. "When was the last time someone lived here?"

"Three years ago."

"No one since?"

"Squatters maybe, but no one on the books."

Morgan nodded. "What do we know about the corpse?"

"Other than he's a John Doe?"

"Yeah."

Prentiss lifted one shoulder in a tiny shrug. "He was stuffed in the barrel postmortem. The UnSub poured lime in to keep the smell down, and to hasten decomposition — of course, that means the UnSub doesn't know that lime actually helps *preserve* a body. I don't know why people think lime speeds decomposition."

"Old wives' tale. Nasty COD?"

She nodded and raised a pale hand to her throat. "Cause of death was strangulation."

Morgan watched Prentiss move to the next window in the front and start poking around the edges with her flashlight beam.

"What are you up to?" he asked.

She stopped and turned to face him. "One thing that wasn't in the report was how the UnSub got inside. The door wasn't jimmied and that barrel got in here somehow."

Morgan nodded. "Right. He had to either have a key or he came in through a window and unlocked the door, so he could wheel the barrel in."

They were already referring to the UnSub as "he" — these murders seemed a man's crime, nothing about it indicated a rare female serial killer, although the lack of sexual assault left that open.

"If the UnSub had a key," Prentiss said, forehead creased with thought, "where did he get it?"

"Or if he came in through one of the windows," Morgan said, gesturing toward one, "why didn't anybody see him?"

She put both shoulders into a shrug. "Late at night, probably. But with that barrel, he had to have it somewhere nearby."

"The cops haven't explained it?"

Prentiss shook her head. "I know it's not supposed to be up to us to gather the evidence, but how this UnSub got into the place might tell us something about him."

"Agreed," Morgan said. "You keep looking here — I want to check something out."

He went into the kitchen, where he turned the knob on a door he thought might adjoin the middle apartment; but he found a short hallway with the middle apartment's door on the right, at the far end, and nearer, on the left, a stairway leading down.

Shining his light ahead of him, he descended ten steps into a dank basement redolent of urine and mildew.

No wonder nobody checked down here, he thought.

Cobwebs drooped everywhere but in the stairwell itself, where they had been removed. A thick layer of dust coated the floor, the furnace, and a few scraps of worthless furniture. He shone his light on the floor and saw footprints in the dust.

He used the light to follow them back to a half window on the far wall. One of two panes had been broken and the latch opened from there. The window was only about twelve inches high and twenty inches across.

Now they knew something about their

UnSub: he was a lot of things, but over-weight wasn't one of them.

Morgan went back upstairs, told Prentiss what he'd found, and told her not to step on the floor. He had left the door open just in case, by some miracle, prints might turn up on the basement side.

He got out his cell phone and called Hotchner and detailed to the team leader what they had found, and suggested Loren-zon get his crime scene team back right away.

July 28
Chicago Heights, Illinois
Dr. Spencer Reid felt a little bit like the kid who had been dumped on his older brother for the day. He rode in back of the SUV with Rossi and Tovar up front. The Chicago Heights detective was behind the wheel, even though it was an FBI vehicle.

Up front, the two men were discussing baseball, the Chicago Cubs in particular, an area of expertise not among Reid's skill set.

Rossi was saying, "You really think this is the year?"

Tovar nodded as he drove them south. "They won the division last year, didn't they?"

"Then got spanked by Arizona."

"Yeah, but the pitching's better now."

Rossi shrugged. "Believe it when I see it."

From the backseat, Reid watched the neighborhood change as they cruised farther south from mostly Caucasian to mostly Hispanic to mostly African-American. By the time they reached their destination, however, the neighborhood had become a middle-class melting pot of variant homes and blacktop streets with no curbs and no apparent storm sewers.

Tovar drove through a neighborhood of well-tended homes that varied from ordinary single-story boxes to brick-faced two-stories that looked like they had fallen off the mansion truck and landed beside the road in the wrong neighborhood.

"Odd mix of houses," Reid said.

"Yeah," Tovar said. "Some of the old houses are being bought up, torn down, and replaced by newer ones. Other oldies are getting the renovation treatment."

"Gentrification," Rossi said. "Gotta love it." But he clearly didn't.

"Oh yeah," Tovar said. "The neighborhood's changing."

Reid asked, "For the better?"

"Matter of opinion," Tovar said. "Certainly isn't better for the Andrews family."

The Chicago detective pulled the Tahoe

to a stop next to a plain but well-maintained one-story tan house surrounded by trees and bushes. "This is where the daughter was parked with her boyfriend when they were shot to death back in April."

Reid looked around, trying to get a feel for the neighborhood. The houses were not terribly close together and they all appeared well cared for, a fairly typical middle-class neighborhood. Across the street, a park spread out before them, a parking lot on the far side of the block.

"Quiet," Reid said.

"Too quiet, like they say in the old movies," Tovar said. "No crimes to speak of, here."

They climbed out of the SUV, each taking a moment to survey the area. Reid couldn't take his eyes off the parking lot across the park. Trees shaded the cars that were nosed in, facing this direction. To see who was or was not inside those cars from there was impossible without binoculars or a high-powered camera lens. The powerlessness gave him an uneasy feeling.

Rossi asked the Chicago detective, "Did the boy and girl park alongside the house and make out, you know, as a regular thing?"

"They had been dating for a while," Tovar

said. "I think it's safe to say that night wasn't the first time they'd sat there and necked, yeah."

Reid nodded across the way. "That park would give someone an easy place to surveil the victims."

"Of course," Rossi said, "but how did he know they would be there on this particular night? Nothing indicates whether this was a randomly chosen couple, or one that the killer had selected and watched over time."

Reid agreed.

Tovar looked blank.

Rossi said, "The boy, Benny Mendoza? His coach had taken Benny and his girl to the White Sox game that night. Benny was a promising young ballplayer. Anyway, the game got rained out late. The boy and girl didn't get back till well after midnight." Rossi made a face at Reid. "How the hell could the UnSub have known that?"

Reid considered that for a moment; then he put some pieces together. "Let's suppose he was indeed stalking the couple."

"Suppose away," Rossi said.

"If he's re-creating Berkowitz's crime, it's the street he's most concerned with — Hutchinson Avenue. What if he was stalking more than one couple along the street, and this one, Andrews and Mendoza, was the couple that happened to show up at the right time?"

Tovar said, "Wrong time, you mean."

Rossi was looking at Reid, hard. "You're saying it could have been anyone along the street?"

"It's possible," Reid said. "Son of Sam shot individuals as well as couples."

"Dr. Reid could be right," Tovar said. "The weather was bad that night. Rained like hell most of the evening. I doubt if there were a lot of people out and about."

Reid said, "This isn't the only house visible from the park."

Rossi said, "It would be easy to watch most of the street from that parking lot."

"There's something else," Reid said.

The other two turned to him.

"Our UnSub is patient. He takes care and exercises a certain artistry, but he's not a perfectionist — he's willing to fudge a little on his re-creations."

Rossi eyed Reid skeptically. "And you've reached this conclusion how?"

Reid shrugged. "He waited."

Rossi chewed on that momentarily. Then he said, "He sat in wait until his victims came along. Yeah. I'll buy that."

"No, I think you miss my point — I mean, he waited past *midnight*."

The other two stared at him.

"Technically," Reid said, articulating something he'd discerned on first reading the report, "he missed the anniversary of the Son of Sam killing. He shot them in the early morning hours of the eighteenth."

"What does that mean?" Tovar asked.

Rossi sighed, gave Reid a little smile that meant, *Nice going,* and said to the Chicago cop, "It means that even though he's re-creating crimes, our UnSub is willing to adapt his crime so that he gets his kill . . . even if it undermines the exactness of his recreation."

Tovar still seemed confused. "And what does *that* tell us?"

Rossi tilted his head just a little, then righted it. "Even though he's patient and highly organized in his planning, he's *going* to *kill* — that's the priority — even if it doesn't fall within the exact boundaries of what he's trying to create."

"Or rather," Reid put in, "re-create."

Rossi nodded, then went on: "Reid used the word 'artistry,' and I think that's right on point: in his own way, probably in his own mind, our UnSub is an artist. Instead of just painting or sculpting the things that inspire him, he's acting them out."

"It wasn't clear until we got here," Reid

said, "but aren't these jurisdictions where he committed the crimes rather far apart?"

"Yeah," Tovar said, with a nod.

"*How* far apart?" Reid asked.

Tovar gestured vaguely. "The Chinatown crime scene is about an hour from here, depending on traffic. The Wauconda crime scene is at least an hour and a half north of here."

Reid's eyes tightened. "That tells us something too."

"Which is?" Tovar asked.

"He's mobile," Reid said.

"He owns a car," Rossi agreed.

"What kind?" Tovar asked, a smile creasing his face. It was a joke.

Smiling back, Rossi said, not joking at all, "Something inconspicuous, probably an older car that would blend in. It won't be anything too flashy and the color will be something neutral or subdued, too. He's been spending a lot of time planning these crimes. He has to've spent a lot of time in the areas where they took place . . . and no one noticed him."

"Okay," Tovar said, impressed. "I can get on board with that."

Reid asked, "Were all the crimes committed at night?"

"This one was," Tovar said. "The other

two, the bodies were found well after the murders, so there's no way to know for sure."

Reid turned to Rossi. "If he's spending this much time in these places, doesn't he have to have some job freedom?"

Rossi nodded, once.

Tovar asked, "Why not just unemployed?"

Rossi shook his head. He patted the SUV near where they stood. "Not likely with the distance between these crime scenes and Chicago gas prices. He's got a job that allows him at least some freedom."

"You're sure of this?" Tovar asked.

"It's an educated guess," Rossi said. "But a very educated guess."

The Hispanic detective mulled that. "Maybe his wife works, or he's somebody that doesn't have to work, 'cause his family left him money or something."

"Possible," Rossi said with a tiny smile. "Not probable."

Mind going a million miles an hour, Reid said, "His job doesn't give him the satisfaction he needs, either."

"Why do you say that?" Tovar asked.

"These crimes are all about getting attention," Reid said. "There's no indication of any sexual aspects to the killings, so the UnSub's doing it for two things: self-satisfaction, a twisted sense of self-worth you might say; and, again, the attention."

Rossi said, "You can't be a performance artist if there's no audience."

Reid and Tovar both turned to look at the goateed FBI agent, his words having hit them both fairly hard.

As Reid digested the idea, Tovar turned toward the house. Following the detective's gaze, Reid turned as well and saw a stocky man of about five-nine striding across the yard in their direction. He had short hair, horn-rimmed glasses and a sad, pouchy face etched with a frown.

Tovar stepped forward, hand extended. "Mr. Andrews."

"Detective Tovar," Andrews said politely. He wore khakis and a tan-and-brown striped Polo shirt. "Good to see you again."

Reid and Rossi let the detective take the lead.

Tovar said, "Vernon Andrews, this is Supervisory Special Agent David Rossi and Supervisory Special Agent Dr. Spencer Reid from the FBI."

"We're sorry for your loss," Rossi said, shaking the man's hand.

Andrews nodded. "Thank you."

"For what it's worth, we're here to help bring the person who did this terrible thing to justice."

"If I can help in any way, don't hesitate."

Andrews was saying this as he shook Reid's hand, the grieving man's grasp limp and cool, a dead man's handshake.

Reid added his condolences.

"Thank you," Andrews said.

"Mr. Andrews," Reid went on, "we'd like to ask you some questions, if that would be all right."

"Will it help find my daughter's killer?"

Rossi said, "We hope so, sir."

"Then please ask. But I'm afraid I don't know what I can tell you that I haven't already told Detective Tovar."

"We know what happened," Rossi said. "Right now, we're more concerned with why it happened . . . and how."

"I'm not sure I understand," Andrews said.

Rossi said, "The police have given us a good picture of the night your daughter and her boyfriend were killed. We want to know what led up to that moment."

"How on earth can I help with that?"

With a small, respectful smile, Rossi asked, "Mr. Andrews, would you call yourself an observant man?"

With a shrug, Andrews said, "I try to be."

"Let me ask you then — did you see

anyone watching your house or the neighborhood in the weeks before your daughter was shot? Someone who didn't belong here?"

The grief-stricken father considered that for a long moment.

Finally, he said, "You know, I never gave it a second thought before . . . but Addie told me one night, last March? That she had thought someone was watching her and Benny, when they were parked next to the house. Actually, it was a kind of accusation — she assumed it was her mother or me, spying on her. At the time, I was so worried about convincing her that she should trust us, that she must've just been imagining things, that I . . . I never took in account that someone might actually be watching them."

Reid asked, "Did Addie say *why* she'd thought you were watching her and Benny?"

"She said . . . said it felt like someone was there in the darkness when they were sitting in the car. With all the trees around the house, she assumed it was Doris — that's her mom. Or me."

"And it wasn't?"

"No. I'm as protective as the next father. But we were young once, we knew the kids needed some time to themselves . . . and, anyway, we trusted Benny. *He* was a good kid, too. We liked him. I'm pretty sure Addie loved him, though she hadn't told us that." He looked at Tovar. "You're a parent, Detective. You understand."

Tovar nodded gravely. "It's a balancing act between trying to protect them and letting go."

"Yes," Andrews said, and swallowed. "I should have protected her more. Did I screw up?"

Rossi said, "No, sir. No . . ."

"Should I have taken what Addie said more seriously, about someone watching her? I screwed up, didn't I?"

Gently, Rossi touched the father's sleeve. "No. You didn't. Let go of that thought. It's no good."

Andrews swallowed again, and nodded. "But I can't help but blame myself, Mr. Rossi."

"We're going to find the one to blame, Mr. Andrews," Rossi said firmly. "And it's not you."

As the four men stood in a loose semicircle, a short, heavyset woman in a blue T-shirt, jeans and tennis shoes emerged from around the house. The blue T-shirt was emblazoned with a white cross next to which the words St. Vincent's Parents Association were printed. The woman's blonde hair was trimmed short.

Reid could easily see the resemblance between mother and deceased daughter.

"This is Doris," Andrews said. "My wife."

She gave them a wan smile. She still seemed shell-shocked from the loss of her daughter, even though months had passed.

Reid also knew that the haunted look would probably never go away, not entirely. He had seen it far too many times in his relatively short tenure with the BAU. Parents never got over the loss of a child. Not really.

They asked her the same questions they had posed to her husband. She, too, shook her head when asked if she had seen anyone watching the neighborhood; she, too, commented that her daughter had accused her parents of watching her and Benny.

Frustrated, Reid turned to Rossi who shrugged. They would get the police to canvass the neighborhood again, but so much time had passed that they would be incredibly lucky if anyone remembered anything.

"I'm sorry," Andrews said. "It looks like we've let you down. And if we've let *you* down, we've let Addie down."

Rossi jumped in. "I know it's natural to

blame yourselves. You have to understand, you didn't have anything to do with what happened to your daughter."

Andrews nodded, but it was clear he didn't believe Rossi. His wife merely appeared dazed.

Reid looked at Rossi and wondered what had gotten into the longtime profiler. Those supportive words were what Reid would have expected from the compassionate Jason Gideon, not the more professionally impersonal David Rossi.

The three of them were about to climb into the SUV and leave what was left of this family to their grief when Mrs. Andrews said, as if to herself, "What about the gray car?"

They all turned to her.

"Pardon?" Rossi asked.

"The gray car," she said. "I remember seeing it last spring, before the . . . before what happened. I thought we were getting a new neighbor, I saw that gray car so much. I saw it around the neighborhood and in the park, oh, three or four times."

"What kind of car?" Tovar asked.

She shrugged. "I don't know cars. Four doors, boxy, gray. That's all I remember."

Rossi asked, "When did you see it last?"

"After what happened . . . the car stopped

89

coming around. I just never saw it again. Or at least I didn't notice it."

Rossi turned to Tovar. "Let's see if we can get tape from any security camera within a five-mile radius. Go back to a month before the crime."

"That's going to be a lot of security video," Tovar said.

"I hope so," Rossi said. "The more video we have, the better chance that someone caught this car on screen."

Mrs. Andrews, vaguely apologetic, said, "It might not be anything."

Rossi nodded. "That's true. Or, you might have seen the assailant stalking the neighborhood."

Mrs. Andrews looked stricken. "You mean . . . I could have *saved* her. . . ."

"No! You had no way to know. What's suspicious about a gray car? And that's the way he wanted it. This is a predator we're dealing with. He's made it his job to blend in . . . and he's good at it."

The mother and father did not appear terribly reassured by Rossi's words.

The profiler seemed to sense it. "Hey, it's our job to catch this guy," Rossi said. "We're good at that, too."

Andrews gave Rossi a stricken look. "But what if he's better than you?"

Rossi gave the man a crooked smile that Reid had previously seen the older man flash only on talk shows.

"Trust me," Rossi said, "he's not."

CHAPTER THREE:
JULY 28
WAUCONDA, ILLINOIS

Nearing five o'clock that afternoon, as Rand Road turned into Main Street to curve around Bangs Lake, Supervisory Special Agent Jennifer Jareau could see, between the buildings, boats and jet skis tearing across the middle of the lake. She could also see, within section areas nearer the beach, swimmers and sunbathers.

Hotchner had the wheel while Lorenzon navigated them through the town of twelve and a half thousand souls. As they eased around to the three hundred block, Lorenzon said, "Over there, on the right. You can park in front."

Hotchner heeled the Tahoe to the curb in front of a one-story, flat-roofed brick building with a big window on either side of the door, a sign proclaiming it the Wauconda Police Department. They got out of the SUV, then made their way toward the building, Hotchner in the lead and Lorenzon pausing in gentlemanly fashion to allow Jareau to go in front of him.

The Midwest, she thought. *Gotta love it. . . .*

When they walked in, Jareau thought the place looked more like a renovated post office than a modern day police station, noting in particular the long black counter dividing the room: most other departments across the country had erected bulletproof glass to separate the police from the populace. This memo had not reached Wauconda.

Behind the counter, several desks were spread out in open bullpen fashion, some with uniformed cops sitting at them, some not. Occasional doors around the perimeter of the bullpen indicated offices, though others obviously led to other parts of the building.

A diminutive brunette wearing a Wauconda PD uniform rose from a desk and approached the counter, planting herself opposite Jareau. The officer, whose name tag read JAMES, asked, "May I help you?" The woman, younger even than Jareau, had her hair tied up and regarded them skeptically with big brown doe eyes that dominated her face.

Jareau flashed her credentials. "I'm SSA Jennifer Jareau with the FBI's behavioral unit. This is Supervisory Special Agent In Charge Hotchner, and that's Detective Lorenzon from Chicago PD."

"The murders," Officer James said, and while her voice had a typical cop matter-of-factness, something hushed was in there, too.

"That's right," Jareau said, keeping it friendly. "How did you know that's why we were here?"

"I've been on the job in Wauconda for over two years, Agent Jareau, and I've never so much as sniffed the FBI. Two girls die, and now I'm looking at two agents and a Chicago PD detective, no less. I don't need a gold shield to do the math on that equation. You'll want Denson."

"Denson?" Jareau asked.

"Jake Denson. He's the lead detective and crime scene analyst on the case."

"He does both jobs?"

James nodded. "We're a small department. Most of the detectives have been to crime scene class. Saves the town money and manpower."

Jareau asked, "Is Detective Denson here?"

"Let me see," James said. She walked back to her desk, and punched buttons on her desk phone. She waited a few seconds, then said, "Jake, it's Ellie, out front. There's some

FBI people and a Chicago detective here to see you."

She listened for a moment, then hung up and said to them, "He'll be here within five minutes. Sit down if you like."

But they chose to stand and, anyway, the wait was more like two minutes before a tall, sinewy man with a shaved head and a prominent nose came through a door to their right, moving with considerable purpose of stride. He swung open the gate at the far end of counter and approached them.

Wearing a blue work shirt, jeans, and black Rockys, Denson looked more like a construction worker than a detective — or he would have if construction workers packed nine-millimeter automatics on their right hips. He had dark eyes set in a perpetual squint and bore the thin-lipped half smirk of someone who was pretty sure he knew something you didn't. His ears were pressed flat against his skull and he carried himself as if every move, every breath, was about something.

He picked out Jareau. "Detective Jacob Denson. What can I do for you?"

Hotchner stepped forward. "I'm Supervisory Special Agent In Charge Aaron Hotchner."

"In charge of what exactly?" Denson asked, eyeballing Hotchner now.

"The Behavioral Analysis Unit team helping investigate."

Denson gave a little chuckle. "Well, now. I've heard of you — profilers. But my understanding is you people have to be asked aboard a case. And, all due respect, I don't remember asking."

Hotchner smiled — Jareau knew of no one who could summon a smaller or chillier smile than her boss. "You've had a killing in your community that fits in with several that have been committed in other nearby jurisdictions."

"Okay," Denson said, and shrugged. "So?"

"We're here to help oversee a joint task force to share information and bring this killer to justice."

"Thanks, but no thanks."

"Maybe you don't understand," Hotchner said. "We're offering our help."

Shaking his head, Denson said, "No, I followed you just fine. Even though you think we're all stumbling around in the dark out here in the boonies, local cops smack dab in Flyover Country — some of us actually understand English, even if we do move our lips when we read."

Jareau's enthusiasm for the Midwest

was fading.

"We're getting off on the wrong foot, somehow," Hotchner said, his hands shooting up in a stop gesture. "I didn't mean in any way to suggest you weren't on top of this crime. It's just that your crime is one of a series of crimes, by the same UnSub, and —"

"Unknown Subject, right? That kind of jargon supposed to impress me, Agent Hotchner?"

"No. Not at all . . ."

"Right," Denson said bitterly. "Well, here's the reality of the situation. I don't put up with the condescending attitude you feds take. And that's not *all* you take — you waltz in, take all our information, all our hard work, then you take something else: all the credit. Bullshit, boys and girls. Not this time. Not on my watch. This is our case, and we'll catch the killer ourselves, thanks very much."

Other cops behind the counter turned their way now, listening to the detective's controlled rant. Some even smiled.

Jareau knew that many cops felt the same resentment that Denson had just articulated. This anger wasn't reserved just for the FBI, either. She had heard similar sentiments expressed about the ATF, DEA, and the Secret Service, even the Peace Corps. No one seemed immune from the wrath of locals who felt they provided the inspiration, perspiration, and dedication, while the feds provided consternation and accepted all the congratulations.

"That's not how we do things," Hotchner said. "We don't take over investigations. We consult."

Denson's grin couldn't have been nastier. "Really? So then, I take it *I'd* be heading up this task force you mentioned?"

Seeing that Hotchner was crashing and burning with the local detective, Jareau decided that maybe this needed a softer touch.

Quietly, smiling gently, she asked, "Detective Denson, is there somewhere more private we could talk?"

He said, "No."

She removed the smile. "All right. Then why don't we meet with you and your chief, and *then* you can make your decision. I left a message about this on the chief's phone, before we flew out — he may be expecting us."

Denson stared at her with something approaching open contempt. She was not used to having a man look at her that way — an attractive woman with considerable diplomatic skills, Jareau had to work not to be taken aback.

Denson was saying, "You want to get to my chief because you think *he'll* be easier to deal with? Well, good luck."

"That's not it at all, Detective."

"Isn't it?" the detective snapped. "Let's see. Come along."

He returned to the short gate and went through, stopped and looked back.

The trio hadn't moved.

"You coming?" Denson asked.

Jareau turned to Hotchner, asked the question with her eyes, and her supervisor nodded.

She led the way, Hotchner and Lorenzon close behind as they followed Denson across the bullpen and through a door leading to a short corridor.

The bald detective led them to the last door on the right, a corner office. The sign on the door said CHIEF LEONARD OLIVER.

Denson knocked, opened it and, as he entered, said, "Chief, FBI's here."

"What do *they* want?"

"They want to talk to you. I don't seem to be able to satisfy them. Supposedly they called ahead, left a message."

Jareau didn't wait for the exchange to go any further, and came on through the door.

The office was good-size, the desk on their left in front of a wide window overlooking the parking lot on the building's east side. Two chairs sat in front of the desk. Various diplomas and other framed citations filled most of the walls, and some framed family photos sat on the desktop, but no decorative touches asserted themselves in this no-nonsense office. Jareau was not a profiler herself, but she didn't have to be one to know that this stark space reflected the personality of its tenant.

Behind the desk sat the chief, his hands flat on the desk, his face a blank mask. The brown hair on his blocky head was parted, laser straight. His eyes were dark blue and clear and moved little as he took in his guests, a doll's eyes. His mouth formed a thin line and he had the pallor common to gamblers and bureaucrats.

Jareau watched with interest as the chief's eyes met Hotchner's, the two men immediately starting to size each other up.

Though her sense of time had slowed, Jareau knew only seconds had passed before the chief rose and stretched his hand across his desk to Hotchner.

"Leonard Oliver," their apparently reluctant host said. "Chief here in Wauconda."

Shaking Oliver's hand, Hotchner introduced himself, Jareau and Lorenzon, the latter having stayed mute through all of this so far. When the ceremonies were over, Oliver offered them each a chair, getting Denson to have two brought in for Lorenzon and himself. Denson's chair ended up next to Oliver's desk, separating him from the others. Soon they were all seated.

"What can I do for you?" Oliver asked, his smile perfunctory.

Sitting forward, Hotchner said, "We were hoping we could do something for you."

"Really," Oliver said, still smiling, though his tone wasn't.

Before Hotchner could say anything, Denson jumped in. "They want to take credit for solving the murders of the two girls we found in the preserve."

"Is that so?" Oliver asked.

Hotchner said, "Have you already solved this case, Chief Oliver?"

"No. Of course not."

"Then perhaps Detective Denson could explain how it is we're taking credit for something that hasn't happened yet."

Not liking where this was heading, Jareau smiled and spoke up. "Chief Oliver, if I might? I'm the police liaison here."

Oliver turned to her, his expression slightly amused. Such condescending looks were something Jareau *was* used to. More than one cop, and criminals too for that matter, had made the mistake of underestimating young, pretty Jennifer Jareau; she no longer felt annoyed about such attitudes, knowing they provided her with an advantage.

She stared at the chief as the man gaped goofily at her. Men, she knew, could at times act like little boys, even men in power like the chief here; and she didn't have to have children of her own to know the look a disgusted parent gave a misbehaving child. Seated across from Chief Oliver, she focused that look on him.

Hotchner, for his part, sat silently, letting his agent establish control so she would be able to do her job when he wasn't present.

Finally, the smile slipped from Oliver's face and his eyes met hers squarely. "Police liaison, yes. Go on, Miss, uh . . ."

"Supervisory Special Agent Jareau. But you can call me Agent Jareau. Or JJ, once we start working together. *If* we start working together. Could I outline what we have in mind?"

The chief swallowed. "Go ahead."

"What we propose," she said, "is to help you and your police force join in with other police entities in greater Chicago to bring to ground a vicious killer who has killed elsewhere in the area."

Hotchner said, "And this is a killer who will continue killing, if we don't join together to stop him."

Oliver nodded. "With all due respect, Agent Jareau, Agent Hotchner . . . we've heard all this before — you scratch our back, we'll scratch yours and so on. What we've gotten out of such collaborations is an extremely itchy back."

Jareau said, "We're sorry you've had bad experiences cooperating with federal agencies before but —"

"You're different," he interrupted.

"We are," she said, the words sounding more defensive than she meant them to. "The BAU operates in an advisory capacity. We don't steal credit. We're not interested in credit, just results."

"That we've also heard before, Agent Jareau. You have to understand, we're a small force and our political decisions must be made on a basis of —"

"This is *not* a political decision," she cut in. "This is about stopping a killer."

Oliver bestowed a patient smile, as if he were the parent now, and dealing with a very slow child. "Agent Jareau, as I'm sure Agent Hotchner would tell you, *every* decision is a political decision."

She glanced at Hotchner, whose expression might have been carved out of a chunk of wood.

"I would think," Hotchner said softly, with no inflection whatsoever, "that it would be politically advantageous for you to catch the killer of the two girls in your town."

"You make my point, Agent Hotchner," Oliver said. "It would be politically advantageous for *us* to catch the killer."

"That's why you don't want our support?" Jareau asked. "So you can do this yourself?"

"You don't seem to understand," Oliver said.

"No I don't," Jareau said flatly. "Neither will the family and friends of the next victims."

The chief ignored that. "We're a small department in a small town. Our budget is a tenuous thing. If the feds solve local crimes, the budget goes down. If we solve them, the budget goes up."

Jareau frowned. "This is about money?"

"Most everything is, Agent Jareau."

She shook her head. "The lives of potential victims can't be measured in dollars and cents, Chief Oliver. Are you prepared to let a serial killer run free over fiscal issues?"

Oliver's face reddened and his eyes narrowed as he rose. "We're not idiots here.

We're not 'letting him run free.' We're going to catch this bastard, and when we do, the community will thank *us,* not *you.* When this perp's been caught, whether you do it or we do it, you're outa here — back to D.C. or wherever the hell you come from. We, on the other hand, will still be right here in Wauconda."

Jareau said, "I don't get your point, Chief."

"If *you* catch him, we look like a bunch of Barney Fifes and our budget goes down. If *we* catch him, we're heroes, and the budget goes up." He was almost shouting. "Because, you see, on the average day in our fair little city, when the high-and-mighty FBI isn't around to 'help' and 'support' us? We *still* have crimes to deal with. And for some strange reason, that's an easier task for us if we have enough money to keep *officers* on the goddamn *street!*"

Realizing he was on a rant, Oliver let out a breath and sat down.

Rising as the chief sat, Hotchner said, "Thank you for your time."

Jareau and Lorenzon also rose and followed Hotchner out of the station and back to the SUV. Hotchner climbed behind the wheel, Jareau next to him, Lorenzon in the back.

As they pulled away, Jareau could hold her tongue no longer. "What was *that?*"

"It's something I've run into more than once," Hotchner said. "Never as extreme, maybe. . . ."

Lorenzon said, "Sorry. I should have warned you about some of these outlying suburbs. They want to cover their asses more than they want to solve crimes."

Trying not to sound too critical, Jareau said to the Chicago cop, "I noticed *you* didn't wade in."

"I just couldn't see getting in a pissing contest with those small-minded jerks."

Hotchner sighed. "That doesn't mean his points aren't valid."

Jareau goggled at her boss. "You're *siding* with Oliver and Denson?"

"Not a chance," Hotchner said, driving along the lake where the two girls disappeared. "We're still the best option for catching this killer . . . but I understand what Oliver said about living here after we're gone. He knows his town better than we do. And he doesn't know we were being straight with him about our willingness to give him and his people the credit."

"What are we going to do, then?" Jareau asked. "We can't investigate without being asked in."

"No, we can't," Hotchner said, pulling the SUV into the parking lot on the lake's beachfront. "But there's no law against stopping for a cool drink before we head back to the city."

The beach was nearly deserted, the sun a ghost on the horizon, the lake looking cool and choppy as an evening breeze rolled in. The July heat still hung in the air, but the crowd had gone home for the night and the kids who ran the refreshment stand were pulling umbrellas out of the few tables outside their boxy little concrete building, stacking plastic chairs.

Jareau gave Hotch a look. "Aren't you breaking the rules? Visiting a crime scene when we haven't been invited?"

Shaking his head, as he pulled into a parking spot, Hotchner said, "I'm just thirsty — aren't you?"

"Well, I don't know about JJ," Lorenzon said from the back, "but I'm parched."

With a little half smirk, Jareau said, "I guess I could use a drink, too, although right now I might prefer something a little harder than what that stand offers up."

"You'll settle for lemonade or bottled water," Hotchner said. "Anyway, I'm buying."

"Better hurry," Jareau said. "Looks like

they're about to close up."

"No problem," Hotchner said. "I don't want to spend a lot of time here, anyway. I just want to get the lay of the land."

They got out of the SUV and strode over to the screen-covered service window of the refreshment stand. Behind the counter, a teenaged girl stood smiling. "May I help you?"

She was blonde and perky, even for the late hour, and Jareau couldn't help but remember her own teenage jobs back at East Allegheny High.

Jareau swiftly scanned the menu on the wall behind the young girl. "Lemonade, medium."

"Medium lemonade," the girl said. "Anything else?"

Hotchner leaned in and twitched a smile. "Make that two."

"Three," Lorenzon said, making the Boy Scout sign.

The girl got their drinks. Hotchner paid the bill, then joined Jareau and Lorenzon and their lemonades next to the SUV. *Fitting,* Jareau thought. *We need to make lemonade out of the lemons Chief Oliver and Detective Denson have tossed our way. . . .*

Jareau gave Hotchner a look. "You're not going to ask her if she was working the day the girls disappeared?"

Shaking his head, Hotchner said, "That *would* be crossing the line."

After a quick sip of his drink, Lorenzon looked back toward the building. "I'm not FBI. I could ask her."

"You're working with us now," Hotchner said. "That would constitute breaking the rules, as well."

"What the hell," Lorenzon said with a smile. "I'll just bend 'em a little — they won't break."

"Not this time," Hotchner said, easy but firm. "If we want to win Chief Oliver over to the side of a joint task force, going behind his back is not the way to get that done."

"What do you call *this?*" Lorenzon asked, gesturing to himself and them.

"I call this," Hotchner said, "three coworkers sharing a nonalcoholic drink at the end of a hard day."

"Riiight," Lorenzon said.

Jareau watched as Hotchner sipped his lemonade through a straw, and for one brief moment she could imagine her stoic boss a young man standing on a beach like this, as human as the next guy or girl. But it was just one brief moment. . . .

Hotch was slowly scanning the lake, then the beach, then the parking lot. A great deal of the lake's perimeter was wooded. On the south and east sides businesses and houses lined the shore and up the west side were a small marina and more homes. The beach was large enough for a couple of hundred sunbathers as well as swimmers, Jet Ski enthusiasts and boaters. The parking lot was smallish, room for maybe fifty cars, tops. As the sun set and the shadows thickened, Jareau could have sworn she felt the killer somewhere out there. . . .

As they loaded back into the SUV, Lorenzon asked, "So, what did we just do?"

"We learned," Hotchner said.

"Learned what?"

Shaking his head as he put on his seat belt, Hotchner said, "Not much."

He started up the Tahoe.

"But *something*," Jareau said.

As they began the long trip back to the city, Hotchner said, "We learned there are something like one-hundred places our UnSub could have observed his prey from."

"A *hundred?*" Lorenzon asked.

"Easily. With high-powered binoculars, he could have been anywhere around the perimeter of the lake."

"And that tells us what?"

Hotchner drew in a breath. Let it out. "It may tell us he was particular. He was trolling for a specific kind of victim — he picked two girls who were at the lake that afternoon, unaccompanied girls. He might have watched all day waiting for just the right set of victims to satisfy his needs."

Lorenzon asked, "What were his needs?"

"Not the normal needs of a serial killer, if the word 'normal' can be applied. Not sex, although obviously murderous rage. He was coolly seeking two young women like Janice Ott and Denise Naslund, the two young women Ted Bundy abducted from Lake Sammamish State Park."

Lorenzon's voice was hushed. "And he found them."

"He found them." Hotchner glanced at the detective. "The thing is, with Bundy, several people saw Janice Ott talking to a well-dressed young man with a cast on one arm. One witness even heard her call him 'Ted.' Did Denson mention to you anything about that? A man with a cast on one arm, spotted at the lake that afternoon?"

Lorenzon said, "Denson didn't talk to me — he spoke to Tovar. But Tovar never said anything about witnesses or a cast, either. Judging from our reception by Denson and the chief, though, I wouldn't exactly be shocked if the Wauconda boys had neglected to share all they knew with Tovar, either."

Jareau shook her head and said, "You would think that *someone* must have seen him."

Hotchner lifted his eyebrows in a sort of shrug. "This guy is very good at his job."

"His *job?*" Lorenzon asked.

"On one level, that's what it is to him. This is what he does, it's what defines him. He is a master at blending in. Someone probably *did* see him, but they don't even know it."

"You have to ask the right questions to find out that kind of thing," Lorenzon said. "And I have no particular faith that Detective Denson did."

"There were probably lots of people at the beach that day," Jareau said. "Still, our UnSub picked out two victims and managed to abduct them, without anyone noticing."

"Which means," Hotchner said, "he's a smooth operator."

Lorenzon said, "He's smart, he's smooth, he plans things well and he blends in. So we do know a thing or two, at that. But how in the hell are we going to catch him?"

Hotchner glanced into the rearview mirror. "If we do our job, we may be able to catch him before he strikes again."

"And if not?"

Hotchner's sigh must have started down around his toes. "Then we have to make sure we're there when he makes a mistake."

Lorenzon was shaking his head. "What if he doesn't make a mistake?"

"He will," Hotchner said. "He will. They all do."

Hotch was right — Jareau's experience told her as much. But experience also told her that an UnSub could take his time, making that mistake. . . .

He sat in his car watching them. They had strolled across the parking lot, got into an SUV and pulled out. He'd let them get out in front, then eased in behind them. They were headed for the city now, but he hoped they would give him a chance to take care of business before they got into the witness-filled streets of Chicago.

Night had fallen and their headlights were on as were his, but in this traffic he knew he would not look suspicious as he trailed them. Once they hit the expressway, things would get more complicated and it would be harder to tail them without their noticing. At least at this hour. During rush hour, when traffic was at a standstill, he could practically take care of business while they were sitting in line waiting for someone to move.

He could tell now, they were headed for the expressway; and he started to wonder if tonight was going to be a missed opportunity. He hoped not, even though he was already following the SUV onto the ramp of eastbound I-90. Trying to keep his karma good, he pulled out his cell phone and hit speed dial number two — home.

She answered on the second ring. "Hello," she said, her voice a little frosty.

"A late job came in, honey — sorry."

"How long will you be?"

He smiled at the thought of what lay before him if things went his way. "It could take quite a while. I'll just get something to eat on the way home later."

"The boys will want to stay up and wait for you."

"Tell them to go ahead to bed. I'll take the day off tomorrow, and we'll do something as a family."

"Really? Do you mean that? Darling, that would be wonderful. . . ."

She sounded almost giddy, like when they first had met. For a moment he felt a twinge of nostalgia. "Sure," he said, trying to sound magnanimous.

"That'll be great. Should I tell the boys? I don't want to tell them if there's any chance you'll cancel. . . ."

The SUV sped up a little and switched lanes. He kept his eyes on the rear bumper but did not change lanes himself.

"Sure, go ahead and tell them."

"I love you," she said.

He mumbled something and pushed the button to end the call. He knew that by the time he got home, much later if he had his way, she would have the whole day planned out.

The SUV was in the fast lane now, pulling away. Switching lanes, he gunned it and his car slowly eased closer, two cars between him and his prey.

He eased right a lane, closing in a little more, but not getting too close. The SUV crossed over two lanes and instantly the killer knew where they were going. They would take the next exit and the SUV would go to one of the three motels that sat on corners of the intersection at the bottom of the ramp.

Happily, he watched as the SUV did exactly as he had supposed it would, as if he controlled the vehicle with his mind. In his mind, he picked one of the three motels as he followed the SUV down the ramp. The vehicle turned right then turned again into the motel he had chosen.

The rush was great — they were following his every telepathic command. He mentally told them to stop and let out the passenger in the backseat. When the SUV pulled under the overhang outside the front door and stopped, he pulled his car around and parked in a nearby spot.

The passenger climbed out of the SUV. He was a white man in his late forties, a little overweight, and he carried a briefcase in a meaty paw. He wore a navy polo and navy blue slacks. He was a salesman of some kind, who had just been wined and dined by customers or vendors or some business contact and they had just dropped him at his motel. He was in motion before the SUV pulled away.

And by the time the SUV was on the same expressway that another SUV bearing two FBI agents and a Chicago detective had taken several hours before, the mark was near the killer's car . . . and before the coworkers who'd dropped the salesman off had reached the next exit, the killer had the victim stuffed in the trunk of his car and was calmly driving away from the motel with his unwilling passenger.

CHAPTER FOUR:
JULY 29
CHICAGO, ILLINOIS

Emily Prentiss, in black slacks and black blouse, knew that by the end of this muggy summer day she would be cursing the choice of color. Nonetheless, she also knew black aided and abetted her sleek professional look and nicely complemented her lithe figure.

Not that she was showing off, but this was her first trip back to the Chicago area since joining the BAU. She knew that more than one agent in the field office here had been against her transfer, seeing it as a promotion she didn't deserve. In particular, some of the Old Boy's Club, who still had issues with women rising in the Bureau, took her making it to Quantico as a personal affront. She would look her best today, and the naysayers could take that as a personal affront, too, if they liked.

The team had rooms at the Hilton downtown because of a favorable government rate and its proximity to the Chicago field office. If her mother had been along, the accommodations would have been at the ritzier Drake or possibly, if Mom was going tourist, the Palmer House. The Hilton was fine with Prentiss; with the BAU, she had checked into such varied inns as Holiday, Ramada and Comfort, and survived just fine.

After clipping her holster to her belt, Prentiss checked her pistol to make sure a shell was in the pipe and the safety was on. She had drawn her weapon in the line of duty only a few times, but this girl abided by the Boy Scout motto: be prepared.

Ten minutes later, seated in the hotel's restaurant, working on her second cup of coffee and the morning crossword (a stress-reliever she had learned from Jason Gideon before his unexpected retirement), Prentiss tried to clear her mind for the upcoming day.

A thought kept intruding, though: she missed him . . . Gideon. Even though Rossi seemed to be fitting in, Gideon was the teammate who had treated her least like the new kid in school when she had joined the BAU. He'd had a warm, compassionate way about him, lending a sort of spiritual center to their relentless work, which was absent from the team now. Even though Gideon had been gone for a while, she still missed his mentoring, his kindness, his presence.

"Did you catch the crossword bug from Jason?"

She looked up to see Hotchner standing over her wearing a gentle smile. Smiling back, she nodded. "Please — have a seat."

Hotchner sat and a waitress came over.

"Coffee, orange juice, and a bagel," Hotchner said.

The waitress nodded and disappeared.

"Not exactly a power breakfast," Prentiss said.

"I don't eat much in the morning."

"I know. Why send the blood rushing to your stomach, when our kind of mornings usually require blood to the brain."

His smile blossomed, a rarity in his grave countenance. "I don't disagree."

Before they'd finished their coffee, the rest of the team joined them. As usual, Reid looked like a refugee from a prep school whose roommate insisted he dress in the dark. Sharper by some distance, Morgan wore a pullover sweater and dark dress slacks, a page out of a *GQ* salute to law enforcement. Meanwhile, Jareau had gone with a gray pantsuit that played up her professionalism (and played down her shape), and work-casual Rossi wore jeans, a sky blue button-down and a red tie under a dark blazer.

Good mornings were exchanged, followed by light talk of how people slept and other such trivia; but no words of work. Yet Prentiss knew every one of the minds in this group was already going over what little they knew about this new antagonist.

Knowing one of these predators was at large, and active, when you were one of the team called in to stop him, presented a variety of stress known to few. If they moved too fast, a perp could walk on any number of technicalities; if they moved too slow, another victim might lose his or her life before the BAU could stop the predator.

Sometimes, *more* than one victim. . . .

So they sipped coffee, nibbled bagels and pretended to be just another group of coworkers about to head in to the office.

Taking the SUVs, they drove west on Roosevelt Road to the field office just west of the University of Illinois at Chicago and the Rush University Medical Center. The FBI was housed in an antiseptic twelve-story monument to glass and steel at 211 West Roosevelt Road.

By the time the team piled out of their SUVs in the parking lot, Lorenzon and Tovar had joined up with them. Soon they were in the lobby, which had a metal detector at the front door (added after the Oklahoma City bombing in 1995) with fire hydrant concrete columns outside (after September 11). Once they had negotiated the building's defenses, they were met by the Special Agent In Charge of the field office.

The SAIC, Raymond Himes, was a tall, broad-shouldered African-American with black hair cut close to the scalp. He wore a gray single-breasted suit over a white shirt with a red-and-blue tie, very sharp, very professional.

He greeted them all with handshakes and smiles, reserving an exceptionally warm smile for his old coworker, Prentiss. Like her, Himes had faced prejudice in his rise within the Bureau and the two had been kindred spirits.

"I'm sorry," Himes said, "that I couldn't arrange to see you folks yesterday."

Hotchner said, "We wanted to get right out to the crime scenes."

Detective Tovar, anxious, asked Hotch, "How did that go, anyway?"

"We'll save that for the meeting," Hotchner said, with just enough of a smile to make that seem less a dismissal.

Prentiss could tell from the detective's expression that he didn't like the tone of that.

Himes said, "I've got you set up in a conference room on the second floor."

"Sounds fine," Hotchner said.

"And if you need anything," the SAIC said, "my office is on the eleventh floor."

"Thanks."

The team followed Himes through the large atrium lobby to a bank of elevators, then rode with him to the second floor. As the doors eased open, they found a young man waiting for them. He was tall, thin, wore glasses and his straight brown hair was parted on the side. To Prentiss, he looked less like an FBI agent and more like a CPA, one barely older than Reid. Behind him, cubicles with busy agents spread out across the floor.

The team filed out of the elevator, Himes remaining inside.

"This is Special Agent Brian Kohler," Himes said, holding a button down to keep the elevator door open. "If you need anything, he's your man."

"Thank you," Hotchner said.

"Brian, show the team to conference room B, will you?"

"Yes, sir," Kohler said, his voice effervescent with youthful enthusiasm.

Prentiss was hoping this wasn't Kohler's first day on the job. . . .

Himes, in the elevator, released the button, and gave them a going away smile. "Don't forget, eleventh floor."

The doors whispered shut and he was gone. Prentiss knew and liked Himes, but her sense was that he'd just rolled out a very tiny red carpet and disappeared. The promise of support from this field office did not fill her with confidence.

With Hotchner at the fore, they followed the young agent down the hall until he led them into a conference room on the left side of the corridor.

"Will there be anything else?" Kohler asked.

He might have been a bellboy fishing for a tip.

"No," Hotchner said.

Prentiss covered for her boss with, "Thank you. Appreciate it."

"Not at all!" the young agent said, and he, too, disappeared. Enthusiastically disappeared, but disappeared.

The room was dominated by a teardrop-shaped table surrounded by a dozen chairs. A white board on one wall, bulletin boards along another one, and a video screen on a third made this an instant home away from home. Windows filled two-thirds of the fourth wall, the view toward the lake. Rossi slanted the blinds, making seeing out hard but allowing light to filter in.

Jareau started filling the bulletin board with crime scene photos. While Reid set up his laptop, Morgan made three columns on the white board and labeled each with the name of the killer being copied.

Prentiss set up her laptop, too, using it to establish contact with the team's digital intelligence officer, Penelope Garcia, back in Quantico. Blonde, pleasantly plump, with dark-framed glasses and a thrift-shop chic fashion sense, Garcia was just a little less quirky than a David Lynch movie, but also a brilliant technician who had frequently come through for them.

"Garcia," Prentiss said.

"Hey," the perky computer expert said, her image on the laptop screen lighting up with her infectious smile.

"Anything?"

"I'm still digging, especially on trying to identify the victim in the barrel. Unfortunately, there are enough missing people in that part of the world to make it tricky, particularly without something more from the Cook County coroner."

"Stay on it," Prentiss said.

"It's what I do," Garcia said, ever chipper in the face of mountains of work.

Prentiss looked up as Hotchner said, "All right, we've settled in — now let's get started."

Taking seats around the table, surrounded by the evidence of the killings of the monster they were hunting, the team hunkered down.

Hotchner began by explaining that the Wauconda PD would not be joining the task force.

"You gotta be kidding me," Tovar said, rolling his eyes. "If they didn't want in, why would Denson give me those crime scene photos?"

Morgan said, "It's the bad company you keep."

The short Hispanic detective blinked at that. "Huh?"

A mirthless grin settled on Hotchner's face. "What Morgan means is . . . sharing information with another cop isn't the same thing as taking it to the FBI. Some law enforcement agencies see us as Big Brother marching in to take over . . . and take credit."

Tovar shifted in his seat. "Maybe if I *talked* to him . . ."

Shaking his head, Hotchner said, "I wouldn't bother. They don't believe we can help them, and that's their choice."

Lorenzon said, "It's a stupid choice." The athletic-looking African-American cop shifted in his seat, a look of disgust on his trimly bearded face. "A rinkydink piddling outfit like Wauconda, turning down first-string help like the BAU? Crazy."

But Tovar sighed and shrugged. His eyes were on Hotchner. "Tate's probably right that the Wauconda PD is foolish not to accept outside help. But, truthfully? I don't know for sure what the BAU can do to help us with this mess. I just know we need help, and Tate knowing Morgan here, well, that's how we came to call on you."

"Understood," Hotchner said. "So let's get on the same page, shall we? . . . Why can we help? Because of one simple truth: behavior reveals personality. The more we know about an UnSub's personality, the easier it is to apprehend him."

"To a street cop," Tovar said, "this all sounds like guesswork mixed in with mumbo jumbo. No offense meant."

"None taken," Hotchner said with a nod. "For all the talk that what we do is new, behavioral science has been around for over a hundred years — in fiction, at least, if not in reality."

"Fiction?" Lorenzon asked. "Aren't we in the fact business?"

Reid joined in. "In 1841, Edgar Allan Poe's protagonist, C. Auguste Dupin, in the short story, 'The Murders In The Rue Morgue,' was a behavioral analyst, even if he wasn't called that. Poe wrote, 'Deprived of ordinary resources, the analyst throws himself into the spirit of his opponent, identifies himself therewith, and not infrequently sees thus, at a glance, the sole methods by which he may seduce into error or hurry into miscalculation.' That's essentially what we do."

Lorenzon's eyes went to his friend Morgan. "What the hell?"

Morgan flashed his killer smile. "We think like they think. And sometimes, *knowing* how they think, we can make them screw up . . . so we can catch them."

"After Poe," Hotchner said, "Sir Arthur Conan Doyle created Sherlock Holmes, who was not only one of the first crime scene investigators, but also a behavioral analyst. And as for fact over fiction, Doyle based Holmes on Dr. Joseph Bell's diagnostic techniques, and later Doyle used these very methods himself in a number of pioneering criminal investigations."

Interested despite himself, Tovar asked, "So, when did profiling come into the *real* world?"

"How old are you?" Hotchner asked.

Tovar gave him an odd look. "Sixty-one, why?"

"You may be old enough to remember. Lorenzon, you're way too young to recall the mad bomber, aren't you?"

Lorenzon blinked. "Mad bomber?"

"George Metesky. In New York, from 1940 until his arrest in 1957, Metesky operated as the so-called 'Mad Bomber.' "

Reid picked right up from his boss. "Metesky planted over thirty devices, some of which exploded, some of which did not. The important thing, from our perspective? Is that the police couldn't catch him. Even though he sent bragging letters, and they had entire bombs to examine — in the cases of those that did not go off — traditional law enforcement could not seem to solve the crimes. Finally, in desperation, they went to a psychiatrist — Dr. James A. Brussel — and gave him the case files."

Lorenzon asked, "And the shrink came up with something?"

Reid nodded. "After combing through the material, the doctor came up with some startling conclusions — he predicted that the UnSub was paranoid, hated his father, obsessively loved his mother, and lived in a city in Connecticut."

"Brother," Tovar said.

Reid continued. "Brussel insisted that the UnSub had a grudge against Commonwealth Edison and was probably a former employee of that firm. And the doctor went on to say that the man was heavyset, middle-aged, foreign born, Roman Catholic, single, and lived with . . . 'brother' is right . . . a brother or sister. Finally, Brussel told the police that when the UnSub was found, he would be wearing a double-breasted suit — buttoned."

Tovar asked, "How close was the doc?"

Hotchner said, "The police came up with a former Con Ed employee: George Metesky. The only thing Brussel missed on was that the UnSub lived with *two* maiden sisters, not one. When they arrested Metesky, he changed into a double-breasted suit — buttoned."

"You're making this up," Tovar said.

Hotchner smiled a little and said, "No. That was chapter and verse from the history of our field. It wasn't until almost twenty years later — 1972 — when the BAU was initially formed with eleven agents. Since then, we've been growing and learning more and more about our craft. Agents like David Rossi, here, built it into what we have today. It's not guesswork, Hilly, or mumbo jumbo, either . . . rather, science based on research, study, and hard-earned field experience. We've had a lot more successes than failures, and I fully expect us to bring this killer to justice as well."

"Okay," Tovar said. "How do we do that?"

"The first question," Rossi said, "is whether or not to suppress the pictures."

"That's a question?" Lorenzon asked, alarmed. "Why in the hell would you even *consider* making them public?"

Rossi said, "To press him. If we can make the UnSub uncomfortable enough, we might force him into making a mistake."

"Okay, I can see that," Lorenzon admitted, "but I don't see how the pictures fit into the catching-the-bastard equation."

"We can use the pictures or not, really," Rossi said, and shrugged. "But if we do, they'll be part of publicizing the mistakes he's already made."

Tovar blinked at Rossi. "He's made mistakes?"

But it was Reid who responded. "Not mistakes that will help us apprehend him — not in the sense of direct evidence, anyway.

But he *has* made mistakes in the sense that his reenactments have been inexact in numerous ways."

Lorenzon asked, "Why's that significant?"

Hotchner said, "It goes back to what I said earlier. Behavior reveals personality."

"Guys." Tovar raised both hands in surrender. "You're losing me. You keep talking in circles."

"We really aren't," Prentiss said and gave the detective a friendly smile. "What we're saying is that this UnSub has gone to great lengths to re-create these crimes — wouldn't you agree?"

"Sure."

"So what does that tell you about him?"

Tovar shrugged. "That he's a goddamn lunatic?"

Morgan shook his head and said, "You're expressing an emotional reaction to the crime."

"You're damned straight I am!"

Morgan gestured with open palms. "Take emotion out of it. Look at the behavior purely for what it is . . . and how it reflects the personality of the UnSub."

Tovar ran a hand over his face, a trail of confusion left in its wake. The older detective looked for help to the younger one, who could only shrug. Frustrated, Tovar turned back to Hotchner. "In English, please."

"If you want to understand the artist," Hotchner said, "you have to look at the painting."

The comparison was one Hotchner had shared with Prentiss, and that he'd probably told them all at some point or other. What Prentiss didn't know was that Hotchner had heard it from Rossi when Hotch first joined the BAU.

Hotchner nodded at JJ, who clicked a button on her laptop, bringing the Chicago Heights crime scene onto the large video screen.

"Set aside any emotional response," Hotchner said. "Now, look at the photo and tell me what you can deduce about the Un-Sub."

Two young people, shot to death in a parked car on a rain-soaked blacktop, a crumpled piece of paper on the road near the driver's door.

Tovar studied the photo for several long moments. "We know he stalked the neighborhood, and probably the victims."

"Which tells us?"

"He's careful?" Tovar asked, a kid guessing at the right answer in algebra class.

"Okay," Morgan said. "What else?"

Tovar thought a while. Then he said, "Dr.

Reid says the perp went to the driver's window, because the male was a greater threat. Another sign that he's careful."

"Good. Anything else?"

"He dropped the piece of paper right where Berkowitz did the same. Means he'd studied the original crime. He mimicked it."

"That's right," Hotchner said. "Which shows?"

"He's . . . detail oriented?"

"Right," Rossi said. "Now, what do you know about most careful, detail-oriented people?"

"Mostly, they're a-holes," Lorenzon piped in.

Rossi chuckled. "And a lot of them are cops — but we'll set aside the chicken and the egg discussion on that point." To Tovar, he said, "What else about detail-oriented types?"

"Well, they're conservative," Tovar said. "Not necessarily in the political sense, but . . . in that they don't usually take big risks."

"I agree," Rossi said. "So, our UnSub is taking a huge risk by shooting two people on a public street. Why would he do that?"

Tovar asked, "Isn't that the question *we* brought to *you?* One of 'em, anyway?"

Nodding, Rossi said, "The big answer will come when we have the profile fully developed. But for right now, in just this Chicago Heights case? He took the risk because he was relatively certain he could commit the deed and escape. He had it well planned out. He had studied not just Berkowitz, but every aspect of *this* attack as well. Escape routes — what to do if things went wrong. He might even have gone so far as to make bogus 911 calls, so he could gauge police response time. This UnSub doesn't blow his nose without planning it out."

"Oh-kay," Tovar said, eyes narrow.

Rising, pacing now, occasionally glancing at the grim photo on the screen, Rossi said, "Even though this careful, detail-oriented UnSub studied and planned every detail of the crime, he made a mistake."

"You keep *saying* that," Tovar said. "What the hell was it?"

Reid stopped and said, "Remember what I said when we first looked at this photo? He went to the wrong side of the car."

"For safety sake, he did."

"But for re-creating a famous crime he didn't," Reid said. "Berkowitz always went to the passenger side — the women were the objects of his anger. He shot *them* first. So our UnSub made a mistake."

"How does that matter?"

Rossi said, "It's something we can use against him."

Shaking his head, Tovar said, "I still don't follow that."

"Go back to careful, detail-oriented people in general. How do they usually react when someone points out they're wrong?"

Lorenzon said, "They get well and truly pissed off."

"Uh huh," Rossi said with a devilish little grin. "And what if the person who points out their mistake is someone that our detail-oriented friend considers an intellectual inferior?"

Lorenzon gave up half a grin. "They get *way* the hell bent out of shape."

Tovar was frowning. "This guy thinks he's *smarter* than us?"

Rossi's short laugh was as bitter as it was humorless. "This UnSub thinks he's smarter than both of you, Detectives Lorenzon and Tovar, and everybody you work with in your PDs. He's smarter than us, too, smarter than the whole FBI, and — perhaps most important — smarter even than the killers he's mimicking. He thinks he can do their crimes *better* than they did. He imagines he'll get away with it. They all got caught, but he won't — in his freedom, that makes him the king, and the famous killers he's imitating are his court."

Hotchner said, "Now, take a person with that much ego, and all the other qualities we've outlined, and how do you suppose he would react to us pointing out his mistakes?"

Tovar said, "But maybe they aren't mistakes. If he's trying to do these murders better than the originals, maybe he views what you call mistakes as improvements."

Hotchner nodded. "That's valid. So these aren't mistakes — they are personal flourishes, improvements. And so how would he react to his improvements being viewed as errors?"

"He'd go batshit," Lorenzon said.

Rossi grinned. "That's as good a technical term for it as I could come up with myself."

Morgan said, "He also made a mistake — or maybe an improvement — with the women in Wauconda."

Lorenzon frowned. "Which was?"

Prentiss jumped in. "When Ted Bundy committed the original crime, he also lured two women away from the lake, killing them, burying them in the woods. The difference is that Bundy placed a body part of a third female victim — one who was never identified — in the grave with the other two.

Our UnSub overlooked that detail."

Rossi said, "Let's call it another mistake."

Tovar sat forward. "And you want to use a public relations campaign citing this madman's mistakes to drive him into a frenzy?"

Rossi shrugged. "Once we figure out how to know when, where, and who he might lash out against, perhaps. If we can force him into the open, and into making a real mistake, we'll catch him. The key is to do it without losing another victim."

The two detectives stared at him.

Hotchner drew their attention, saying, "That's why we're not suggesting any publicity campaign at this time. When we know more about our UnSub, we may want to try that, to draw him out. Not yet, though."

Rossi said, "I *can* tell you a couple more things about him, however."

The detectives looked up at Rossi expectantly.

"Even though this UnSub is copying crimes, his rage is as real and as great as those who originally committed them. It would be a mistake to read this as a cold-blooded killer playing copycat from a prepared script."

"If it's rage," Lorenzon said, "why the elaborate re-creations? Why not just lash out?"

"This rage is nothing new to our UnSub," Rossi said. "He's felt this fury for a long time, possibly his whole life. But now something has fueled him to act out that fury. If we find the stressor that triggered all this, we find the beginning of the chain."

Tovar frowned. "Are you saying he's killed more than these five people?"

"It's possible," Rossi said.

"Oh hell," Lorenzon said.

Rossi looked from one local detective to the other. "I've also seen enough of these cases to know this UnSub is a cop buff — the type that thinks he's smarter than all of us cops combined. So the next thing to be aware of is that almost certainly he'll be injecting himself into this investigation."

"How so?" Lorenzon asked.

"That, I have no idea," Rossi said, then added: "*Yet* . . . But, trust me, he'll find a way. He'll want to know what we know, and he'll want to prove to himself that he's smarter than we are."

Hotchner added, "By insinuating himself in the investigation, the UnSub gains a feeling of power. This reassures his feeling of superiority, when we can't figure out it's him, and he's been right in front of us."

Tilting her head, Prentiss asked, "Were

there gawkers at the Chicago Heights crime scene?"

"There are always some," Tovar said with a nod. "Mostly neighbors."

"Possibly the UnSub, too," Prentiss said. "Did you get pictures of the crowd?"

"No . . . I never even thought of it."

Prentiss didn't give him a hard time about that, just asked, "How about Chinatown? Any gawkers there?"

Lorenzon said, "You know there were. Half of Chinatown came around, and a bunch of walk-ups who just happened to be in the neighborhood eating Chinese and buying trinkets."

"Photos of the crowd?"

"I didn't take any, and I didn't specifically ask that any be taken. Someone else might have. Possible TV news footage might cover that. I'll look into it."

"Thanks," Prentiss said. "We might get lucky. If the UnSub shows up to check out what's going on, we might catch a picture of him. If we spot a face at more than one scene, with the locations this far apart? It might just belong to our guy."

"No shit," Tovar said.

"It would be nice if it was that easy," Hotchner said dryly. "My guess is it won't be."

Lorenzon's cell phone chirped. They all turned to him as he yanked it off his belt and checked the number. "My boss," he said. "Better take this." He rose and left the room, all their eyes still on him.

Before Hotchner could start up again, Garcia spoke through the computer. "Emily?"

Prentiss looked at the screen, where Garcia was staring at her with wide, bright eyes. "What?"

"The Cook County ME has just ID'd your body in the barrel."

Garcia had the attention of everyone in the room now.

"Who is he?" Prentiss asked.

"His name is Bobby Edels. He was twenty. The ME had to identify him through dental records."

Hotchner asked, "What do you know about him?"

Garcia said, "He worked at a Fix-It Mate in Mundelein."

"Fix-It Mate?" Reid asked.

"Small chain of home-repair stores," Tovar said. "Dozen or so across the Midwest."

Jareau asked, "And Mundelein?"

"Far northern suburb," Lorenzon said. "No telling how he got from there to Chinatown."

Reid said, "The starting point is *when* he disappeared."

"March twenty-first," Garcia said from the computer. "He was last seen when he clocked out from work that day."

Prentiss frowned. "Almost a month before the shooting in Chicago Heights . . ."

Hotchner said, "He's been at this even longer than we thought."

"Sunshine," Morgan said, looking toward the computer (he and Garcia had a close, joking relationship), "have you got anything else on Edels?"

"His parents live in North Barrington. Cook County has sent officers to inform the family."

"Nothing else?"

"Still digging," Garcia said.

"That's my girl."

Hotchner said, "All right, let's get to work. David, you and Reid visit Edels's parents. Maybe they know something that can help."

Half out of his seat, Tovar said, "I'd like to go with them."

"Fine," Hotchner said. "Prentiss, you work the victimology."

"Yes, sir."

"Morgan, you and Detective Lorenzon hit the Fix-It Mate. Interview Edels's coworkers. See if they have security video of the parking lot that might tell us something."

"You got it," Morgan said.

"JJ, try to keep the media at bay a while longer, and meantime I'll keep going over the material we have, to see if we missed something."

Except for Prentiss and Hotchner, they all rose at once and emptied the conference room to work their assignments. Sneaking a glance at Hotchner, Prentiss noticed that his typically serious expression seemed even more grave.

They were going full bore now, and there would be no rest and not just for the wicked: the team would push from now until they brought the UnSub down.

It was going to be a very long day.

And probably just the first of many . . .

CHAPTER FIVE:
JULY 29
NORTH BARRINGTON,
ILLINOIS

Though Supervisory Special Agent David Rossi had visited scores of families of victims, he found the task never got any easier. Unlike the first round of uniformed officers, detectives and crime scene analysts, profilers arrived after the loved ones had begun to deal with their loss, meaning wounds that were still healing or even recently healed requiring picking at.

On occasion, though, a profiler on the front line of a case could appear in the early hours, when wounds were fresh and so was the information, the latter a plus no matter how painful the former. But the distress of the families could be so severe as to cloud the inquiry, and distract even a hardened investigator.

The air-conditioned car had provided relief from the relentless Midwestern heat and humidity, but as Rossi stepped out into the punishing bright sunshine, he could almost feel his sports jacket's dark color soaking in every ray.

Detective Tovar, who had driven the unmarked Ford, came around to the passenger side as Dr. Spencer Reid got out of the backseat and stepped up next to Rossi.

"Normal middle-class neighborhood," Reid said.

Tovar shook his head. "The more normal the neighborhood," the Hispanic detective said, "the weirder it seems. I mean, you find somebody shot in an alley with his pockets turned inside out, where's the surprise?"

"Every smooth rock in the world," Rossi said, "has worms squirming under it."

Tovar thought about that. Reid just nodded.

They were poised in a quiet neighborhood whose streets were nearly deserted on this Tuesday morning. The worker bees of this middle-class enclave, with their trimmed lawns, well-maintained homes and backyard barbecues, had long since departed to go sit and wait on the freeway, enduring their daily commute to the hive. Theirs was a lifestyle that Rossi, much as he might respect the hard work and good hearts behind it, could never have maintained himself.

Rossi had craved something more, a career that made a difference, a path that included less sameness to each day. That craving had brought him here, to the front door of yet another family who had lost someone to the pointless violence. And in such moments, he could only envy the worker bees.

No police car out front. No family vehicles, either — maybe no one was home. The two-story white clapboard, with green shutters and a single car garage tucked up the driveway on the left-hand side, would have made a nice house to grow up in. A silver maple on one side and an oak on the other flanked a sidewalk that divided a freshly mowed front yard.

"Another Pleasant Valley Sunday," Rossi muttered.

"What?" Tovar said. "It's Tuesday."

Reid said quietly, "Monkees. Goffin and King. 1967. Got to number three on the *Billboard* chart."

Rossi gave Reid a sideways look that said, *Stop that.*

Tovar got out his cell phone and made a quick call. He spoke for a moment, then clicked off. Turning to Rossi and Reid, he said, "The ME says the family's been notified."

"That's a small blessing for us," Rossi said and started up the front walk, the other two behind him. "But it still won't be easy."

The house had a three-step porch up to an aluminum front screen door with an old English "E" embedded into scrollwork.

Rossi rang the bell.

They waited a long moment and, just as Rossi was about to press the button again, the inside door swung open and a pale, pouchy male face peered out.

The man was about Rossi's age, somewhat taller than the FBI agent, his hair grayer, his body softer, his eyes red-rimmed from crying. His thin lips quivered as he said, "You gentlemen look official."

"We are," Rossi said and smiled just a little. "Mr. Edels?"

"Yes, sir."

Holding up his credentials, Rossi said, "David Rossi with the FBI. This is Supervisory Special Agent Dr. Spencer Reid, and that's Chicago Heights police detective Hilly Tovar."

Edels nodded at each as the introductions were made.

Rossi asked, "May we come in, sir? We need to talk to you about your son."

"Please do." Edels held the screen door open for them.

The central air was on and the house cool, the entryway dark though Rossi could easily make out stairs to the second floor, at right, beside which a hallway led to the back of the house. The law enforcement group went through the handshaking ritual with their host, then Edels led them off to the left, into the living room, which was not large but homey and inviting enough.

Against the wall to Rossi's right was a long, well-used sofa with family photos scattered across the wall above it. The wall at left was mostly windows onto the front yard, flimsy curtains covering them now. Beneath the windows crouched a coffee table flanked by wing chairs. The wall directly before him held shelves with a television, some electronic equipment, a row of DVDs and quite a few CDs. This was no formal living room but a lived-in room.

Edels said, "Have a seat, gentlemen," then sat on a recliner near the sofa, perching on its edge.

Rossi sat in a wing chair while Tovar and Reid took the sofa, sitting forward.

Their host seemed clearly in shock to Rossi, who asked, "Are you here alone, Mr. Edels?"

"No, no," Edels said, wiping away a tear with the back of his hand. "My wife is in the kitchen with Karen."

"Karen?"

"Our daughter."

"I'm sorry to have to ask," Rossi said, "but would you get them, please? We need to ask them these questions, too."

Edels nodded, got up and walked in zombie fashion back through the entryway. When he returned, he was followed by two women — the younger one, obviously the daughter, high school age, was rather tall and thin, wearing navy blue shorts and a gray T-shirt with NOTRE DAME in navy blue letters over a green clover leaf; her dark hair was trimmed short.

"This is my daughter, Karen," Edels said.

In better circumstances, the high-cheekboned girl would have been attractive; but right now her eyes were red-rimmed and her jaws clenched as she shook hands with each of them. She, too, had a zombie air.

Tovar and Reid rose and gave the sofa over so Karen Edels and her mother could sit down.

In a dark robe and slippers, Mrs. Edels — Phyllis, her husband told them — was the shortest of the three, but even so was probably five-seven. She had dark hair like her daughter, cut even shorter, and an athletic frame; the mother/daughter resemblance was strong. She twisted a handkerchief between her fingers.

"We're terribly sorry for your loss," Rossi said to them, panning across their shell-shocked faces.

Mrs. Edels, in a voice knife-blade thin but with a quiver, asked, "Are you going to catch the animal that did this to Bobby?"

"We're going to try," Rossi said.

"Try?" She stared at him, her green eyes burning.

"We have a very good track record, Mrs. Edels," he said. "If anyone's going to stop this killer, it's us."

That seemed to calm her slightly.

"There's no easy way to do this," Rossi said. "So, with your permission, I'm just going to get into it."

Mr. Edels nodded and then so did his wife, and finally their daughter.

"Did Bobby have trouble with anybody in his life? Someone you might call an enemy?" Rossi tilted his head. "Or if that's too strong, someone he'd had a conflict with, a bad argument, for example."

The family exchanged glances, then Mr. Edels said, "Everybody liked Bobby. I know every parent probably says that kind of thing, but really — he was a good kid and a hard worker."

"And he worked at the Mundelein Fix-It Mate, isn't that right?"

Edels nodded. "Since he was sixteen. He loved carpentry. He probably caught the bug puttering with me in the garage since he was a boy."

"Did he go to college, or was he planning to?"

"No. He was hoping to work his way up at Fix-It Mate. And there was talk of being a contractor some day."

Rossi nodded. "Any trouble at work?"

"No, sir. Everybody there liked Bobby, too."

"If I may, what do you do for a living, sir?"

"I teach school," Edels said. "Wood shop."

"And you, Mrs. Edels?"

"I teach at Lake Zurich Junior High, too," she said. "English."

"How about you two, as teachers? Any problems with staff or students for either of you?"

They both said, "No," at once.

"All right," Rossi said. "Did Bobby have a girlfriend?"

"Never had the time," Mrs. Edels said, a little too quickly. "He worked hard. Someday the right girl might have come along, but —"

"Mother," Karen said, a little too sharply considering the situation. The thin girl

stared right at Rossi and said, "Bobby was gay."

She might have slapped her parents, judging by their stricken expressions.

Rossi said, "If that's true, Mr. Edels . . . Mrs. Edels? We need to know. It could be significant in finding the person responsible."

Mrs. Edels became very interested in her hanky and Mr. Edels studied the floor for maybe fifteen seconds before slowly raising his head. Tears clung onto his eyelids like passengers on a sinking ship.

Then he said, "My daughter . . . speaks the truth."

The odd formality of that struck Rossi as particularly sad.

"Robert," Mrs. Edels gasped, and it *was* a gasp.

"Phyllis," her husband said, "we can't keep something that important away from these men, something that might help them bring Bobby's killer to justice."

Mrs. Edels looked at her husband for a long time, almost as if she were trying to see through him; then, slowly, she nodded.

Rossi said, "I assure you, Mrs. Edels, we'll make every effort to keep this information confidential."

"I appreciate that," she said.

Karen Edels turned to her mother and said, "If us being open about Bobby's sexual orientation helps their investigation . . . if people *knowing* helps some other 'Bobby' out there keep from being victimized . . . then, Mother, we *have* to do it."

"I *know!*" her mother snapped.

Rossi took a few moments for everything — and everyone — to settle.

Then he said, as casually as he could, "Was there someone special in Bobby's life?"

Both parents turned to Karen, and Rossi realized at once that the sister was the only one who'd been privy to this part of Bobby's life. These were parents who hadn't wanted to know such things and, accordingly, had never asked.

"No one in particular," Karen said. "To the general public, Bobby was in the closet. He was working in what was kind of a hardware store, and that's a pretty conservative environment. Of course, I knew, and our folks knew, but it was 'don't ask, don't tell,' around here."

"Karen," her mother said sharply.

"Well, it is. It was. Mother, Dad — can you imagine Bobby bringing somebody home for you to meet?"

They said nothing.

Rossi asked, "Did he have a lot of friends? Straight? Or gay?"

"Hardly any," Karen said.

"Where did he hang out?"

"Either here or at work, mostly," Karen said. "If he was going anywhere else, if there was somebody or somebodies he was seeing, he kept it to himself. He knew I was supportive, and he appreciated that — but he was very private."

"Did he have a fake ID?"

"Not that I know of. I never even saw him drink."

Rossi turned to the parents and asked about the fake ID and they both shook their heads. Looking past them, he glanced at Reid, standing on the periphery with Tovar. The younger man's eyes held a silent question and Rossi gave him the barest hint of a nod.

Reid took a half step into the room. To Rossi, the young man always looked as if he was about to raise his hand and ask permission to go to the bathroom. And yet this eternal nerd also happened to be one of the smartest men Rossi had ever met. If not *the* smartest . . .

Tentatively, Reid asked, "Would it be all right if we looked at Bobby's room?"

Mr. Edels nodded, but Mrs. Edels asked, "Why?"

Reid said, "The more we know about your son? The more information we have to try to understand how he came to be singled out by this UnSub."

"Unknown subject," Rossi said. "The killer."

Frowning, working the hanky in her hands furiously, Mrs. Edels asked, "Shouldn't you be learning about this monster instead of Bobby?"

"Everything we learn about Bobby," Rossi said, "tells us something about that monster."

Any reservations the woman had melted away and she rose, to lead them up the stairs to the second floor. The hallway was long, the bedrooms of the kids on the left, the bathroom and the master bedroom on the right. The corridor contained a few more family photos on either side wall: Bobby in Little League, Karen in a cheerleading uniform (probably junior high), a family portrait of the four when the kids were still in elementary school. They passed Karen's bedroom and she opened the door for them to enter Bobby's.

The room was small and dark. Mrs. Edels opened the curtains wide and let the sun in, then — without a word — left Reid, Rossi, and Tovar alone in the room, closing the door behind her.

The window took up most of the wall opposite the door, the bed against the wall on the right; the floor was hardwood. A desk and chair squatted beneath the window, the chair neatly pushed underneath a desk that was home to a small pile of books (novels, *Tales of the City* on top) and a laptop computer.

"Reid," Rossi asked, "can you get into his computer?"

"Possibly," Reid said. "But I'd still feel better calling in a computer tech."

"All right," Rossi said.

Shelves on the left held a TV, a few books, a video game console and assorted games and CDs. A poster over the bed was of a pasty guy with long, unruly hair with only the words "The Cure" at the bottom to give Rossi the slightest clue what the poster was supposed to represent. Another poster above the shelves and TV was of another musician, this one with black hair and pale skin as well — "Nine Inch Nails," it was labeled. He wondered how one man could be a whole band (all nine of them?), but rock music had left Rossi behind some time ago. Around "Pleasant Valley Sunday."

Tovar said, "Seems normal enough."

"We can only hope the computer gives up something," Rossi said. "Or maybe his car —"

The word was barely out of his mouth when Rossi realized they had all skipped a major potential clue. Opening the door, he went into the hallway. The Edels were standing there expectantly, father, mother, daughter, like a party waiting to be seated in a restaurant.

Rossi asked, "How did Bobby get around?"

"Well, his car," Mrs. Edels said.

"Which is where?"

"We wish we knew," Mr. Edels said.

Rossi frowned. "How's that?"

"It hasn't turned up. God, it seemed like every day after he disappeared one of us thought we *saw* that car, and phoned the police. I think they finally got tired of us bothering them, but they never found it. Must be a lot like it out there."

"What kind of car is it?"

"Ninety-five Honda Civic."

"Navy blue," Bobby's sister added.

Rossi said, "Thanks," and got out his cell phone and hit a number in the speed dial.

"Hotchner."

"It's Rossi. We need to find Bobby Edels's

car. It went missing when he did."

Hotchner was ahead of him. "The local cops up there ran it when he disappeared. They came up empty."

"Well, hell, let's put Garcia on it. We need to know what happened to that vehicle."

"I'd like to know myself, but we don't gather the evidence, Dave."

"With all due respect, Aaron, remove the stick from where you're sitting and get real: Bobby Edels disappeared. Wherever he disappeared from, he got there in his car. That car is a clue that we need to find so we *can* interpret it."

"Agreed," Hotchner said. "I'll get Garcia on it right away. Anything else?"

"Not yet," Rossi said, "but you'll be the first to know when there is." He clicked off.

With a curious frown, Mrs. Edels asked, "If the police haven't been able to find Bobby's car, what makes you think you can?"

Rossi gave her a half smile. "Because we have a secret weapon."

Named Penelope Garcia.

Supervisory Special Agent Derek Morgan and Detective Tate Lorenzon had spent the last three hours interviewing Fix-It Mate employees.

They started with the assistant manager

and worked their way slowly through co-workers of Bobby Edels. The assistant manager, highest-ranking person on duty, had shown them security videos of the parking lot. They had watched Bobby Edels get behind the wheel of his Honda Civic and pull out of the parking lot.

Then Bobby disappeared down the road, out of sight and, seemingly, off the planet.

Even after twenty-two employee interviews, the agent and the detective knew no more than what they'd seen on that video.

They were in the employees' break room now, where they had conducted the interviews, and Lorenzon got up to pour them what seemed like their twentieth cup of coffee. Or maybe thirtieth.

"Do we know *anything* new?" Lorenzon asked as he returned to the table and set their cups on the table.

"Sure," Morgan said, sipping the coffee.

"Such as?"

"We know that Fix-It Mate coffee sucks ass."

They both laughed. As they drank the wretched brew, young, dark-haired Stan Schultz, assistant manager, wandered into the break room. He wore a blue Fix-It Mate shirt and navy blue slacks. The slightly taller, middle-aged man who followed him in wore khaki shorts and a white Cubs T-shirt. He had brown hair, pale skin, horn-rimmed glasses and a small beer belly under the shirt.

Schultz said, "Officers, this is Alan Bellamy, our store manager — he's come in on his day off."

Introductions were made and hands were shaken all around.

Then Bellamy said, "Bobby was a good employee — hell, *everybody* liked him. How can we help?"

Lorenzon listed what they had already done at Fix-It Mate.

Bellamy's eyebrows rose. "I don't know what else I can add. Kinda hoped, comin' in like this, I could do Bobby's cause some good."

"Maybe you still can. We've talked to people about how he got along with his fellow employees — how did he get along with customers?"

Bellamy didn't hesitate. "In the store, he was great. First-rate people skills, that kid — surprising, since he was on the quiet side, kept to himself. Far as customers go in the store, I never heard a complaint about him."

"You said, 'in the store' twice," Morgan said. "Does that mean there were complaints *outside* the store?"

Bellamy shrugged. "Bobby was part of our installation staff — part of the team that does everything from layin' carpet to building garages. He'd been doing that for us, oh, hell, ever since he graduated from high school, for maybe two . . . two and a half years? I mean, every team had complaints. Some customers are . . . hard to please."

"Were any of these complaints in writing?"

"Sure."

"May we see them?"

Bellamy's smile was a frozen thing that just hung there for a while.

Finally he said, "Normally, we keep those to ourselves. We dispose of the letters, and any phone message and such, but we do keep a list of customers who've said they were dissatisfied with a team's work, with a little write-up of their specific complaint or complaints."

"It might help, as you said, Bobby's cause."

"Well, if it can help you find the son of a bitch who did this thing, hell — we're glad to help any way we can, here at Fix-It Mate."

That little commercial made Morgan smile, but he merely said, "Much appreciated, Mr. Bellamy."

Bellamy led them up to his office, printed

off the list and, ten minutes later, the agent and the detective were back in the car. Lorenzon pulled out of the parking lot as Morgan snapped on his seat belt and glanced over the list of only eight names. Nothing familiar stood out.

"Anything good?" Lorenzon asked as he wove through traffic, headed back toward the expressway.

"Eight names," Morgan said. "Abbott, Benavides, Denson . . ."

"Wait a minute," Lorenzon interrupted. *"Denson?"*

"Yeah."

"*Jake* Denson?"

"There's a Jacob Denson. You know him?"

"He's the Wauconda detective who didn't want you guys helping him. I was with Hotchner when we visited the PD up there. The guy's a complete and utter asshole."

Morgan felt a chill. "He's more than that, Tate."

"Yeah?"

"He's a complete and utter asshole with a connection to at least three of the victims."

Morgan's first call was to Hotchner to tell the SAIC what they had learned. Hotchner ordered them to Wauconda to talk to Denson. His second call was to Garcia.

"Office of Omnipotence," she said.

"Love of my life," Morgan said, "I need some help."

"Do I have to say you've come to the right place?"

He grinned at the phone. "No. Hey, I need you to find out all you can about a Wauconda, Illinois, detective named Jake Denson."

"Checking up on one of the good guys?"

"Checking to see if he *is* a good guy."

"Gotcha," she said.

"Catch you later, sweetheart."

He clicked off.

Lorenzon, behind the wheel, glanced over at Morgan. "Was that intelligence you called, or your latest girl friend?"

"Best computer tech on the planet. We're just friends. We kid around."

"That kind of kidding around gets you written up where I come from."

Morgan gave him a look. "Tate, this serial killer is an aberration in your life, right? Not saying you don't face tough stuff, day in and day out, but this is off the rails, wouldn't you say?"

"Way off."

"Well, that brilliant and gentle soul I was just talking to? She needs a little TLC sometimes, to take the edge off the horrific garbage we face day in and day out."

Silence.

"So, then, she's just a friend?" Lorenzon asked lightly.

Morgan and Lorenzon had been needling each other since they were kids.

"She's a good friend."

Lorenzon grinned. "Damn, if I had a nickel for every time I heard you say that over the years . . ."

"Hey, hey, I picked that up from you, baby."

The detective's eyebrows shot up. "When did *I* ever tell you some woman of mine was just a friend?"

"How about . . . every woman I ever saw you with?"

Lorenzon laughed. "You know, come to think of it? That's right. That's right. . . ."

Traffic being what traffic always was in Chicago, the better part of an hour dragged by before they got to the Wauconda PD HQ.

Morgan had spent the time reading the Fix-It Mate report of the complaint Denson had made against Bobby Edels's construction team. The complaint had no allegations against Edels per se, but Denson had claimed that the team, at his house to construct a two-car garage, had practiced shoddy workmanship and left behind a mess in his yard. Not the sort of thing that would normally draw a red flag, but in a city of over three million, one detective having ties to three of five murder victims in different jurisdictions certainly was. Flags did not come much redder. . . .

After he parked the car, Lorenzon led the way into the police department, where Morgan felt he'd stepped through some sort of time warp.

Police stations just didn't look like this anymore. Hotch and JJ had both commented on the place as a security nightmare and were they right: no bulletproof glass, three officers within sight of the front door, making easy targets. A female officer, who had probably stood on her tiptoes to meet the height requirement, paused on the other side of the counter from them.

"May I help you?" she asked.

Before either man could say a word, a door to their right swung open and a tall man in jeans and a blue work shirt sauntered in. He had a shaved head and dark eyes that clouded with anger when he spotted Lorenzon.

"What the hell," he said, his voice carrying through the nearly empty room, "are you doing back here, Lorenzon? Don't they give you any crimes to solve in Chicago?" He moved through the swinging gate.

Unshaken, Lorenzon turned to Morgan. "Supervisory Special Agent Derek Morgan, meet Detective Jake Denson, Wauconda PD."

"*Another* goddamn fed?" Denson asked, making no effort to shake hands as he drew closer.

Morgan grinned, refusing to rise to the bait. "Yeah, I know you must feel invaded. But we need to talk to you. . . ."

"What about?" Denson demanded, really putting on a show for his buddies now.

". . . in *private*."

Morgan removed his grin and gave Denson a hard stare.

"You strut in here and tell *me* what to *do?*" Denson said. "Suppose I don't feel like *talking* to you?"

Morgan took a half step closer and dropped his voice so only the detective could hear. "That's cool. Then I'll have the supreme pleasure of disarming you, cuffing you, and, with the help of my friend Lorenzon here, dragging your ass out in front of all your pals, and all the way down to the FBI field office to question you there. If that's how you want this to play out, hey, it's your call."

A tense silence hung in the room as Denson's eyes bore into him and Morgan let the detective see the calm determination that told the local boy he meant every word.

"All right," Denson said. He nodded behind him. "The chief's office."

"Lead the way."

Denson took off quickly, Morgan and Lorenzon keeping up. A minute later, they were behind the closed door of an office.

"Where's Chief Oliver?" Lorenzon asked.

"Family vacation," Denson said. "He won't be back for a week. Now, what the hell are you two doing, coming on my turf and threatening me?"

"I didn't threaten you," Morgan said coolly. "I was just providing you an option."

"Fuck you, fed! You can't come in here and bully me like I'm your dog and I just crapped on the rug. This is *my* house. We don't want to join your god-damn task force, so you're wasting your time coming back around trying to bully me into it."

Morgan laughed, once. "That's why you think we're here?"

Denson's face turned crimson as his hands balled into fists.

Lorenzon stood close to their host. "You better dial it down a notch or two, Jake, because my friend here will break your ass in public or private, doesn't matter to him. And you definitely want to scale back the fuck-you rhetoric."

Morgan, not really wanting a fight in either place, said in a businesslike way, "We're here to talk to you about Bobby Edels."

Denson's face morphed from anger to confusion. "Who the hell is Bobby Edels?"

Is that genuine surprise? Morgan wondered. *If it's an act, it's damn good. . . .*

"Bobby Edels," Lorenzon said, "is the kid who ended up dead in a barrel in Chinatown — I showed you that picture."

"*That's* his name?" Denson asked. "You didn't give me a name."

"We didn't have one at the time."

Again, Morgan wondered if they were being put on. "He was identified this morning, Detective Denson."

"Doesn't mean diddly to me."

"It should — you filed a complaint against him and the crew he worked with at Fix-It Mate."

"What? This vic was on that worthless crew?"

"That's right."

"Hell, I didn't know any of those guys," Denson said, with a dismissive wave. "Did it say I singled out this Edel or Edsel or whatever? 'Cause I don't think I did. I remember complaining about the entire

167

crew, because they did a lousy-ass job and left a humongous mess behind."

Morgan studied the man. "That's all it was? Just some bad craftsmanship?"

"Hey, come home with me now, if you don't believe me," Denson said, his voice rising as his agitation grew again. "Look at my damn garage and make up your own mind about the 'craftsmanship.' "

Looking to keep his quarry off balance, Morgan asked, "Aren't you investigating the murders of Donna Cooper and Casey Goddard?"

"What of it?"

"I was just curious — did you know either of them before they were murdered?"

"Yeah," Denson said. "I knew them both — they worked at the convenience store up around the corner. It's a small town, in case you didn't notice. That's why I'm working so hard to catch the bastard that did this. What are you getting at?"

Morgan held Denson's eyes. "There have been five bodies in this case and you've got ties to three of them."

"Wait a minute," Denson said, his eyes narrowing. "Wait a minute. . . . You're not trying to muscle us into joining your damned task force? You're here because you think I'm a *suspect?*"

"You're a detective," Morgan said. "Look at the facts — what would you think? Person of interest, certainly."

Denson pointed at the door like a father banishing a wayward daughter in an old-time melodrama. "I think you need to get the hell out! And I'm not going to talk to you again without a lawyer present."

Morgan and Lorenzon didn't move.

"You think I'm bullshitting you?" Denson demanded, eyes and nostrils flaring. "Get the hell out of here! You're not dragging me into your shit."

They surely didn't have enough to bring Denson in, so — having no choice — they left before the confrontation degenerated any further.

As they pulled away slowly from the PD, Morgan thought he could feel Denson's eyes on him through the chief's window, but he did not turn to look. He kept his focus on the windshield, looking for the convenience store Denson had mentioned.

He asked the Chicago detective, "What's your gut telling you?"

Lorenzon stopped at a red light. "My gut believes him, and so do I. I think it's a coincidence."

"You have any idea, bro, how many serial killers have tried to join law enforcement over the years? The mental test can't screen them all out."

"I hear you," Lorenzon admitted. "But I just don't think anybody's *that* good an actor."

"I'll give you that," Morgan said. "But we'll see."

They traded a look.

"Do me a favor," Morgan said. "Take a right and stop at that convenience store on the next corner. I want to get something to drink."

Lorenzon shook his head. "Your boss is going to kick your ass, and I'm going to get mine fired."

After a chuckle, Morgan said, "Is that all? Tate, I want a damn Coke. Is that against the law in Chicago?"

"We're not in Chicago. We're in Wauconda."

"Do they sell Cokes at convenience stores in Wauconda?"

Lorenzon shook his head. "Damn. This is about as bad as when you wanted us to steal that car when we were kids."

"Hey, we never did that."

" 'Cause you got *scared.*"

"Bull," Morgan said. "I got smart. We rolled up on that heap and I just got this flash we'd get caught and go to jail and then to prison and —"

Interrupting, Lorenzon said, "Funny, I just had that flash now."

He turned the car to the left, away from the convenience store. "You can get a damn Coke when we get to the expressway."

Morgan patted his friend's arm. "Yeah, I'll settle for that. Right before we get on the expressway. I'm buying."

"You're all heart, bro. Gonna buy me dinner too?"

"I might at that." Morgan took his phone off his belt and punched the speed dial and got an answer after only one ring. "Mom, how are you?"

"Derek! Fine, fine — you're in town?"

"Sure am. You and the girls free for dinner?"

"We can be, if you're coming by. I can cook us something, real quick, and —"

"No sale, Mom! Home-cooking another night. We're going out. Tate's driving, and we'll be by to pick you up in . . ."

He glanced at Lorenzon who mouthed, "An hour or so."

". . . an hour or so," Morgan said. "Can you call the girls?"

"I'll take care of it," his mother said. "It'll be good to see Tate! He's been way too long a stranger."

"An hour then. Love you, Mom!"

He ended the call.

"That woman loves me like I was her own, you know," Lorenzon said. "Always treated me like family."

Morgan chuckled. "Much as you were eatin' our food, maybe she thought you *were* family."

"Ain't my fault she kept inviting me to stay for dinner."

She had done that many a night because Tate's mother wasn't always home. Both Morgan's mom and Tate's were single parents working hard to make a better life, but Mrs. Lorenzon worked a lot more nights than days and Tate had done more than his fair share of homework at Morgan's. They had also found lots of ways to get in trouble together.

Glancing at his old friend, Morgan decided they had both turned out pretty well. They could easily have wound up going down the wrong path, but thanks to their mothers — and each other — they had stayed true to the way they'd been raised.

Morgan knew that very likely their UnSub's family life had been far worse than either his or Tate's. People who mistreated their kids raised people who mistreated others — sometimes such people took their rage out as verbal and even physical abuse on their own families; but sometimes that rage became something even more monstrous and reached out into the world, to make the world suffer, too. . . .

But one thing was certain: UnSubs usually had a lot more trouble in their family histories than Tate Lorenzon and Derek Morgan.

And as they wove through traffic, Morgan couldn't help but wonder what kind of home life Jake Denson had had.

CHAPTER SIX:
JULY 30
CHICAGO, ILLINOIS

Supervisory Special Agent Aaron Hotchner had his back to the laptop screen when Garcia's voice behind him called, "Sir?"

Hotchner turned to the flat screen, and for one odd moment he recalled watching the old *I Dream of Jeannie* show on TV as a child — their computer tech's pleasant, pretty face on a laptop screen somehow made her the BAU's resident genie, capable of modern magic.

"You have something, Garcia?"

"Yes, sir. I think I found Bobby Edels's car."

"Where?"

"There's a navy blue 1995 Honda Civic," Garcia said, "with a vehicle identification number matching Edels's in a lot owned by a towing company in Lincoln Park."

"And where is that?"

"It's an area of the city that runs from Lincoln Park Zoo on the east to Clybourn on the west, from Diversey Parkway on the north to, fittingly enough, North Avenue on the south."

Hotchner couldn't help but smile; Garcia always overdid it a little with him, and was more formal than with anyone else on the team, since she'd embarrassed herself in front of him, a few times, with her chummy, even flirty relationship with Derek Morgan.

"I'm sorry, Garcia. I meant where's the towing company?"

"Oh. Sorry, sir. On Lincoln Avenue between Armitage and Dickens."

"Do we know how the car got there? And how it escaped notice of the local police?"

Garcia brightened. "Yes, sir. It took a little digging, but I tracked that down."

"And?"

"Bobby Edels disappeared on March twenty-first. The North Barrington police ran his plates the next day and came up empty. The car disappeared until this morning, when the company, Buccaneer Towing, filed to get the title of the car, so they could sell it. That's how I found it. And that's where it's sitting — in Buccaneer Towing's lot."

"How could they file for title? What's that about?"

"That means the vehicle has gone unclaimed for one-hundred-twenty days. And that gives Buccaneer the right to file title claim."

"They're an aptly named company."

Her face on the screen froze a little; he could almost see a dozen quips passing behind those eyes, but because it was Hotchner, she wouldn't share an "Aye aye, matey" or "Arrrrrr" with him. He was tempted to share one with her, but, truth be told, he preferred her in this more business-like mode.

So he just told her, "Good job," and signed off.

The area detectives were out in the field with Rossi, Reid and Morgan, running down leads. Jareau was upstairs with SAIC Raymond Himes going over logistical matters. That left only Prentiss, hard at work on the victimology of the crimes, in the conference room with Hotchner. He considered not bothering her and going upstairs to request an agent from the local office, but talked himself out of it.

Turning to Prentiss, who was hunkered over her laptop computer, Hotchner asked, "Interested in taking a break?"

Prentiss stretched. "When the boss suggests I take a break, I take a break. What did you have in mind?"

"How about taking a ride?"

Prentiss displayed her dazzling smile and said, "Let me guess — this is not an invitation to enjoy a gently breezy day in the Windy City. You have somewhere you want to go, and you don't know your way around the city."

Shrugging, Hotchner said, "It still qualifies as a break."

"A break, or work away from this conference room," Prentiss said. "Either way, I'm in."

"Do you know where Lincoln Park is?"

"Yes, sir. Piece of cake."

An hour later, they'd made the jog up Lincoln Avenue, past the Lincoln Park Zoo, and the legendary Second City comedy club just off Lincoln on Wells. Cruising northwest now, as they passed Armitage, Prentiss started looking for a parking place.

They were a block up and around a corner before she found one. The Buccaneer Towing lot would have been hard to miss, with its sign painted on the side of a junked car sitting atop a twenty-foot-high steel pole. The lot was surrounded by a seven-foot cyclone fence with canvas attached on the inside, in an effort not to be a neighborhood eyesore — meaning, someone figured a square block of seven-foot green canvas was somehow less of a blight than a lot full of parked cars.

A mobile home next to the lot's front gate served as the office of Buccaneer Towing. Hotchner held the glass door open for Prentiss, then followed her in.

The interior design was 1980s metal desk chic. They stood temporary sentinel between the front door and a twelve-inch color TV and a coffee urn that were perched on a table against the back wall. Louvered windows were just clean enough to let in light but little more.

The desk on the left, nearer the door, was occupied by an Hispanic woman in her early twenties, her long, black hair pulled up in a bun; she had the high cheekbones of a model and the world-weary smile of not a model, and wore a black sleeveless button-down blouse and jeans. One the desk itself were a huge logbook, a telephone with five lines, a computer keyboard and monitor. The computer tower resided on the floor next to the desk, a mouse on the pullout leaf.

The desk at right was recessed a foot or two from its twin and Hotchner's reading of the setup was that the woman had secretary/receptionist duties, while the male occupant of this other desk actually ran the place. The male's desk had a stacked in-and-out box, a newspaper open to a cross-word puzzle, a pen next to it, and a phone. On the back wall, a two-way radio perched on a shelf.

The boss, maybe fifty and balding, had a squat, troll-like look, as if he'd hopped off a tall building, landed on his feet and compacted himself. He wore a white short-sleeve shirt and what was probably a clip-on tie, red-and-blue stripes.

Prentiss showed her credentials to the probable receptionist, who immediately glanced over at the boss.

"That's okay," Hotchner said to her with a trace of a smile. "We'll introduce ourselves."

Turning to the heavyset man behind the other desk, Hotchner again displayed his credentials. "FBI — Supervisory Special Agent In Charge Aaron Hotchner and Supervisory Special Agent Emily Prentiss."

The squat little man made no move to stand or to offer a handshake. His eyes held a cold but unconcerned suspicion. In an undistinguished second tenor, he asked, "What can I do for you?"

Putting away his credentials, Hotchner said, "To start with, what's your name?"

The troll shot a look at his secretary/

receptionist, then said, "Jake Guzik."

Hotchner nodded. "Any relation to Jake 'Greasy Thumb' Guzik, the mobster who died in 1956? Sharing a name with a felon is no crime, of course, but maybe we should take you down to the field office, so we can fingerprint you just as a precaution."

Prentiss was smiling just a little.

The guy patted the air in front of him. "Whoa, whoa, I was just havin' some fun with you guys."

Prentiss said, "Do we look like we stopped by for the matinee?"

"Sorry, sorry. Bad joke. Stupid joke. We don't get the FBI around that often."

Hotchner arched an eyebrow and asked, "But sometimes you do?"

Now their host *was* worried. "I was just kidding around. I am glad to help you people. What do you need?"

The secretary turned away, possibly stifling a laugh, albeit probably not the laugh her boss had hoped to get out of her.

"Let's start again," Hotchner said. "Name?"

"Marshall — Art Marshall."

"Good," Hotchner said. "That wasn't so hard, was it?"

Marshall smiled feebly.

Prentiss said, "Would you mind if we sat down?"

"No. That'd be fine."

"Do you have any chairs?"

"Sure. Absolutely we have chairs. Consuela, couple of chairs for our guests!"

She said, "Yes, sir," and rose and got them chairs.

The agents sat down.

Then Hotchner said, "Now, let's talk about a car."

"*Which* car?" Marshall asked, suddenly finding himself on more comfortable ground.

Actually, that was a good sign: if Marshall were up to anything illegal with this business, Hotchner knew, the question would have unnerved him, not relaxed him.

Prentiss said, "A 1995 Honda Civic, navy blue."

"Consuela, bring it up."

The young woman, back at her desk, ratty-tat-tatted at the computer keyboard and the screen on her monitor changed to display a table.

"We have three 1995 Honda Civics," she said.

"Three?" Prentiss asked, obviously surprised. "All navy blue?"

"All navy blue."

Hotchner said, "This one was registered to a man named Edels."

Consuela nodded, checked the screen, then took a sideways look at her boss. "We just filed the paperwork to sell that car."

"We know," Hotchner said to her. To her boss, he said, "Did you know the police had run this plate number as a missing car?"

Marshall shrugged. "I can't keep track of every car that the cops are looking for. I stop at due diligence."

Hotchner had not expected above and beyond the call of duty from the manager of a business self-dubbed Buccaneer.

Prentiss asked, "When was it towed?"

"March thirty-first," Consuela said.

"Ten days after Bobby Edels disappeared," Hotchner said to Prentiss. He asked the secretary, "Where was it towed from?"

Consuela read the screen again. "A private lot north of Davis Square Park, down by the railroad yards."

"What was the car doing there?" Hotchner asked, as much to himself as anyone.

Marshall was shaking his head. "Not much down that way."

Hotchner stood. "We'll be calling in a crime scene team to take the car."

Marshall frowned. "What about my money?"

Prentiss said, "You'll have to settle for the satisfaction of knowing you may help catch a murderer."

"You can't eat satisfaction."

Hotchner, with no expression whatsoever, said, "Skip a meal."

They nodded good-byes to the manager and his secretary, and stepped out onto the lot.

Prentiss said, "That was pretty funny."

Hotchner gave her a look. "Don't tell anybody."

Using his cell phone, Hotchner phoned SAIC Himes at the Chicago field office and arranged for someone to come tow the Civic to the FBI garage.

Hotchner said, "We'll need somebody to fingerprint all the Buccaneer tow truck drivers, too."

"Not a problem," Himes said. "What *is* a problem is we just got a call from the police department in Des Plaines. They've found a body in the crawl space of a vacant house at 8213 West —"

"Summerdale," Hotchner said, finishing the sentence.

"How in the hell did you know that?" Himes asked.

"That's where John Wayne Gacy lived."

"You have got to be shitting me."

"I wish I were," Hotchner said. "We're on our way." He clicked off and punched in Rossi's number, knowing all he had to do was give David the address, and the significance would be obvious.

Rossi said, "Morgan and I can be there in . . ."

Hotchner could hear Rossi conferring with the Chicago native.

". . . an hour."

"I'm with Prentiss," Hotchner said. "We're farther away, but we're coming too."

In a Tahoe a few miles away, Supervisory Special Agent David Rossi clicked off and pocketed his cell phone.

Shaking his head, Morgan said, "Gacy?"

"Yeah. The clown prince himself. Let's shake it."

Along with Lorenzon (who rode in the back), they had been in Chinatown canvassing the neighbors along Twenty-fifth Street, looking for anyone willing to talk about the house at 213. They had been there over an hour and were pitching a shutout — not a single person thus far had let them get past showing their credentials before the door closed in their faces.

The midafternoon traffic was light and Rossi watched with some admiration as

Morgan wove expertly through it; in forty-five minutes, they were pulling up to the house of death.

Although untold misery had been perpetrated within, from the outside this was an unprepossessing brick-front bungalow with a picture window left of the propped-open front door, and a long, narrow driveway running up the left side. The gateway to hell had rarely looked more benign.

Several police cars, both marked and unmarked, sat on either side of the street, an ambulance backed into the driveway. The yard had been cordoned off with crime scene tape and several officers milled around outside. A nearly constant parade of personnel, both uniformed and plainclothes, made its way in and out of the front door.

Morgan parked and the two agents and the detective climbed out of the SUV. As they crossed the street, a plainclothes guy, obviously a detective, came out of the house and saw them. He was tall and broad-shouldered, with a block-shaped head with thinning gray hair. This obvious old-timer wore a suit that screamed Sears-off-the-rack, barely disguising the gun on his hip, and Rossi would have pegged the guy a cop even without his erect posture and swagger. Right behind the plainclothes veteran came a slightly shorter guy with brown, curly hair and a digital SLR camera hanging on a lanyard around his neck. He wore a maroon polo, black jeans, and black sneakers and appeared pretty fit. Another lanyard around his neck held a plastic ID.

The Old School detective instantly nodded in their direction and cut across the lawn toward them.

"Lorenzon!" he called in a husky baritone, as he neared them, the photographer trailing slightly.

"Andy Wallace," Lorenzon said. "Haven't seen you since that crazy asshole on the expressway, couple years ago."

"That crazy asshole you *shot,* you mean."

Lorenzon shrugged. "He *did* shoot at me first."

"There is that. But tell me, Tate — was it worth enduring the shooting board?"

Lorenzon managed a grin. "You know, I think it was."

"So much for nostalgia. What are you doing out here at *this* crime scene?"

"FBI investigation," Lorenzon said. "Task force. And speaking of nostalgia . . ."

Wallace grimaced, glanced at the Gacy house. Then he nodded toward the photographer. "This is Daniel Dryden. Crime scene photographer with Cook County.

Helping us out today."

Lorenzon made introductions to Rossi and Morgan and they shook hands all around. Rossi explained to Wallace and Dryden about the copycat serial killer, the snail-mail photos to departments, and the investigation in general.

Rossi said, "We'll talk to your chief about joining the task force. In the meantime, maybe you can get us caught up on what happened here."

"Hell of thing," Wallace said, shaking his head. "What kind of sick fuck thinks copying *Gacy* is a good idea?"

Rossi said, "That's what they pay me to find out."

They were about to get down to business when Wallace's cell phone trilled.

He stepped away from them, answered, said, "No shit," a couple of times, then clicked off.

He turned back to the task force members and said, "You guys were right. That was my captain — he told me he just got a picture in the mail."

"Jesus," Rossi said. "He's not even paying any attention to the dates anymore. . . ."

Morgan said, "Definitely escalating."

"This task force is growing faster than I'd ever want it to," Rossi said. Then to Wallace he said, "Who found the body?"

Wallace said, "Meter reader. The house still has an old-style gas meter. Inside the house, in the laundry room. Reader had a key to get in and noticed the cover off the crawl space. He shone a flashlight down there, saw what he saw, then called us."

"How did the killer get in here with the body?"

"Window in the kitchen in the back of the house," Wallace said, gesturing. "He cut a hole in the window, slipped in, then unlocked the back door. It's a quiet neighborhood. If he did it late at night, no one would have even noticed."

Rossi asked, "Have you identified the victim?"

"White male, early twenties, no ID, still dressed, partially buried in the crawl space under the house."

Morgan nodded toward the innocent-looking, nondescript bungalow. "House is vacant?"

"Has been, off and on, since Gacy," Wallace said. "No one with even a vague idea of what went on in there has ever wanted to live in that house. Of course, there's nothing vague about *this* killing — looks like it was done by someone who knew about the original crimes."

"What makes you say that?" Rossi asked.

Wallace jerked a thumb at the bungalow. "I was a rookie when this went down back in 'seventy-eight and 'seventy-nine. I hadn't been on the force six months when the excavation started. I hate this god-damn house. The body? To me, it looks like the killer, to pull this off? *Had* to've been in the house with us back then."

Rossi said, "It could be as simple as he saw photos. This thing was heavily covered."

"Yeah, well, what we saw didn't make the papers or any of the magazines or even the books about the case." Wallace's tone and his expression were grave. "He must've seen the actual crime scene photos."

"Who had access to those?"

Wallace shrugged. "Really, just cop shop people."

"From just around here, or Greater Metropolitan Chicago?"

"You know how it is, Agent Rossi. Cops cooperate. Somebody wants a look at famous crime scene photos, you show 'em."

"But there'd be no record of who looked at them."

"No. Nothing like that."

Rossi and Morgan traded a wary glance. Rossi figured their UnSub would be a police buff, but maybe he was more than just a buff. He had never met this Wauconda detective, Jake Denson, but Hotchner had told him about the encounter. Now, Rossi wondered if Denson had some tie to their new John Doe, too. . . .

"Excuse me," Dryden said. "But . . . *I've* seen them. The photos?"

They all turned to him.

"And so have a lot of people all over the country, who have no connection to Chicago."

Rossi frowned. "How's that?"

"Well, I've seen the Gacy shots at forensic photography seminars, crime scene analyst seminars, and, frankly . . . if you know where to look . . . some of 'em are even on the Internet."

Rossi sighed, shook his head. This news did not make their lives easier.

"We canvassed but got bubkes," Wallace said. "This guy's a ghost."

Rossi laughed humorlessly. Then he said, " 'Even then the cock crew loud, and at the sound it shrunk in haste away and vanished from our sight.' "

Morgan's forehead frowned and his mouth smiled as he said, *"Hamlet?"*

Rossi gave up a rumpled grin. "It was either that or 'I ain't afraid of no ghosts.' "

■ ■ ■ ■

After her meeting with SAIC Himes, Jennifer Jareau had returned to the conference room to find it empty.

This was not unusual. Though much of the public, and even some cops, thought what the BAU did was hocus pocus and that they sat in an ivory tower divining their profiles from crystal balls or tea leaves, the truth was they spent most of their time out in the field . . . which meant the media/police liaison spent a great deal of her time alone, or at least away from the rest of the team.

None of the agents had ever made her feel like anything less than a one hundred percent participant in the BAU, but it still nagged her, sometimes, that they were off busting their humps while she was sitting here in the office.

In her worst moments, she felt like the team mascot or the little sister who wanted to tag along and rarely got to. She worked hard and contributed to the effort, she knew that. Still, they were out in the field now.

And she wasn't.

Going to her laptop, she hooked up a video feed with Garcia.

191

"What's up?" her friend asked.

Jareau shook her head. "Everybody's in the field."

"But you," Garcia said. "Listen, while you were —"

"Meeting with SAIC Himes?" Jareau offered.

"Yeah, while you were doing that, they got a call about another body."

Jareau straightened, surprised she hadn't been alerted. "Where?"

Garcia's eyes widened, and — with much more melodrama than a mere address would seem to warrant — she said, "8213 Summerdale in Des Plaines."

Jareau shrugged. "Oh-kay — what am I missing?"

Garcia stared at her a long moment. "That's the former address of John Wayne Gacy."

A momentary wave of nausea passed through her. "Great. Just swell. . . . All right, I better sign off, then. It's going to get ugly around here. Uglier."

"Sometimes," Garcia said, "I'm very happy to be sequestered in my little domain."

Then she was gone.

Jareau wondered why her cell phone wasn't ringing itself crazy already. She snapped it off her belt to see if it was turned off or the battery'd gone dead. But the phone was on and the battery indicator read full.

The police, the media, *someone* should be calling her for help or a comment or something.

She continued to eyeball the device, confused by why it remained mute. She was concentrating so hard, she couldn't help but flinch when the thing vibrated in her hand, and she almost threw it, reflexively, against the wall.

"Jareau."

"Hotchner. You heard?"

"Yes, Garcia told me. I'll get right out to the scene. . . ."

"No — sit tight. The Des Plaines Police are waiting for your call — they're going to join the task force."

"Yes, sir."

"The victim at this crime scene is a John Doe, male, white, early twenties. Garcia's working on the identification."

"All right."

"I guess I don't have to tell you. . . ."

"That the media's going to run wild with this? No. You don't."

Hotchner said, "Just a heads-up. I wouldn't wish this on anybody, but I know we're in good hands."

"Thanks, Hotch."

"We should be back soon," Hotchner said, and clicked off.

The phone remained silent for almost ten whole seconds before it rang again. "Jareau."

"Supervisory Special Agent Jennifer Jareau?"

She didn't recognize the voice. "Yes. May I help you?"

"My name is Logan Brinkley. I'm managing editor of the Chicago *Examiner*."

That didn't take long, Jareau thought as she said, "What can I do for you, Mr. Brinkley?"

"I think it might be what I can do for you, Special Agent Jareau."

"Please explain."

A momentary pause. "I just received several photos via e-mail."

"Yes?"

Again Brinkley hesitated before continuing. "They are very . . . disturbing."

Jareau felt another wave of nausea, only this one hung on a while.

"They were photos of murders that have occurred in the Chicago area over the last few months — homicides that the involved communities have no idea are related. And it's clear the *police* have known."

Jareau wondered how many other media outlets had been sent the pictures. The *Trib*? The *Sun-Times*? The television stations? The potential media onslaught was almost too much to consider.

The overriding factor, however, was that she had to tell Hotch. Not just to alert him that the media was going to be more intrusive now, but to tell him that the UnSub's behavior had escalated.

Taunting the police was one thing; sending full-color press releases another. . . .

Managing editor Brinkley was saying, "The publisher wants to run all the photos in tomorrow's edition, despite their . . . graphic nature. I can't blame him, since the police behavior here is certainly questionable. Still, I managed to convince him that we should call the FBI first. So, here I am."

"Running those photos," Jareau said, "could seriously impede a federal murder investigation."

"Please, Agent Jareau. How many times has a government flack uttered those words?"

"I can't deny that," Jareau said coolly, though the harshness of the word "flack" offended her. "I can't comment directly on an ongoing investigation, of course . . . but it would be safe to say that any killer who sends pictures of his crimes to a newspaper is looking for attention."

"Agreed. But perhaps, if we give it to him, he will stop."

"Mr. Brinkley, how long have you been in the newspaper business?"

"Thirty-two years."

"And in all that time? Have you ever heard of a serial killer stopping *because* he got attention from the press?"

Several moments crawled past. Then: "You make a reasonable point, Agent Jareau."

"Thank you," she said. "You seem like you want to do the right thing here, Mr. Brinkley. Perhaps we can work something out."

"You'll give us an exclusive?"

She wanted to say: *How many times has an editor of some tabloid rag uttered those words?*

But what she did say was, "I can't make that promise, Mr. Brinkley — not where the public safety could be jeopardized. I do have an idea of how you can sell papers and not interfere in our investigation . . . and you can do a service to your community as well."

"I'm listening," Brinkley said.

"I can give you a twenty-four lead on one thing. Did you get a photo of a young man partially buried in a crawl space?"

"Yes," Brinkley said.

"The victim is a John Doe. You can run a photo of his face with a plea for anyone who knows him to come forward and identify him."

"I don't *have* a picture of just his face."

"You will. Our digital intelligence officer will send it to you while she investigates the path the killer's e-mail took to get to you."

Brinkley considered that. "And if I fight to keep your agent out of our computers?"

"First, our tech is smarter than you and smarter than me and you couldn't keep her out with Bill Gates's help. And second, you want to help us catch this killer — I know you do. That, Mr. Brinkley, makes for favorable press . . . and it won't be limited to just your own paper."

After a moment's thought, Brinkley said, "Special Agent Jareau, I believe you have yourself a deal."

"Thank you, Mr. Brinkley. Now, I have one more question for you."

"Yes?"

"Did he send the photos to the other media outlets?"

Brinkley's voice was subdued. "I don't think so. Mine was the only name in the address box and there were no others in the courtesy copy box either. If he *did* send the pictures to all the media outlets, would he have taken the time to send a copy to one person at each outlet, individually? That would take a lot longer than just spamming us."

"I agree."

"And if he did send mass copies, why send a *single* copy to me? No, Special Agent Jareau, I think it's possible that he only sent them to us. Then again, it's not like any other media outlet would tell me if they had copies of these things."

"Thank you, sir."

"You might put your computer whiz on it."

"I might at that."

"Now, Agent Jareau, if I may . . . one bonus question?"

"All right."

"You haven't told Chicago that there's a serial killer out there — why?"

"It's a policy of the FBI and the BAU not to discuss ongoing investigations."

"Yeah, right, that's the officialese," Brinkley said. "But how long have you known?"

"Off the record?"

"I could do that," he said.

"Because of the jurisdictional considerations, and the involved departments not sharing information until now? Two days."

"Oh hell," Brinkley said.

Jareau sighed. "That kind of response I've been hearing a lot lately. . . . Our digital intelligence officer, Penelope Garcia, will be in touch within the next half-hour. She'll send you the picture and start tracking the e-mail, Mr. Brinkley. I want to thank you for your cooperation."

"We're not all in it just to make money, Agent Jareau. I've seen the photos and I would do everything I could to keep them out of the *Examiner,* but the last word here is seldom mine. As a concerned citizen, though, I want you to catch this monster and relegate him to some dark hole forever."

"We're trying to do just that."

"Well, good luck."

"Thank you, Mr. Brinkley."

"And, uh, Agent Jareau?"

"Yes?"

"Sorry about that 'flack' remark. That was uncalled for."

"That's all right. I almost called your paper a tabloid rag."

He laughed. "You wouldn't have been the first."

CHAPTER SEVEN:
AUGUST 5
CHICAGO/AURORA,
ILLINOIS

Six days had passed since the last murder and — although the BAU team had been working sixteen-hour days, and sometimes longer — they were no closer to finding, and stopping, the UnSub.

As for the UnSub, he seemed to have taken a very long weekend after re-creating the Gacy murder. While he rested, they had worked. And worked.

For her part, Supervisory Special Agent Emily Prentiss was exhausted. They had already put in eight hours, and now as she stood with Hotchner and the rest, before an expectant audience, she could only wonder if her teammates felt as spent as she did. They were about to present the profile they had developed over the last week.

Their audience consisted of not only the officers from the task force and the affected jurisdictions, but representatives of neighboring communities, as well. So many had been invited (and so many more had asked to attend) that the conference room in the FBI building on West Roosevelt Road would not hold them. Instead, the BAU had borrowed a lecture hall at the University of Chicago.

Three quarters of the seats were filled as the five members of the BAU team gathered on a low stage, Hotchner at the lectern, the others fanned out around him. As usual, the team leader wore an immaculate dark suit. Rossi, to Hotch's right, wore a charcoal sport coat over a light blue dress shirt with a navy tie and jeans. Beyond him, Jareau wore gray also, a business suit with sensible shoes. To Hotch's left, Prentiss wore one of her classiest dark business suits and to her left Morgan wore a white button-down with dark tie and slacks, but no jacket. Even Reid, next to Morgan, had his tie snugged in place.

They were the top professionals in the profiling field, and they looked it.

They were all such imbeciles.

The cops, the FBI, the pathetic public, none of them had any idea about him and who he was and what made him tick. The public feared him, but they still didn't respect him. That would change, as the media fueled the

201

fire. The cops knew only what he wanted them to know, and the FBI even less. And none of them could touch him.

As for the individual citizens who made up this city, they were so goddamn dim that, right now, one of their pitiful ilk was driving him away from a downtown bar, *thinking he was a woman.*

Oh, he had the requisite attire, a black dress, naturally. His freshly shaven legs looked even better than he had anticipated. Once upon a time, he had created beautiful women from lesser material than this. His wig had been appropriated from home, a prop from that past life, and the makeup had been applied perfectly (tricks of his former trade) in the motel room he had taken for the night — he explained to his wife that he would be at a conference.

His mark was now, ostensibly, driving him to another motel, one that catered to clients who might not necessarily need the room for the whole night.

Hotchner said, "This UnSub has killed six innocent people who appear to have no connection with each other."

Except for the three who had a connection to Detective Jake Denson, Prentiss thought.

"Three women and three men," Hotchner

said, "with no sexual evidence in the crimes, even when there was in the original crime being mimicked."

He was a chubby guy, Tom Something, who had picked "her" up in a crummy, dark bar downtown. A salesman from Peoria, Tom had been a no-sale at a factory here in Aurora before he entered the bar, where he'd been taken by the cool blonde at the end of the bar.

"I don't normally do this sort of thing," Tom said.

Balding, with thick-lensed wire frame glasses, Tom wore a K-mart dress shirt, a tie with a tomato sauce stain, and polyester slacks that had long since lost the battle with his ample belly.

"I do it all the time," "she" said huskily.

Hotchner said, "Our UnSub is a chameleon, able to be different things to different people — an actor of considerable skill. The Chicago Heights murders were a blitz attack — an assassin personality. Yet, the Wauconda murders required him to charm two women into leaving with him, without anyone noticing — a sexual predator personality. The Chinatown killing could have been either, since we have yet to establish the circumstances of his death. That victim,

Bobby Edels, was treated as if he simply disappeared."

Hotchner glanced at Reid, who came forward and said, "Jeffrey Dahmer, like Ted Bundy, was a sexual predator. The difference between the two was gender of victims. The key factor here is that the UnSub displays an impressive ability to appear as whatever facilitates his gaining control of his intended victim . . . and reenacting the next famous murder on his list."

"What did you say your name was?" Tom asked.

"Aileen, with an A."

"Really," Tom said, his speech slightly slurred from several Rob Roys (and a little something extra supplied by "Aileen" when he had been looking at "her" legs instead of his drink).

Night had fallen and traffic was thin as they moved deeper into the darkness. They were gliding west on Galena Boulevard.

Tom's hand slid over and touched "her" knee, then slid farther up the thigh.

"Aileen" playfully slapped the hand away. "Let's not get ahead of ourselves, big boy."

"It's just I can't hardly wait — you're so foxy, it's unreal. . . ."

■ ■ ■ ■

"This killer," Hotchner said, "like many serial offenders, thrives on manipulation, domination and control. He feels that he has no control in his normal life, and this is the only way he can get it."

"Turn right here," "she" said.

Tom did as he was told. They now traveled north on Hankes Road, not another car in sight.

"You sure there's a motel out this way?"

She rubbed Bob's leg reassuringly. "Just another maybe ten miles up this road — that's all."

"Ten miles? I don't know if I can *wait* that long. . . ."

Which was exactly what Tom was supposed to say.

Smiling, "Aileen" said, "Well, if you're in that much of a hurry, why not just pull off up there . . . into the forest preserve."

"Where?"

"It's right up on the right. To tell you the truth, lover, I don't know if I can wait, either."

"Really?"

"Really. Baby, baby . . . am I *wet* for you. . . ."

"Even though he has an inadequate personality, don't be fooled," Hotchner said. "His IQ is probably well above normal."

Hotchner glanced at Rossi, who said to the crowd, "This is a very organized offender, capable of almost anything. He's convinced beyond a doubt that he's superior to the police, the FBI, and of course his victims. He began by sending these photos to the police, and now he's going to the media to gain even more attention."

Hotchner, nodding, picked back up: "He's certain we can't catch him, and he's demonstrating his arrogance."

Following directions, Tom turned off the road onto the blacktop of the Aurora West Forest Preserve. A short distance in, a gravel parking lot loomed on the right.

Tom pulled in, killed the lights, and shut off the car.

As he turned to kiss her, "Aileen" withdrew a gun from "her" purse and leveled it at Tom, whose eyes went wide with fear.

"What the hell?"

"Oh, Tom, Tom, Tom . . . you're such a fool."

■ ■ ■ ■

Hotchner continued: "This UnSub is cold and calculating and devoid of compassion or mercy. He is a textbook sociopath."

"What the hell? You want money?"

"She" pulled the wig off and the "female" voice dropped to its normal, deeper timbre. "I don't want your money, Tom."

His face went pasty. "You . . . you're a *man?*"

"And to think I called you a fool, when you're clearly such a perceptive observer."

He flicked the safety off the .22 automatic. Not a big gun, but big enough.

"Please . . . *please* don't kill me! Please, I . . ."

The first shot hit Tom in the face and he sagged back against the door. He groaned once and two more quick shots silenced him.

"Now you're wet for *me,* Tom."

"The UnSub," Hotchner told the assembly, "is highly organized — he plans ahead and, so far at least, he seems ready for pretty much any situation he encounters."

Working quickly now, he got out the passenger side, came around to the driver's side, opened the door and watched as Tom flopped out of the car into a heap on the ground.

From the purse, the killer got a handkerchief, then got back into the vehicle to wipe down everything he had touched. The wig, purse, and gun, he took with him. Outside, he plucked a Mini Maglite from the purse, clicked it on, and sent the beam, narrow and pointed low, out ahead as he made his way to a pile of leaves at the far end of the parking lot. After shoving the leaves aside, he pulled out a backpack he'd buried in the underbrush.

Next, he picked the corpse up under its arms and dragged the thing into the woods, where he tossed it into a shallow grave. Using the camp shovel with which he'd dug it, he filled the hole in quickly.

Changing out of his "Aileen" apparel, and into his regular clothes, took barely any time even in the near-pitch darkness of the forest. All the while he dressed, he strained to hear any sound. He knew he was in the middle of nowhere, but the possibility that someone had heard one of the shots, or seen the flash as they drove by, had to be considered.

"The photographs serve a couple of purposes," Hotchner told the attentive group. "First, they function as a souvenir, giving him a way to relive the crime later. The Un-

Sub can re-create the excitement for himself with the pictures. Secondly, they are his instrument to communicate with us . . . and to *taunt* us."

After packing his female clothes in the back-pack, he got out his camera. As he set up the first shot, he wondered if he should send it straight to the FBI. The idea amused him.

They knew about him now, these so-called "profilers." Taunting the police was easy, almost too easy, but the feds — these *particular* feds — made a new challenge.

Perhaps it was time to say, "Hello, and welcome to *my* world."

He snapped the photo, flash strobing the night; then another, then changed angles and took a few more. Then, in a burst of inspiration, he realized that a bigger, more spectacular introduction was needed for the profilers.

And he knew just what to do.

When he had finished shooting his photos, he squatted outside the passenger side of the car. Looking through the windows on each side, he could see the moon hanging just above the trees, the mark's blood black on the driver's side window in the moon glow.

He took a couple more photos. He loved the black blood. It took every ounce of strength he possessed not to touch it.

But a real artist knew not to touch a master-piece when it was still damp.

A voice from the audience called out: "What he's telling us now?"

Prentiss detected a note of sarcasm in the question, but Hotchner answered it straight.

"That he's in control. That he's smarter than us. That he can strike any time he wants . . . and there's nothing we can do to stop him."

Rising, he strode to the backpack and put away the camera, then swung the pack onto his shoulders.

He had known he would not want to walk back to town, and a hitchhiker would be noticed. Deeper in the woods, not near any trail, he had taken a secondhand bicycle he bought this morning and chained it to the trunk of a tree, before covering it with leaves and dirt. Even in the blackness, the arithmetic was simple: just count his steps from the concrete block that held the trash bin across the parking lot to the spot one-hundred-fifty steps into the woods where the bike lay waiting.

Ten minutes later, he was on the road, pedaling toward town, nothing more than a silhouette in the night, "Aileen" as dead as Tom.

■ ■ ■ ■

Rossi stepped forward. "What is he *saying?* He's saying 'Go screw yourselves.' "

This got a few laughs in the big hall.

Rossi continued: "But, just for the record? He's not limiting that sentiment to the five of us on this stage. He's saying it to every man and woman here. This UnSub thinks he's smarter than all of you and all of us, put together. And, so far, folks . . . he's been right."

No one laughed at that. The auditorium fell silent and Rossi stepped back, nodding to Hotchner to continue.

He did. "There are some other things we're pretty sure about, too," the team leader said. "He's white. Serial killers hardly ever cross racial lines. He's between thirty-five and fifty."

All across the audience, pens were scribbling furiously in notebooks; here and there, mini–cassette recorders were held up.

"These are not the crimes of a young offender," Hotchner was saying. "These murders are too sophisticated, too organized, the fantasy too well formed, to have been committed by someone who hasn't had years to develop it. He also has patience.

Some of these crimes took a long time to set up . . . and evidence suggests he's even stalked some of the victims."

Morgan said, "That's a patient man. He's going to have a job that allows him freedom to come and go as he pleases, as well."

"He's single?" one cop called out.

"Not necessarily," Prentiss said. "It's just as likely we'll find that he's married. He might even have kids too."

Morgan nodded. "He's not acting out the sexual aspects of the crimes on his list, and that is a major, significant omission. No sexual evidence has turned up in these crimes. So there's no reason to think that he's married or not. Remember Dennis Rader, the BTK killer in Wichita, Kansas? Married and with two kids."

Reid added, "Andrei Chikatilo, the Russian serial killer, was also married and had two children."

Taking back the reins, Hotchner said, "Also like Rader, who had a job with a security company for fifteen years, our UnSub will be a police buff or work in security or he could have applied for the police and been turned down. He could, presumably, even be a current officer."

No mention of Detective Denson would be made today, however; Hotchner had made that clear to his team.

Rossi said, "But he is very likely to find a way to inject himself into this investigation. Further, he's got his own car. These crimes have taken place around the city, and they're too far away from each other for him to walk or take public transportation."

Hotchner picked back up: "His car will be either a police-type vehicle, like a Ford Crown Victoria, or something larger, perhaps. That fifty-five-gallon drum got to Chinatown somehow. The vehicle will be nondescript and probably a dark color, navy blue, gray, maybe black. He's moved in and out among people both at Bangs Lake and Chinatown, yet no one seems to have noticed him."

An audience member asked, "You really think it could be a cop?"

Rossi stepped forward again. "We're not saying it's a cop any more than we're saying it's the night watchman at Navy Pier. This is a *type* of person. We put all the pieces together, and we narrow down the list of suspects from everybody in the United States, to everyone in the Midwest, to men in Illinois, to white men in the greater Chicago area, to cop buffs with too much time on their hands."

Morgan said, "Eventually, we'll get down

to one guy and the sooner, the better. We can do this, but we need your help." He pointed at random faces in the audience and tapped his finger, *bing bing bing bing.* "You're our eyes in the streets, guys. *All* of you. Which is why we're trying to help you know what to look for."

The briefing lasted another half hour and, when they were through, a few officers and detectives hung around to ask even more questions. By the time the BAU team left the university, it was after nine at night and any reasonable person would be heading home; they, however, grabbed a quick snack at a diner, and were soon back in the field office and at work on the case.

Prentiss had hoped to go back to the hotel to get some laundry done. They'd packed for only a few days and had now been here a week. If she didn't get some laundry done soon, all the perfume in the world wouldn't prevent her from being mistaken for a Cubs player after an extra inning game.

She continued to work the victimology, trying to discern why one potential victim was chosen over another.

Addie Andrews and Benny Mendoza had probably been nothing more than victims of opportunity on that rainy April night. The UnSub had chosen the time and place for a reason — mimicking Berkowitz — making the identities of the victims less significant. Killer needed a necking couple and, on that particular night, few couples would have been out. The weather had seen to that.

With the two girls at Bangs Lake, the story had been different. They were two among hundreds that day. *Why them?*

Donna Cooper was a brown-haired, straight-A student, and a cheerleader in high school. Her friend, Casey Goddard, had also been a brunette young woman going to college part-time and working two jobs to pay for it. She, too, had been a bright girl and a good student. Of the hundreds of girls who had been at Bangs Lake throughout that sunny June day, why had these two been chosen over all the others? Certainly more than two bikini-clad brunettes had been on the beach that day.

Prentiss was still puzzling over that when a face appeared on the screen of her laptop: Penelope Garcia.

"I've got news," Garcia said.

"Try to make it good news," Prentiss said.

"You'll have to decide that from your end. First, rain washed away any fingerprints on the outside of Bobby Edels's car."

"How about the interior?"

"Wiped clean. Even Bobby's fingerprints

were gone."

Prentiss said, "The car was missing a long time — they might have just evaporated."

"The crime scene tech I talked to said there were signs that the car had been wiped. The killer might have been in the car."

"Or even moved it," Prentiss suggested. "Have you come up with any good reason for the car being dumped in that neighborhood?"

"Sorry. Could be the UnSub moved the car from wherever he abducted Bobby. But this much we know: the car didn't have plates, and was wiped clean. If the towing company hadn't filed for the title with the Vehicle Identification Number, we still wouldn't know where it was."

"Meaning no offense whatsoever, to a valuable member of our team? Nothing you have said sounds even remotely like good news."

But on the little flat screen, Garcia was smiling. "Well, I do have one more thing. . . ."

Noting the glee in the computer expert's tone, Prentiss sat forward. "Spill."

"Our friend Detective Jake Denson," Garcia said, with triumph in her tone, "had a connection to one of the young women who disappeared."

Prentiss felt the air go out of her. More worthless information. "Garcia, we knew that. It's a small town, they worked at a local convenience store Denson frequented, and now he's investigating their disappearances. End of story."

"Here's a brand-*new* story," Garcia said. "Casey Goddard used to babysit for Denson's kids, before his divorce. His ex-wife and the kids? Moved away."

"You wouldn't tease me, would you? Make things up?"

"This is as real as real deals come. I was combing newspaper articles that were written not long after the women's bodies were identified. Emily Goddard, Casey's mom, gave an interview to the *Lake County Witness* where she was quoted as saying, 'I have faith in Detective Denson. He's dedicated and he's been a good friend over the years. Casey used to babysit for his children — I know he will find my daughter's killer.' "

Prentiss's eyes darted around the room searching for Hotchner. *Everybody else was here — where was the boss?* Finally, she said, "Garcia, hang tight. I can't find Hotch."

Turning to the room, she asked, "Anybody know where Hotch went?"

With a vague gesture, Reid said, "He's in one of the back offices, trying to catch an hour's sleep."

"Wake him," Prentiss said.

Shaking his head, Reid said, "He doesn't want to be disturbed. He said —"

"Whatever he said, he's going to want to hear this. Wake him."

Her tone carried enough weight to propel Reid out of his chair and out of the conference room.

Almost simultaneously, Morgan and Rossi turned toward her and asked, "What is it?"

Prentiss held up a steadying palm. "Hotch'll be here in a second," she said to them (and Garcia, still online and on screen).

Their bleary-eyed team leader came in quickly, jacket off, necktie loosened, short hair managing to look mussed, and said to Prentiss, "Please tell me this is a major break."

"Might well be," Prentiss said. She nodded to Garcia's face on the flat screen.

He leaned in at Prentiss's laptop. "What is it, Garcia?"

The zaftig blonde reiterated what she'd told Prentiss.

Hotchner's alertness sharpened even as his irritation vanished, and ice was in his voice as he said, "Garcia, tell me you have Denson's home address ready."

She said nothing, just punching some keys to give him the information almost instantaneously.

Hotchner's eyes went to Morgan. "Morgan, get hold of Lorenzon. I want the two of you to pick up Jake Denson and get him in here ASAP."

Rossi shrugged. "I could go with Morgan."

Hotchner shook his head. "This might be nothing, but it might also mean the apprehension of an offender who's armed and dangerous, and knows law enforcement tactics."

"Right," Rossi said. "So I'll go with Morgan."

"No. Lorenzon's a street cop, Dave. You're a profiler."

"What, I'm not up to this collar?"

"It's not a collar yet — we're just bringing Denson in for questioning. But I want one of the locals in on this, not just the big bad feds."

That mollified Rossi.

Just after midnight, when they should have been asleep in their hotel rooms (or at least, Prentiss thought, back doing their laundry), the BAU team was still in the conference room as Morgan and Lorenzon came in accompanying a very pissed-off Jake Denson.

The detective with the Yul Brynner haircut wore jeans, a Cubs T-shirt and sneakers. He looked like he hadn't shaved since morning and he still had his gun on his hip.

Hotchner, pulling his tie tight as he rose to meet them, glanced at Morgan, asking a question with his eyes.

"He wasn't at home," Morgan said. "He was working — caught up with him at the Wauconda PD."

Hotchner turned to the detective and said, "You always work this late, Detective?"

"Do you?" Denson said. "What the hell is this all about?"

"Have a seat," Hotchner said.

"I'll take a pass," Denson said, folding his arms. "You see, I'm not going to be here that long. So I'll just stand."

"We need to talk about your case — the murdered girls from Bangs Lake." Hotchner gestured to a chair at the nearest table. "You'll be more comfortable if you sit."

"How many times," Denson said, "and how many ways, do I have to tell you where to stick your task force? You're not getting my case, boys and girls. I started it, and I'll finish it."

Hotchner said, "We don't want to talk to

you about *your* investigation."

"No?"

"No. We want to talk to you about *our* investigation."

"What about your investigation?" Denson asked, confused. "You think I'm gonna let you pick my brain so you can —"

"We're investigating *you*, Detective Denson."

"Me?"

Hotchner's hands went to his hips, elbows winged. "You haven't been entirely forthcoming with us."

"Why should I be?"

"Thing is, in keeping things from us, Detective, you've helped us develop a suspect."

"I have? Who?"

Several seconds passed before he realized that everyone in the room was staring at him. "Me?"

"You lied to us," Hotchner said.

"Like hell I did!"

"Casey Goddard was a babysitter for your family."

Denson swallowed. "Not telling you that doesn't make me a liar."

Rossi asked him, "Would you let a perp get away with that line of bull?"

Denson turned toward Rossi.

But it was Prentiss who spoke: "Didn't your mother ever tell you a sin of omission is the same as a lie?"

Denson spun toward her.

Only Reid commented next: "Holding that back makes you seem like someone with something to hide."

Denson swivelled to face Reid.

Then Morgan, shaking his head, said, "I can't believe we haven't busted your damn ass already."

Denson's final turn had brought him back to his initial position. No one said anything else but all of their eyes were on him and his hands went to either side of his head like he was trying to hold his skull together.

"All right, goddamnit — I *loved* her!"

If Denson was expecting looks of revulsion, he didn't get any. The profilers were studying him, yes, but clinically.

And Hotchner pulled out a chair for him and the detective finally sat.

"She wasn't underage or anything. It wasn't like that. We'd known her for years, she was my kids' babysitter since she was in junior high, and was like . . . like one of the family. I went through a rough patch of drinking and running around, and finally my wife asked me for a divorce. Before my wife moved out, with the kids, Casey was still baby-sitting for us. This one night, I drove her home and she knew I was upset about something and we sat and talked and . . . I guess she'd had a secret crush on me or some such, because it . . . it turned into something."

Hotchner asked, "Did your wife know?"

"No. Christ, if she had, she'd have used it to beat me up even worse in the divorce."

"How about the girl's parents? Did they know?"

"I don't think so."

Morgan moved in. "How about the other girl? How about Donna, did *she* know? Is that why you killed them both?"

"No! Hell, no." Denson was shaking his head, furiously. "I didn't kill either of them. I *told* you. . . . I loved Casey. When my wife moved out, Casey and me, we started sneaking around, because she was still in high school at the time, and her parents would've gone ape shit, and who could blame them? Finally she got tired of me, I guess . . . novelty wore off. I think I'd have stayed with her forever, if she'd've had me. All in all, it lasted maybe . . . six months."

Hotchner said, "She didn't love you, anymore. But you still loved her?"

Denson shook his head. "No. No, I'd moved on, too. I wasn't some old perv stalking her, if that's what you mean."

"And you tried to keep us out of the Bangs Lake investigation so we wouldn't turn this up?"

"Maybe. Maybe that was part of it." He looked up helplessly at Hotchner, then his eyes searched out every other face. "But mostly I wanted to solve this thing, solve it myself! Why do you think I've been working so hard? I want to get the bastard that did this awful thing to that lovely, lovely girl."

And he hunched over and cried. He didn't even bother bringing up his hands to cover his face or catch the tears. He just sat there and wept.

Finally Hotchner said, "Go home."

"What?"

"While we're wasting our time with you, we're losing ground to the real killer."

"You . . . you believe me?"

Morgan said, "Shouldn't we?"

But Hotchner was shaking his head. "I don't believe you and I don't disbelieve you. We'll check out your story. But if you're on the level, and all you want is Casey's killer to be brought to justice, here's what you're going to do."

"Anything," Denson said.

"First, you're off the case. Second, you convince your chief to share all information that you and anyone else on the Wauconda PD have gathered on this. Then your chief is to send someone over to join our task force. *Not you* — someone else."

"I'm the one that knows the case!"

Hotchner's smile was like a cut on his face that had refused to heal. "You're still a suspect, and we have a policy here at the BAU — suspects don't work on the investigation."

Morgan said, "If you're looking for a choice, we could lock you up till this thing's over."

Denson sighed. "I'll do everything you said. I'll cooperate fully. You have my word. Just . . . just catch the son of a bitch."

Rossi said, "You have our word. We will."

When Denson had gone, Hotchner wheeled to Jareau. "Get SAIC Himes to give us bumper-lock surveillance on our fellow law enforcer, Detective Denson. I want to know his whereabouts twenty-four/seven."

Jareau nodded, cell phone out already, and headed off.

Rossi was frowning. "You think our friend from Wauconda is the UnSub?"

Hotchner breathed deep. "We'll tail him as such. Who knows? Maybe we'll save him from himself."

CHAPTER EIGHT:
AUGUST 6
CHICAGO, ILLINOIS

Here and there around the conference room table, the BAU team members were lost in their individual pursuits, heads buried in evidence, reports, laptops, crime scene photos. They'd had scant sleep since their interview with Denson, but with the addition of the information from the Wauconda crimes, they should now have a bigger knowledge base to work with. And — a basic tenet of profiling — the more information you have, the more accurate your profile.

Despite these long hours, and mainlining coffee to keep going, they had renewed energy, knowing that they had more information on the two women.

Problem was, for Supervisory Special Agent Derek Morgan, this so-called new information wasn't helping. The Wauconda police, despite Denson's avowed constant attention to the case, appeared to know little more than the BAU team.

"I've read the file cover to cover," Morgan said, shaking his head. "I'm not sure Denson isn't still our best suspect. He hasn't dug up anything we didn't already know."

Reid leaned back in his chair and gave Morgan narrow-eyed regard. "I noticed that, as well. But I had the opposite reaction."

"How so?"

"If Denson *was* the killer? He could have planted false evidence and red herrings. He could have even used the report to build a frame for another suspect. These files, and the report he wrote up for us, are scant but accurate. I believe he's telling the truth."

Prentiss said, "Reid makes a good point."

"Or," Rossi said, "Denson could be withholding evidence."

Morgan frowned. "Because he's our Un-Sub?"

Rossi shrugged facially. "Possibly. Or because he still wants to wage this investigation himself, as a vendetta."

But Hotchner was shaking his head. "It doesn't mean anything one way or the other at this juncture. We've still got to work the case as if he's a suspect."

Morgan glanced at Hotch. "As if . . . ? Does that mean you agree with Reid that

Denson's telling the truth?"

"It means I don't care," Hotchner said. "We work the case. That means we read the evidence, work the victimology and study the UnSub's behavior — nothing more, nothing less."

Nods all around.

Then they lapsed into silence and got back to work.

Morgan knew Hotchner was right: they had a killer to find, and Denson was just another person of interest now. The only thing to do at this stage was concentrate on the work in front of them.

After another quarter hour, Lorenzon popped in, a skinny, bushy-haired white guy trailing him. The man had a long, sharp nose, even white teeth and a pointy chin. Taller than the African-American detective, he wore a blue, collarless shirt with buttons down the front, navy blue slacks with narrow maroon suspenders and black loafers. Lorenzon instructed their guest to wait by the door, and approached Hotchner, who was seated at the head of the conference-room table.

Lorenzon said softly, almost whispering, "I think you're going to want to talk to this gentleman."

Around the table, they all looked up.

"Why?" Hotchner asked, also sotto voce.

Lorenzon's eyebrows rose. "Because he's identified your John Doe . . . and recognized the picture of another of the victims from the newspaper."

Hotchner said, "I think we want to talk to this gentleman."

Lorenzon ushered the guy over, gesturing to him the way a car salesman in a showroom indicates a shiny new model. "This is Paul Grant. Mr. Grant is a bartender from a club called Hot Rods."

"*Not* a car club," Rossi said, with a puckish smile.

"No," Grant said, with a nervous smile in response. "It's a gay bar."

Hotchner stood and gestured to an open chair. "Sit down, Mr. Grant. Join us, Detective Lorenzon."

Morgan knew his boss might have preferred a private meeting with Grant, but the field office was laid out so that conference rooms and interrogation rooms were not even on the same floor, much less near each other. And taking this witness upstairs and ushering him into a cubicle might create the wrong impression.

The chairs Lorenzon and the bartender took were near Hotchner. Reid and Prentiss slid their chairs down in the direction of

Morgan, at the far end of the table, to give their boss a semblance of privacy. Rossi, however, stayed put.

Hotchner asked the bartender, "You know our John Doe?"

"I didn't 'know him' know him," the bartender said. "But I *knew* him."

Though the other agents had mostly moved down, they were all, of course, listening in on this interview. And that particular response made Prentiss's eyes widen while Morgan tilted his head just a shade (the equivalent of anybody else rolling their eyes). Meanwhile, Rossi looked like he was trying hard to digest something, with only Reid seeming perfectly comfortable with Grant's chasing-its-own-tail answer.

Hotchner asked, "Could you break that down?"

Grant shrugged. "Well, it wasn't like we were friends or anything. We just both knew some of the same people."

"You knew his name, then?"

"Yeah. Sure. Of course. Stevie."

"Do you know Stevie's last name?"

Grant considered that. "Pretty sure it was Darnell. Stevie Darnell."

"You didn't know him well."

"No."

"How *did* you know him?"

"From the club, mostly. You work the bar, you get friendly with regulars."

"He was a regular, then."

"Oh, yes."

"Was that the extent of it, your friendship?"

" 'Friendship' overdoes it. I ran in to him at a couple of gay events, once or twice at the movies, but that was pretty much it. He was one of those people you know well enough to say 'hi' to."

Rossi asked, "You say he was a regular. Was he in the club a lot?"

"Some."

Hotchner asked, "How much is some?"

Grant scratched at his bushy head of hair as if that might unearth the answer. "Twice a week, maybe?"

"Pretty regular, then," Rossi said.

"A lot of the guys are. Not Bobby though."

Rossi said, "Bobby?"

"Bobby Edels," Grant said, and shrugged. "The other guy that got killed. That's why I'm here, isn't it?"

Prentiss moved her chair back closer; so did Morgan and Reid.

Morgan said, "So you knew Bobby Edels, too?"

Grant nodded. "A little. Not even as well as I did Stevie. Bobby, he came into the club a couple of times, but he wasn't out yet."

"Still in the closet," Rossi said.

Grant nodded again. "Still in the closet. It was like, you know how it is, he was still trying to put the pieces together. Stevie, *he* was out — *way* out."

For once the profilers were at a loss for words: a major break had just walked into the conference room and sat down at the table. Hard to know even where to start . . .

Detective Lorenzon finally spoke up: "Tell them what you told me, Mr. Grant."

Glancing from the cop to Hotchner, his voice barely above a whisper, Grant said, "On different nights, I saw them each leave the club with the same guy."

Rossi frowned. "The three were together?"

"No! The first night Stevie left with the dude, the other night Bobby left with him."

Hotchner asked, "Did you know the man they left with?"

"No. I saw him around once in a while, but not often. He's struck me as kind of a creep, frankly. A user."

"Of drugs?"

"Well, maybe. But definitely of people."

Hotchner nodded. "Did anybody else in the club seem tight with him?"

Grant shrugged. "I wouldn't know. I pick up on things, sure; but I'm also busy working. That's something I never noticed."

Jumping in, Rossi asked, "Think you could you identify this guy if you saw him again?"

"Oh, yeah, sure. Absolutely. In a heartbeat."

Hotchner turned to glance around the room. "Where's JJ?"

Prentiss said, "Dealing with the editors of the newspapers, I believe."

"Would you get her, please?"

Prentiss got up and went out.

Returning to Grant, Hotchner asked, "Does the club have video security?"

"You bet it does. Inside and out."

"Good. Now, I want you to sit down with a forensic artist — are you willing to do that?"

"To stop some bastard who's killing gay men? Hell, yeah. Anything. Name it."

No one bothered to point out that the UnSub wasn't just killing gay men — this was a monster without prejudice.

Prentiss came back in, Jareau in tow.

Hotchner made quick introductions, then said, "JJ, we need a forensic artist ASAP. Mr. Grant is going to give us a description of a possible suspect."

"I'm on it," Jareau said with a smile and a nod, and was gone again.

Hotchner turned to Prentiss and told her, "We need the security video from the club and we need to stream them to Garcia. Once the forensic artist is finished, Garcia can scan the tapes looking for our UnSub."

"Yes, sir," Prentiss said. "Do you want me to interview the employees of the club?"

"Let's hold off on that until we've got a suspect sketch. After that? Make it a top priority."

"Yes, sir."

"Morgan," Hotchner said, shifting, "you and Reid stick with that Wauconda material and see if there's anything we missed the first time."

Reid nodded, and Morgan said, "If there's anything, we'll find it."

Turning to Rossi, Hotchner said, "David, you and I will go back to victimology. We'll add in the two gay male victims and see how that changes things."

"Right," Rossi said.

Hotchner thanked Grant, and Lorenzon took the witness to a break room for coffee while a sketch artist was rounded up. But the team leader would ask Tovar to check Grant out — their cooperative citizen could be the UnSub insinuating himself.

Three and a half hours later, the profilers

were again gathered around the table, but now with fresh copies of the composite drawing made by the forensic artist and from Grant's description. Detective Tovar, back from running down some stray leads, had taken the bartender home and had just gotten back again. He and the other task force detective, Lorenzon, were sitting in.

"Did a copy of this sketch go to Garcia?" Hotchner asked.

Prentiss nodded. "She's already working on the video."

"Good. Nice work."

"This was fast," Rossi said appreciatively, eyebrows up, a copy of the sketch in hand. "How about the bartender's boss? The club owner? Any fuss from him over handing over the security vids? That's a pretty insular world."

"Yes it is," Prentiss said. "And a serial killer who might be targeting gay men is bad for business in that world."

Morgan said, "If the clientele is too afraid to leave home, they won't come to the club. No patrons, no money."

Prentiss was nodding. "That's what I pointed out to him. After that, the impresario behind Hot Rods couldn't wait to hand over the videos. We got everything for the last six months."

"Free enterprise," Rossi said. "Gotta love it. Self-interest, the keystone to good citizenship."

Hotchner asked, "Morgan, did you and Reid come up with anything new out of the Wauconda material?"

Tossing the file, Morgan said, "Zip. Seems for all his bluster, Denson's investigation was stalled. For no more progress than he was making, he might as well have gone door to door asking for a confession."

Rossi's brow was furrowed as he stared at the suspect sketch. "In two of the crimes our UnSub has chosen to imitate, he's gone out of his way to find gay victims. He's duplicating crimes on a level I've certainly never seen."

"Fast and loose with details," Reid said, "but the overall scenario he mimics with exactitude."

Hotchner asked, "And what does that tell us about him?"

"He's obsessed," Morgan said. "He wants the attention the original killers received. The closer he comes to replicating their crimes, the closer he comes to replicating their fame . . . he thinks."

Reid said, "He believes that if he replicates what the original serial killers did, as precisely as possible, and doesn't get caught —

and they *did,* remember, all get caught — then he's better than all of them." The young profiler shook his head. "This is a *massive* ego."

Rossi chuckled mirthlessly. "And yet, still an inadequate personality."

"About the victimology," Prentiss said, sitting forward. "How do we get out in front of this guy? There's a hundred serial killers he could pick to imitate next. How do we figure out which one it will be, and try to protect the appropriate potential victims?"

That was a question none of them had an answer for.

Their mood, uplifted by the gay bar breakthrough, turned somewhat glum at the grim reality Prentiss had pointed out. They went back to work and the day dragged along with precious little progress. The long hours of hard work and little rest were wearing down both body and spirit.

Morgan knew they needed another breakthrough, and they were all poring over material looking for it; but Morgan was wondering if Rossi's idea of drawing out the UnSub was not the most reasonable course, after all.

He was about to say something when Garcia's face popped up on his computer monitor via a video link.

"You do not look like a happy man," she said.

"Girl, tell me this isn't just a social call."

"It isn't. I have a little something for you."

He straightened. "You found something?"

"Just possibly the identity of your Un-Sub."

"You're a doll." Morgan turned and said, "Hotch! You need to hear this."

The entire team huddled around Morgan's laptop and gave their full attention to the genie in the box.

"I may have found him," she said, "on the security video from the bar."

Prentiss asked, "How could you identify him from that? Was he in the company of one or more of the victims?"

"No, but the suspect sketch gave me somebody to look for, and the face from the security video I fed into my facial recognition software, which ran those parameters against all the mug shots in the Cook County database. That's how I came up with a less than sterling citizen named Eddie Minchell."

"Good," Hotchner said. "What do we know about him?"

"A thoroughgoing lowlife," Garcia said. "Twenty-four with arrests and convictions for procurement, misdemeanor possession of marijuana, and one battery charge that got dropped when the complainant didn't show up in court."

His expression perplexed, Reid said, "And now he's imitating some of the most evil serial killers in American history? He doesn't fit our profile."

Nodding, Morgan said, "Either we're completely off base or this isn't our guy."

"One way to find out," Hotchner said. "Garcia, do you have a current address on Mr. Minchell?"

"Last one was an apartment on Clark," she said, "near the bus station."

She read off the address.

"I *know* that building," Lorenzon said, sitting up. "It's an old hotel that devolved into a flophouse. We busted a bunch of junkies there, last few years."

"All right," Hotchner said. "You and Morgan go get him."

The African-American detective nodded.

Rossi said, "I'd like to go along."

"Fine," Hotchner said. Then he asked Lorenzon, "Can Chicago PD provide backup?"

"No problem," Lorenzon said.

Tovar stood up. "I'm in too."

The two profilers and two local detectives

took two vehicles: a Tahoe, with Morgan behind the wheel with Rossi riding; and Lorenzon's unmarked, which the detectives shared.

Less than a half hour later, they pulled up and double-parked, lights flashing, at the run-down building housing Minchell's apartment. Each man donned a bulletproof vest, Morgan's and Rossi's with FBI stenciled in white on front and back, while the detectives' vests said CHICAGO POLICE. The heat today was sweltering, all four sweating profusely.

The neighborhood was busy, sidewalk heavy with pedestrian traffic going or coming from lunch. None of the four were distracted by a need for lunch: the aroma of the neighborhood was a bouquet of fried chicken, car exhaust, Burger King, cigarette smoke and urine. Of course, an old Chicagoan like Morgan felt right at home. . . .

As they checked their weapons, Lorenzon said, "Look, uh . . . you know how I told your boss backup would be a piece of cake?"

"Uh oh," Rossi said.

"Uh oh is right," Lorenzon said. "I radioed in on the way over and got informed SWAT is wrapped up in a hostage crisis in Wrigleyville."

"Cubs fans out of control again?"

Lorenzon grinned. "Hey, wouldn't surprise me; but actually I think it's a robbery gone bad."

"What about patrolmen?"

"Cleaning up a chain reaction accident on Lake Shore Drive."

"There's four of us." Rossi shrugged. "One nonviolent offender, I think we can handle it."

"He *did* have a battery charge," Tovar said with half a grin.

Morgan gave him the other half of the grin. "What are you saying, Hilly? Want to wait for SWAT because the guy got frisky once?"

Tovar shrugged. "What if he's the killer?"

Rossi said, "Then we better make sure he doesn't get away." He made a face, eyebrows climbing. "Of course, if this really is our UnSub? Once we get back, Morgan and I can start updating our résumés."

Tovar bit. "Why?"

"Because we'll be looking for work once Hotchner sees out how far off we were on the profile."

They stood at the rear of the double-parked Tahoe and discussed tactics. Morgan and Lorenzon would go in the front, Rossi and Tovar down the alley next to the ten-story brick building, to find a back entrance or a fire escape, just in case.

They were about to execute their plan when Morgan looked up and saw Eddie Minchell less than half a block away, walking toward them, smiling to himself, the poster boy for the Ignorance Is Bliss Society.

With this many citizens around, Morgan couldn't risk yelling; he could only hope Minchell would just keep coming, oblivious to their presence on the sidewalk.

A medium-sized guy with a plastic bag of groceries dangling from one hand, Minchell was a ringer for the forensic drawing: floppy blond hair, lively blue eyes, high cheekbones, and a sharp chin. He wore a green T-shirt with the words ALL-BEEF WIENER, jeans with holes in the knees, and canvas sneakers.

Morgan willed himself to become invisible in the throng. The two detectives and the other profiler were turning now, to go to their stations, and had no idea that their quarry was approaching them from their right. Wanting to alert them, but knowing he'd have to yell to be heard, he didn't, as Minchell would hear him, too. . . .

"Don't see me," Morgan muttered to himself as he closed the rear door of the SUV. "Don't see me, don't see me, don't see me." Morgan stepped up on the curb, the muttering now his mantra, his eyes riveted to Minchell.

Hand snaking toward his pistol, Morgan took another step . . .

. . . then their eyes locked.

And in a split second, everything went to hell.

Minchell made him as an officer, and the blissful smile dissolved as he froze, staring at Morgan. And in his next breath, Minchell took off in the opposite direction, pitching the grocery bag.

"Minchell!" Morgan bellowed. *"Freeze!"*

Rossi, Lorenzon and Tovar all turned, but Morgan was already in motion, heading up the block in pursuit, struggling through the mob on the sidewalk. His eyes still on Minchell, Morgan instantly decided to cut between two parked cars and move into the street.

Within seconds, Morgan heard footsteps pounding the concrete behind him and knew the others had joined pursuit. Minchell was still struggling to make his way on the sidewalk, shoving people out of his way, running as best he could, occasionally looking back to check on the progress of his pursuers.

Running in the street, weaving in and out of cars, getting sworn and honked at, Morgan closed the distance on his prey rapidly. The space between them narrowed from twenty yards to ten yards, then to five yards as Morgan again cut between two parked cars and hopped up onto the sidewalk, and closed the distance to ten feet.

"Federal officer!" Morgan yelled, but the crowd didn't cut him much slack.

Still, Morgan managed to get within five feet of his man, and then Morgan drew even closer, stretching his arm to reach for Minchell, who suddenly veered left out of Morgan's grasp, down an alley.

Morgan overshot, and had to bump his way back to the opening, the other three — Rossi, Tovar and Lorenzon — turning down the alley, ahead of him now.

No pedestrian traffic in the alley, but parked cars sat here and there on either side. The four officers followed their man down the narrow canyon of brick and concrete.

"Freeze!" Rossi yelled.

Tovar followed that with, *"Stop!"*

Soon Lorenzon — younger than Rossi and Tovar — took the lead while Morgan quickly caught up with the other two. On his way, Minchell tipped over a metal trash can and it caught Lorenzon across the shins, sending him in a somersault that landed the detective in a heap, the others dodging around him to keep from piling on. Rossi and Tovar slowed, Morgan bursting past them, continuing the chase as he heard Lorenzon yelling, "*Go! Go!* I'm *fine!*"

Instead of turning at the next corner, Minchell charged straight into the street, sidestepping left to keep from running broadside into a passing Volkswagen Passat. Lurching right, Minchell avoided a second car, drawing horn blasts from several drivers as he sprinted across the street, Morgan closing in again.

Hearing the screech of brakes, Morgan looked right to see a yellow Hummer bearing down on him, and he dove out of the way, rolling and popping up again, but having lost ground with his suspect.

Morgan was in top shape but he still felt as though he were breathing liquid fire. Sweat rolled down his cheeks and his back felt sopped under the Kevlar, his legs aching like flu had suddenly set in. Even as he pursued his quarry, a part of his brain was processing just how bad his balky knee would feel tomorrow. . . .

Still, he pounded after Minchell, determined that the bastard was not going to get away. They were nearly to the end of the second block's worth of alley when Morgan saw a pile of garbage bags on the right. Veering left, he launched himself, his arms encircling the legs of his target, and he and Minchell flew as one into the garbage bags and crashed with a sickening, smelly squish. Then they both rolled back into the alley, rising together, facing off, Minchell getting a short-bladed knife from somewhere, like Bugs Bunny producing a carrot.

As Rossi and Tovar caught up, drawing their weapons as they saw the knife, Minchell lunged at Morgan, the blade extended.

Pirouetting, allowing the blade to miss down his side with a swish, Morgan grabbed Minchell's right arm, the knife arm, in his own right hand.

The suspect was behind him now, and off balance. As Minchell kept coming forward, helped by Morgan pulling his right arm, Morgan threw his left elbow backward, catching Minchell in the face with a crunch. The blade fell from the suspect's hand and clattered on the concrete as the man seemed to slowly melt into a puddle at Morgan's feet, his nose a crushed, shapeless thing.

Standing over the suspect, wearing the nasty smile of big city cop, Tovar said, "You have the right to remain silent. . . ."

Minchell's eyes rolled up into his skull and he passed out.

". . . oh the hell with it. I'll Mirandize his ass when he wakes up."

At Morgan's side, Rossi asked, "You okay?"

"Yeah. I wish he hadn't done that, though. Knives aren't my favorite."

"Maybe he had the knife," Rossi said, looking down at the bloody face of the unconscious Minchell, "but he got your point."

Lorenzon finally came limping up and looked down at Minchell. "That's what you *get,* fucker!" he told the unconscious suspect. The big detective leaned down and rubbed his shins. "*Damn* it, that hurt. Everybody else okay?"

"Well, except for this lazy jackass," Rossi said, nodding toward the slumbering Minchell, "yeah."

Getting out his cell phone, Lorenzon called for an ambulance, then phoned a judge to get a search warrant for Minchell's apartment.

"A search warrant?" Tovar asked. "On what basis?"

"Running from federal officers is probable cause," Lorenzon said, "don't you think?"

Tovar had no argument.

Four hours later, the four found themselves in the curtained cubicle of the nearest emergency room, a bandaged Eddie Minchell in a hospital bed, hooked to a saline IV. The two cops, Rossi and Morgan, fanned out around him, Lorenzon holding up a fat bag of marijuana confiscated from the suspect's apartment.

"A pound of trouble, Eddie," Lorenzon said, looking into the bloodshot eyes of the suspect.

"How the hell did you know I had that?" Minchell asked, frowning with the hurt look of a betrayed child. "Did Boo Boo rat me out?"

Rossi looked at Morgan. "Boo Boo?"

Morgan couldn't help it — he laughed.

"Hey, is it my fault that's his fuckin' name?" Minchell said, through bandages that made understanding him a trifle tricky.

"Pound of dope and attempted murder of a federal officer," Lorenzon said. "Little man, you've had a busy day."

"No shit," Minchell said; then he lapsed into a surly silence.

"You happen to know about these murders going on in the city?" Tovar asked. "I assume you can read the papers or watch TV."

Minchell glared at the Hispanic cop, but said nothing.

"We're not DEA," Morgan said. "We're FBI. We came to see you about the killings."

His eyes huge with fear, Minchell blurted, "I want a lawyer. Now!"

"That's smart," Morgan said, patting his arm. "That's what I'd do if I was in your shoes. Or your hospital bed, anyway."

Rossi stepped closer to the suspect's bedside. "My colleague's right. If you have a lawyer, you can't get in any more trouble. It's just that it's going to take a lot longer to clear all this up."

"What? Why?"

Rossi gave him a rumpled, seen-it-all smile. "I mean, hell, Eddie — we been through that rattrap where you live. We know you're not the killer, and we just had a couple of questions for you; but yeah, sure, right, having a lawyer makes more sense. You don't want to take any chances aiding an investigation."

Minchell stewed for a long moment.

Then, as Lorenzon plucked his cell phone off his belt, to make the call to the public defender's office, Minchell said, "I guess I could probably answer a couple of questions, without, you know, an attorney."

"Good," Morgan said. "Cooperation is a good thing. That might help me forget what happened in the alley."

Minchell stared cross-eyed at the bandage on his nose.

"Yeah, I know," Morgan said, his voice matter-of-fact, no malice at all. "I broke your nose. But remember, you did try to knife me. Attempted murder of a federal officer? Kind of makes a pound of grass seem like so much shit."

". . . Okaaay. What do you wanna know?"

Rossi said, "We need to talk to you about a couple of your friends."

Minchell shifted excitedly in the bed. "You didn't say anything about me ratting anybody out!"

Rossi shook his head. "These friends aren't worried about getting ratted out, Eddie. These friends are dead."

Minchell looked surprised. "No friends of mine died lately. That I know of."

"How about Bobby Edels and Stevie Darnell?"

His brow tightened. "Never heard of 'em."

Rossi and Morgan traded a look.

"We were told different," Morgan said.

"Who the hell said so? Somebody yankin' your chain, is who. I never heard of *either* of those guys."

"A bartender from Hot Rods says you knew them," Rossi said. "In fact, he says that on one occasion, Bobby left the bar with you, and on another, Stevie did."

Minchell shrugged. "I go to that bar

sometimes, yeah. It's an okay place. I've even left with guys from time to time. I'm what you call bi-curious. But I don't remember either of those names. Of course, sometimes names don't enter into it. . . ."

Lorenzon withdrew pictures from a pocket and passed them to Minchell. "You recognize one or both of these men?"

Minchell studied the photos for a moment. "Well . . . yeah, actually I do. Yeah, I remember both these dudes . . . but neither of them was ever with me."

Rossi frowned at him. "Are you saying that neither of them left the bar with you? Or are you saying that you didn't sleep with either of them? Be specific, Eddie."

Minchell had to think about it, but finally he said, "I didn't have sex with either of those guys. Both were dudes I picked up for this *other* guy — uptight character who didn't want to be seen going into a gay club. Paid me good money to help him out and serve as sort of . . . an intermediary."

"Pimp," Tovar chimed in.

"Hey, I performed a service and was tipped for my trouble. I told each of 'em a really good-looking guy was interested, but he was shy, a closeted type, you know? But he was hot, and he had money to burn. They both went along. That isn't pimping where I come from."

"The important question now," Rossi said, "is not what we call your activity, but the name of your client."

"Hell, I don't know," Minchell said. "Swear to God, I don't."

Lorenzon held up the bag of weed. "This is not simple possession, you know. This much weight is intent to deliver — a felony."

Minchell threw up his hands, nearly pulling out the IV. "Bust me for the pot, bust me for the knife, hell, what can *I* do about it? I don't know the guy's goddamn *name!*"

Rossi patted the air in a calming fashion, then asked, "Could you identify the guy?"

"How?"

"If you *saw* him," Rossi said, as if to a slow child, "would you *know* him?"

Minchell nodded. "Like I said, good-looking guy. He's not very big, though. Still . . . there's something kind of . . . *off* about him."

Morgan asked, "How many other times did you . . . troll for this guy?"

"Just those two times. Never saw him but on those two occasions."

"If we brought in a forensic artist," Rossi said, "would you be able to help develop a picture of this man?"

Minchell's eyes and nostrils flared. "If this

guy's some kind of killer, and he found *out* . . ."

Lorenzon dangled the bag of dope. Morgan watched as Minchell silently calculated how long he would be spending in the Joliet state pen. To nudge him in the correct direction, Morgan got out the evidence bag that held Minchell's knife.

"The dope is column A," Morgan said, and then wiggled the bag with the knife. "Column B is federal time."

Rossi said, "Both is the all-you-can-serve buffet."

Minchell's face turned as white as the bandage on his nose.

Then he said, "Sit down with one of those sketch artists? Sounds like fun. Sure. Glad to help."

Chapter Nine:
August 7
Chicago, Illinois

The man some were calling the UnSub prided himself on his planning, on never leaving any detail untended.

Yet here he was doing something simple, checking to make sure that dolt was still buried if not dead, and now, looking down at the road, he could see that he was about to be interrupted, some moron butting in on his private business. . . .

Headlights turned into the gravel driveway and started up the long hill to the house, toward the back of which the UnSub had, prior to this intrusion, been heading. The sultry night (actually early morning — the time was one fifteen a.m.) offered up only a few lonely clouds that drifted like lazy smoke, blotting out the moon and a thousand stars. His own car was safely hidden in the barn, so the property should still look vacant.

So who the hell could be wandering up the driveway?

As the vehicle drew closer, he could make out a Ford Bronco. . . .

"More the merrier," he said with a shrug, then chuckled, and headed to the backyard just as planned.

There, he saw at once that the grave seemed fine, undisturbed, and the man beneath the earth made no sound. The UnSub found his shovel behind the bushes where he'd left it, then leaned it against the back wall of the house — couldn't set a trap without a carrot.

Moving back along the far side of the abandoned house, keeping the structure between him and the approaching vehicle, he came around the front as the Bronco eased up into the side yard.

The UnSub had his gun drawn as he knelt next to the corner of the old house, waiting to see who his caller was. If this was some lost tourist seeking directions, who knocked on the door, got no answer, and then headed back to the Bronco, who knows? He might just choose to be merciful. After all, his strong suit was not improvisation, but carefully calibrated performance.

And if this wasn't some poor traveler seeking assistance? Well, that was different, wasn't it?

A man climbed down out of the Bronco.

When he appeared at the front fender, he was clearly no lost tourist, not with a pistol drawn and a face as clenched as a fist. The UnSub could barely make out the man, who wore a T-shirt and jeans, and — other than a shaved or possibly bald head — the intruder's features couldn't be made out, not distinctly.

The intruder headed cautiously around the back of the house while the UnSub reversed his direction and circled around behind. As surmised, the bald man had spotted the pipe in the ground, and the propped-up shovel, and immediately holstered his weapon, grabbed the implement and started digging.

The UnSub let him dig a while.

Then, coming up behind the intruder, the UnSub said, "Don't turn around."

"It's over, asshole," the bald man said, stopping his work, leaning on a shovel full of dirt. "Denson, Wauconda PD. You're surrounded."

"Am I?"

"I *knew* it was you. . . ."

"If you knew —"

That was as far as the UnSub got before Denson spun, throwing the shovelful of dirt toward him. The UnSub had anticipated this move, however, and sidestepped, and shot the bald cop in the belly before the man ever got his gun back out. The bald man did an awkward little pirouette and dropped facedown into the shallow hole. He was breathing heavily, but whether conscious or not, the UnSub couldn't tell.

"Gut shot like that," the UnSub told his guest, who could possibly hear him, or possibly not, "it should take a while for you to die. Maybe half an hour, maybe an hour. Although, it's likely you'll suffocate first."

Picking up the cop's gun from the ground, sticking it in his waistband, the UnSub whistled "Whistle While You Work" and he casually started refilling the grave on top of the intruder who now lay on the very slightly exposed plywood casket, from which perhaps could be detected the tiniest whimpering.

Smiling as he casually tossed a shovelful of dirt to plop onto the man's back, the seeping exit wounds turning the dirt damp, the UnSub said, "Don't you fools know? I'm always a step ahead."

That gunshot, before, would have sounded like a cannon going off out here in the middle of nowhere, so it was best to finish fast and leave.

That's just what the killer did.

Once the burial was complete, the ground patted down hard around the pipe, he returned the shovel to its place behind the bushes, pulled his vehicle out of the barn, pulled the cop's in. The last thing he did, before shutting the barn door behind him, was remove latex gloves that prevented him from leaving finger-prints on anything; these he threw into a corner of the barn.

He got into his car and drove away. Here he was in the middle of the night — actually, the early hours of morning — and he still had work to do.

Who was it said, no rest for the wicked?

Supervisory Special Agent Spencer Reid knew he was blessed in his ability to get by on short sleep. On the BAU, that was as valuable to Reid as his intelligence or his memory.

Hotchner had phoned just before six a.m., barely four hours after Reid had finally crawled into bed, and told him to be in the hotel lobby, ASAP. Fifteen minutes later, mildly disheveled, hair still damp from a hurried shower, Reid exited the elevator into the lobby to find Hotchner, Prentiss and Rossi waiting.

Hotchner, newspaper folded under his arm, his countenance perhaps even more tense than normal, looked typically impec-cable in his navy blue suit, as did Rossi in a gray suit of his own. Prentiss too seemed to have taken more time than Reid getting ready, and Reid wondered if he had been the last one called or whether the others were just better organized.

The next elevator car opened and muscular Morgan emerged looking like he'd walked out of a magazine ad in black loafers, slacks, and a T-shirt that might have been spray-painted on.

Only Jareau was MIA, and Reid wondered where the normally hyper-punctual JJ was until he spotted her through the hotel's glass doors. She, too, was impeccable in a gray pants suit, though her hair swung animatedly as she paced a small patch of sidewalk, cell phone pressed to her ear, engaged in a heated conversation with someone.

Seldom had Reid seen JJ this upset — she was naturally cool and her liaison role required her to be cooler than that; but now and then she lost it, though judging by her gestures, she was as worked up now as he'd ever seen her. As she marched back and forth beyond the door, her expression said that whoever was on the other end of the call had not informed Jareau she'd just won the lottery. . . .

Reid turned to Hotchner. "What's going on? That's not JJ's normal style."

"*This* is going on," Hotch said tersely. The team leader took the paper from under his arm and handed it to Reid like a summons he was serving.

And as tentatively as someone who'd just been so served, Reid opened the newspaper — the Chicago *Daily World.* Not in a class with the *Trib* or the *Sun-Times,* the *Daily World* ran a distant fourth in what was, essentially, a four-paper circulation race. What the paper lacked in readership and integrity, it made up for in sleaze and salaciousness.

The headline read, "Artist's Grisly Tableau." Then, below that, in a slightly smaller font, it said: "Serial Killer Claims Seventh Victim."

"*Seventh* victim?" Reid asked no one in particular as he continued to read.

Under the headlines, just above the fold, was a color photo of an empty car with blood on the seat and windows.

"This is our UnSub's work?" Reid asked.

"Seems to be," Hotchner said.

"How did that paper get this before we did?"

"The UnSub sent it to them," Hotch said, biting off the words. "That and the photos from the other crimes. The other three papers are cooperating and not running them, but the *Daily World* is going all out. . . . On page three, you'll see the rest."

Frowning, Reid asked, "What about consideration for the families of the victims?"

Shrugging, Hotchner said, "Evidently, the *Daily World* feels the public's 'right to know' trumps that."

Reid blew out air. "These must be all over the Internet, already."

Until now, Jareau had done a yeoman's job of keeping the murders off the front page and off the lead story of nightly local newscasters. The murders had been covered by the newspapers and TV, of course; but thanks to her efforts, the copycat aspect had been kept out, as part of the ongoing investigation.

That minimized citywide panic and, as Hotchner and Rossi had reasoned, put the killer on edge as the news coverage did not feed what they already knew to be a hungry massive ego. Of course, a possible downside of that strategy was that it might speed up his kills, as the UnSub sought to garner media attention through sheer volume. Now, thanks to the *Daily World,* that point was moot.

Reid held the paper up and pointed to the grisly photo. "Do we know where this crime scene is?"

Morgan said, "Lorenzon and Tovar are working the phones — we're assuming the photo was sent to the local PD, as well, although if it went snail mail, it might not have shown up yet." He gestured with open hands. "But it's just about got to be one of the outlying suburbs — none of the nearer ones have claimed it."

Prentiss added, "The area in the background appears to be woods, but . . ." She shrugged. ". . . there are lots of wooded areas around Chicago. Garcia's also on the job, trying to track down the police department. This time the UnSub used e-mail to send the photos to the newspaper. That's new."

Morgan said, "So an area PD may have received the photos via e-mail attachment already."

Reid frowned in thought. "Then this is a fresh kill. . . ."

"Probably sometime last night," Rossi said. "Possibly the night before, but I doubt it. E-mail tells us he's looking for more immediate gratification."

Reid's eyes tightened. "Do you think he's devolving?"

"How could he not be?" Rossi asked. "He abducted the first victim in March, at least the first one we know about, and made sure that body wasn't found until July. Now, he kills another in the last twenty-four to forty-eight hours and can't even wait for the mailman to deliver the picture, he's so proud of his work — for the first time, he e-mails it to speed up the process. Not only do I think the UnSub's devolving, I think he may be in spree mode and won't stop killing until we stop him. Every day, hell, every *hour* that we don't have him in custody puts another innocent in danger. How long did Cunanan take?"

Rossi was referring, Reid knew, to notorious spree killer Andrew Cunanan, who killed five people, then himself.

In case any of the others weren't as familiar, Reid said, "Cunanan threw himself a going away party in San Diego on April 24, 1997. His first two victims were in Minnesota — Jeff Trail in Minneapolis and David Madson in Rush City. Next, Cunanan turned up here in Chicago, where he killed a prominent real estate developer named Lee Miglin. Then he drove Miglin's car to Pennsville, New Jersey, and killed a cemetery caretaker named William Reese. That was May ninth. He didn't show up again until he shot the famous designer Gianni Versace in Miami on July fifteenth. The police finally found him in a Miami houseboat on July twenty-third, where he had shot himself to avoid capture. Almost exactly three months after his 'going away' party."

Rossi was smirking at Reid. "You could at least credit me with a footnote."

"Your spree-killing book *is* the standard reference," Reid said, with a shrug.

Rossi's eyes widened in the way they sometimes did when Reid made a point.

Then Rossi said, "Well, this guy's not going to be *around* in three months. At the rate he's going, he's not going to last three *weeks.* I think he's got the fever, and I think his temperature is still going up."

Hotch nodded grimly. "No question he's accelerating. But let's not get too far out in front. Let's deal with things as they come."

Reid glanced back through the glass doors as Jareau snapped her phone shut, then came through the main lobby door and marched toward them, heels firing off like gunshots on the marble lobby floor. Her anger was so extreme it almost cancelled out her prettiness. Almost.

Hotchner asked her. "What did the editor say?"

Jareau took a deep breath, then let it out, and seemed to will herself into a more calm state. "I asked the gentleman how he thought the families of the victims would react to these photos, and he said, 'Read tomorrow's edition. We'll be interviewing them all today.' "

Hotchner chuckled but there was no humor in it. "Did he say anything about knowing where the crime scene is, or the name of the victim?"

"If he has that," Jareau said, "he's not saying."

Reid frowned. "He ran the photo of a murder victim, without knowing whether the family had been notified or not?"

Jareau, her eyes hot in her cold face, said, "I don't think he's the type to care."

"All right," Hotchner said, taking control. "Back to the office — we need to get started. He's not slowing, so we need to speed up."

Half an hour later, they entered their conference room to find Lorenzon and Tovar waiting, the older detective talking on the phone, while Lorenzon sat punching keys on a laptop.

Tovar wore loafers with no socks, jeans, a white shirt with a navy blue knit tie, loosened at the neck, and a gray sport coat. Even though he was balding, what little hair he had looked slept on.

Lorenzon, on the other hand, looked like a page out of the Derek Morgan fashion field manual — a black polo with a Chicago police shield over the left breast, black slacks and socks and black loafers with rubber soles and tassels.

"Anything?" Hotchner asked as they entered.

Lorenzon shrugged toward Tovar. "I think Hilly's got something."

"Thank you, Chief," Tovar was saying into the phone. "We'll have someone out to talk to you ASAP." He clicked off.

"What?" Hotchner asked.

"That was the Aurora chief of police," Tovar said. "Far west suburb. The crime scene is in their jurisdiction. Killer shot the victim three times in the chest, and left him in a place called the Aurora West Forest Preserve."

Tovar rose and went to a map on the wall and stuck a push pin into the area he'd referred to, making it one of five pins, each representing a crime scene.

Reid considered the five pins — one way up north in Wauconda, another way south and east in Chicago Heights, then in Chicago's Chinatown, on to the Gacy house also on the north side and now, this latest one, far west and on a line halfway between the two easternmost pins. He struggled to divine a pattern, mentally connecting the dots, first this way, then that, going through the various possibilities until he was certain there was no help there.

Hotchner asked, "Anything with geographic profiling?"

Reid shook his head. "This is a huge area. The UnSub's safety zone could be any of a hundred places without him ever having to hunt in or even near it."

"What about a pattern with the crimes?"

"None that I can detect," Reid said. "There's certainly no geometric pattern evolving. But when Luke John Helder was dropping bombs in rural mailboxes, to make a smiley face on the map of the U.S.? No one saw that pattern until he told them."

"All right," Hotchner said. "Prentiss, you and Tovar head to the Aurora PD and talk to the chief."

"Right," Prentiss said.

"Morgan, get with Garcia — try to ID the victim if the locals haven't."

"Yep," Morgan said.

"Rossi, you and Reid go with Lorenzon and hit the crime scene. Much as I hate its existence, it's nice to get a fresh look for a change."

"Talk about mixed blessing," Rossi said, getting up.

Reid merely nodded.

"And you, Aaron?" Rossi asked.

"We've only got one suspect," Hotchner said. "Our colleague Detective Denson — I'm going to try to figure out where he's been lately, without tipping to him we're looking."

"Good luck," Rossi said. "It's a whole different deal when a suspect is a cop — they have access to the playbook. Be nice if we had a *real* friend in the Wauconda PD."

"Would at that," Hotchner said.

Even with the majority of rush hour traffic headed into the city, the drive to Aurora took the better part of two hours.

The forest preserve sat on Hankes Road, west of Aurora and just east of a little town called Sugar Grove. The promise of another hot, humid day made a haze of the air as they followed a blue-and-white around a bend to the preserve.

As the FBI Tahoe pulled in, the squad car pulled off to the right and behind another squad. Three more blue-and-whites and a couple of unmarkeds were along the other side of the blacktop drive. A last squad was parked across the entrance, its occupant climbing out as they pulled to a stop a few feet short of the obstruction.

Rossi glanced around. "No ambulance?"

"They took the body away already," Lorenzon said. "Funny — the victim wasn't in the car, but in a shallow grave in the woods. They found it pretty easily."

The uniformed officer came to the driver's side and Lorenzon showed his ID.

"And these two?" the officer asked.

"FBI," Rossi said, showing his credentials. Reid followed suit.

"Park over there," the officer said, pointing to the unmarked cars. "You'll have to walk in. It's not far."

Lorenzon pulled the car up the road and off onto the shoulder. They walked back, passing the car blocking the entrance and, as they did, three men came walking from the other direction, the first with a camera, the second carrying a crime scene kit, and the third obviously a detective.

The photographer, shorter than the other two, stood maybe five-ten and weighed in at about one-seventy. He had a heart-shaped face, ruddy cheeks and blond hair. The crime scene analyst was an African-American with a shaved head. Maybe forty, he was building a little belly despite an otherwise muscular build; he wore wire-framed glasses and walked with a slight limp. The detective, blond and blue-eyed, tall and wide-shouldered, had walked off a recruiting poster for the Aryan Nation; he wore a navy blue suit and dark glasses.

Lorenzon and Rossi nodded to the photographer.

"Jerry Peters," the photographer replied, shaking hands with Rossi and Lorenzon.

"You on the Aurora PD?" Lorenzon asked.

"Freelance," Peters said. "Too many crimes, not enough cameras. I'm all over the suburbs." He shrugged. "You help where you're needed."

They turned to the detective.

"Detective Henry Karl," the cop said, extending his hand. "Aurora Police Department."

Rossi introduced himself and they shook hands. The senior agent then introduced Reid and Lorenzon.

"Glad to meet you," Karl said with a wide smile. "Thanks for pitching in. This big guy is our crime scene tech, Orlando Ramirez."

The African-American with the crime scene kit shook hands all around, then took a step back, his limp exaggerated a little.

"Football?" Lorenzon asked, nodding toward the leg.

Speaking with the barest trace of a Spanish accent, Ramirez said, "I wish. Nine mil in Cuba, when I was a boy."

"Ouch," Lorenzon said.

Rossi nodded toward the crime scene. "What have we got here?"

"A nightmare," the photographer said.

The cop and CSA nodded and shook their

heads, in accidental synchronization.

"We don't usually have anything like this out our way," Karl said. "We're far enough from the city that not much of the slime rubs off. Hell, we would have thought it was just a robbery gone bad without that photo . . . plus Detective Tovar calling us to tell us this was part of a serial crime."

"This isn't just far from the city," Reid said, looking all around. "This preserve is at least five miles from anywhere. Any idea how the UnSub got out? Are there tire tracks?"

"Ay, *mierda,*" Ramirez said. "This place has more traffic than you would think, Agent Reid. Sightseers, picnickers, nature lovers, people looking for a little privacy in God's great green world. Are there tire tracks? What does a bear do in the woods? We've been here since before sunup, and most of what we've done is take tire impressions and pictures of tire tracks. Your suspect, though, he left another way."

Reid cocked his head. "What other way?"

Ramirez gave a harsh single laugh. "On a damn bicycle."

Rossi said, "I've seen weirder."

"Come with us back to the scene," Karl said. "Orlando and Jerry found some good evidence, I think."

The six men followed the blacktop a quarter of a mile into the woods to where a gravel parking lot filled a small clearing on the right. The victim's car sat at the far end.

The car — a newer, green Honda Accord — had Illinois plates.

Rossi asked, "Is he a local?"

Karl shook his head. "We traced the plate to a Peoria guy named Vern Latham. Salesman for a company that deals with Mastodon, local company that makes tractors and earthmovers."

"So," Rossi said, "here on a sales call?"

"Yeah," Karl said. "We're trying to retrace his steps, but it's hard, since no one seems to have seen him since he left Mastadon yesterday afternoon."

Rossi shook his head. "*Someone* saw him."

Reid studied the car and its position. He leaned inside to look at the bloodstains.

"Three shots," Karl said. "Probably a .22. I doubt he ever saw it coming."

Reid said to Rossi, "It's as we thought — Aileen Wuornos."

The others had come over by now.

"Who?" Karl asked.

Rossi turned to them. "You haven't seen this morning's Chicago *Daily World*?"

Karl grunted. "I wouldn't wipe my ass with that rag."

Ramirez said, "They don't sell it out this far."

Rossi nodded. "Okay, I better bring you fellas up to speed."

Quickly the profiler did so.

"Son of a bitch," Peters, the photographer, said. "He's copying famous *serial* killers?"

"Yes," Reid said. "This one is Aileen Wuornos, and it's a frankly audacious choice for a male UnSub. Wuornos was a prostitute in Florida who shot seven men. Six were found and identified. Peter Siems's car was found, but his body never was. This crime was supposed to match that. Except he didn't think you'd find the body so quickly."

"You're sure about this?" Karl asked.

Reid said, "Call it probability."

Rossi put a hand on Karl's shoulder. "Trust us," he said. "If Dr. Reid says it's Wuornos, it's Wuornos."

Reid's eyes narrowed to slits. "This may mean we have a male UnSub whose physicality lends itself to a remarkable masquerade."

Rossi said, "Dr. Reid means the UnSub probably pulled off a drag queen routine that fooled his victim."

Eyes wide, Karl said, "Posed as a woman, and what? Picked him up somewhere, a bar maybe?"

"As a working hypothesis, yes."

Reid faced the Aurora detective. "Where was the body buried?"

"Over here," Ramirez told them, and led them to an area not far into the woods.

The grave had been shallow, blood still visible in the bottom.

Reid shook his head. "He couldn't have thought this would fool anyone. . . ."

Peters said, "Maybe he wasn't trying to hide the body."

"He *should* have," Reid said. "That was part of the Siems crime. He got the date wrong too — that crime was July 4, 1990. He missed by over a month. This is, generally, the Siems scene . . . but he's getting sloppy."

Peters frowned. "How many has he killed?"

"Seven, that we know of."

"How sloppy can he be, if he's at large after seven of these atrocities?"

Reid said nothing. Turning to Ramirez, he asked, "Any evidence from the grave?"

"Just that he used a camp shovel to dig it. The marks on the sides aren't wide enough to've been caused by a full-sized shovel."

Looking back toward the parking lot, Reid asked, "How did you determine the UnSub left by bicycle?"

"I came across something," Peters said, and led them over to a spot past the other side of the parking lot.

Soon they stood around a bare area of grass surrounded by piles of leaves.

Peters pointed. "He had something buried here under the leaves. Could have been a bike."

Then Ramirez and Peters led them further into the woods to another area that had been cleaned away, this one larger than the first.

Rossi, hands on hips as he looked down, asked, "What do we have here?"

Ramirez said, "The escape route."

"Yeah?"

Ramirez pointed to thin ruts in the grass. "Tire tracks from a mountain bike."

"Could it have been a motorbike?" Lorenzon asked. "Kind of out in the boonies for a bike, aren't we?"

"Maybe, but it's not motorbike tracks. The killer had a bicycle snugged here and did his thing and just pedaled away."

Rossi was nodding. "This guy's organized," he said.

Karl's eyes went from Rossi to Reid and back again. "One of you says he's organized, the other says he's getting sloppy. Do you guys *really* know what the hell you're doing?"

Rossi gave the detective a sly smile. "Hard to believe, maybe, but we do. The UnSub has been organized in how he *plans* the crimes, but he's becoming more disorganized in his actual carrying out of the crimes."

"Isn't that a contradiction?" Peters asked.

Rossi's smiled broadened. "Isn't making murder an art form a contradiction in itself?"

Hotchner was livid.

He had spoken on the phone, personally, with the editor of the *Daily World,* who had gone on and on about the first amendment and freedom of the press when obstruction of justice was more like it. The team leader knew he should have left this critical work to Jareau and got off the phone as soon as he realized how futile the effort.

Shortly thereafter, Jareau came into the conference room. "I've got the court order! I found a federal judge who will let Garcia into the *Daily World*'s e-mail account."

"Take Prentiss," he said. "Go serve it to that editor."

"You don't want to go yourself?"

Shaking his head, Hotchner said, "I

don't think I can be in the same room with that defender of the freedom of press right now."

Jareau smiled. "All right. But I intend to enjoy myself telling him to move over and let us in."

"Enjoying yourself is allowed, if the job gets done."

Jareau and Prentiss left.

Only Morgan remained in the room with Hotchner. Bent over his laptop, Morgan seemed deeply involved in something. Hotchner made himself put his anger aside and get back to work. Letting out a long breath, he rubbed his forehead and sat down at his computer.

This day was shaping up to be another long, bad one and he knew that the clock was ticking. With the UnSub back in business, and spreading news of his deeds to an even wider circle of the media, before long a full-blown panic would grip the nation's Second City.

Even though Denson's story had checked out — at least according to the cop's ex-wife and his associates — the man had seemingly disappeared. The tail Hotchner had set up with local agents had lost Denson — hard to tail a cop, at least for long — and now no one could find the detective. In fact, no one had seen him since he'd turned over the Bangs Lake files to the BAU.

Hotchner hoped that was because Denson had taken his advice to stay away from the case, that the man was taking it easy somewhere and staying out of trouble.

Morgan looked up from his laptop screen to ask Hotchner, "Did you ever get the second picture from the forensic artist?"

Hotchner swung around in his chair. "After you left yesterday, the Demerol they gave Minchell for his broken nose kicked in, and he passed out before the artist could even get started. Artist is back over there now."

Reid and Rossi entered, fresh from the latest crime scene. They took seats around the table and filled Hotchner and Morgan in about the new murder.

Hotchner wadded up a piece of paper, which was about as much emotion as he was willing to show. When he looked up, the others all stared at him.

"Sorry," he said, and twitched a smile. "Frustration. We've been a step behind this UnSub since we got here. We still don't know how he picks the victims, and we don't know which killer he's going to imitate next. How do we get out in front of him until we figure out how he's choosing the killers and victims? He's gone right down the line, Berkowitz, Bundy, Dahmer, Gacy, Wuornos . . . there's no way to know who's next."

"Alphabetical order," Reid said quickly.

All eyes went to Reid.

"Simple," Hotchner said. "And I noticed that a long time ago, Reid; but it doesn't help us. Obviously not every serial killer in history is on his list — we could fill in plenty of others between all of those names. . . ."

Very quietly, Rossi said, "He skipped a chapter."

They all turned to him.

"What?" Hotchner asked.

"He *skipped* a goddamn *chapter*," Rossi said, and pounded the table with a fist. "Damnit. I didn't put it together, Aaron, till you listed them just now."

"Put what together?"

Rossi's laugh was bitter. "I know how he's picking which killer to imitate next. I was fooled because he skipped a chapter. Literally."

Frowning, Morgan said, "Dave — what are you talking about?"

"Max Ryan's book, *Serial Killers and Mass Murderers: Profiling Why They Kill.* Max Ryan, Jason Gideon's mentor, my colleague. The UnSub, he's doing the chapters of the book . . . in order." Rossi held up a forefinger. "Except for one — he skipped Herman Kotchman. That's probably what took me so long to put this together. He's done them all, in order of the chapters in the Ryan book . . . except Kotchman."

Reid said, "Herman Kotchman was a serial killer in the early seventies infamous for abducting middle-aged men who reminded him of his sexually predatory father, and burying them in coffins in his backyard. Dubbed 'The Premature Burialist' by the media, he claimed innocence, since he always gave his victims a 'fighting chance,' burying them with a hammer, a gallon of water, and a vent pipe for air."

"Right," Rossi said. "I helped catch the sick bastard."

No one said anything — not even Reid.

Quietly, Rossi said, "One of our first cases — hell, we weren't even the BAU back then. We were just a bunch of guys who thought that if you studied enough offenders, you could learn things from their behavior. Things that would help you stop them."

Hotchner said, "You were right."

Rossi said, "You know, at his trial? Kotchman said, 'They had at least a week before they died of thirst. I'm innocent. If they died, it was because they decided not to free themselves.' We might not have caught him at all, but his last victim *did* get free, and led us right to Kotchman's damn door."

A sick feeling ran through Hotchner's gut. "Kotchman's crimes took time — a long time. What if he *hasn't* skipped a chapter?"

Rossi frowned. "What?"

Hotchner's intensity heightened. "What if he's *already* committed the crime, and hasn't mailed a picture because the victim is buried out there somewhere, and isn't dead yet?"

His teammates' expressions did nothing to alleviate Hotchner's queasy stomach. In fact, they all looked a little ill.

Rossi said, "We have got to catch him — *right now.*"

Morgan snapped his fingers, and all eyes went to him. He said, "Rossi, you said you know which one he's doing next. Who is it? Who is the next chapter in the book about?"

"Richard Speck," Rossi said.

Reid said, hollowly, "Speck killed eight nursing students in one night. Right here in Chicago . . . but what happened to alphabetical order?"

Rossi said, "Max's book was divided in two sections — serial killers first, mass murderers second. Speck as the first of several of the latter discussed."

"My God," Morgan said. "The son of bitch built acceleration into his overall scenario!"

"Eight young women," Prentiss said, the whiteness of her face heightened by her bloodred lipstick. "Facing a death sentence . . ."

As Hotchner's eyes traveled the conference room, the faces looked back at him with the same obvious concern.

Did they have enough time?

CHAPTER TEN:
AUGUST 7
CHICAGO, ILLINOIS

Finally, things were moving.

The UnSub would re-create the Speck murder next. That much the BAU team knew — but not the killer's identity or where precisely he would strike, much less when.

But they had taken the first step in the thousand-mile journey and, with any luck, the next step would be easier.

They began with Dr. Spencer Reid filling them in on what had happened the day Speck committed his atrocities.

"July 14, 1966," the young agent said. He was on his feet, the others seated at the conference table. "Richard Franklin Speck entered the two-story townhouse at 2319 East One-Hundredth Street in the Jeffrey Manor neighborhood of Chicago. Speck claimed his intention to commit a simple burglary. Nine student nurses shared the dwelling, and Speck took them all prisoner, as each returned home. Then he brutally stabbed and killed seven of his captives. The eighth and final victim, he raped, then stabbed to death. The ninth woman in the house, Corazon Amurao, escaped by hiding under a bed. Famously, Speck seemed to have lost count of his hostages during the murders, and left thinking he had killed them all."

Even these hardened profilers could only fall into a grim silence, hearing of the madman's spree.

Reid continued: "At nineteen, Speck went to a tattoo parlor and had the words 'Born to Raise Hell' applied to his left forearm. This was one of the things police used to identify him when Speck was arrested on July seventeenth, three days after the crime and his own attempted suicide. In an interesting sidebar, when he was in prison, Speck once found an injured bird. He nursed it back to health, tied a string to its leg and let the bird ride around on his shoulder. When he was told he couldn't have the bird, because the prison had a policy against pets, Speck threw the bird into a running fan. When a guard said, 'I thought you liked that bird.' Speck replied, 'I did, but if I can't have it, no one can.' "

"Well," Morgan said, "that's a little self-ish."

"Speck is generally categorized as a mass murderer," Reid went on, "but he was a suspect in the deaths or disappearances of eight other women other the years, as well as an individual rape. So other experts classify him a serial."

Reid looked around for any questions, then lifted his eyebrows and twitched a smile, like a nervous kid who'd just finished a school report. He took a seat at the conference table.

Hotchner asked Rossi, "Do you remember the other names in the mass murderer section of Ryan's book?"

Rossi's eyes were tight with thought. "The emphasis was on serial killers, with a relatively small section on mass murderers. I know Howard Unruh, first of the so-called lone gunmen, and Charles Whitman, the University of Texas tower sniper, were written up. I believe there was one other, but I don't recall who."

"Byran Uyesugi," Reid said. "The Xerox murderer."

Rossi chuckled dryly. "That memory of yours does come in handy. But we could still use a copy of that book. If it's the UnSub's bible, having it around could be helpful."

Hotchner dispatched Reid to a track down a local bookstore with a copy of *Serial Killers and Mass Murderers: Profiling Why They Kill.* The book was not available for download, and it wasn't as if they could print a copy from Reid's memory. No one said so, but they all knew that if they failed to stop the Speck reenactment, they would need every tool available to prevent the next performance on the UnSub's list.

Morgan felt great respect for Max Ryan, David Rossi, Jason Gideon and the other pioneering pro-filers; they had built all this up from nothing. The BAU had worked a case with Ryan several years ago, helping the retired agent crack an old unsolved case that had haunted him. With the exception of Rossi, the old guard was gone now. Hotchner led a new generation of behaviorists. Mind hunters, the press called them.

The mind they were hunting this time belonged to an utter sociopath bent on killing as many people as possible in his sick bid for power and recognition. And knowing that the reenactment of individual killings was headed toward re-creations of mass murder was a chilling thought, even to a seasoned veteran like Morgan.

While Jareau dealt with the media, Prentiss stayed in touch with Garcia, who sought to locate groups of nursing students living together who might mirror the configuration of Speck's original atrocities.

Reid was out getting the Ryan book, and Hotchner was searching for the missing Jake Denson via phone and computer. Rossi, along with detectives Tovar and Lorenzon, was headed for One Hundredth Street, the site of Speck's invasion.

Meanwhile, Morgan dug into the Herman Kotchman case. Born in California in 1948, Kotchman grew up with an alcoholic mother who turned a blind eye to the abuse of her two sons by her bisexual second husband, perhaps because that lessened his presence in her bed, sparing her to some degree the man's physical and sexual abuse. One night the abuse turned to murder, when the stepfather killed Herman's brother, who had dared try to escape his grasp, and the boy was buried in the back-yard of their rural home in what was forever referred to as "a terrible accident" and "our family secret."

In 1966, the same year Speck was making a name for himself, Herman Kotchman, not content to wait for the draft, had joined the army. With the Vietnam War escalating, the army seemed willing to take just about anybody. Kotchman, however, couldn't make the grade even with lowered standards, and was mustered out on a dishonorable discharge, after savagely beating another soldier in the shower. Seemed the man had been looking "funny" at Kotchman's penis.

Once back home, Kotchman chose not to return to the house of his mother and stepfather. Instead, he took an apartment in nearby Modesto, California. A year later, the stepfather died of cirrhosis of the liver, and his grief-stricken drunken mother's first call had been to Herman. To help keep his mother from starving, the dutiful son entered into a plan with her to bury the stepfather in the backyard and continue to cash his social security checks.

The stress of all those years of abuse and secrets finally cascaded over into Herman's reality once he was living in the house again. His pent-up fury at his late stepfather consumed him and he began trolling gay bars and nightclubs for victims that reminded him of the balding, pudgy man. He would bury them in the backyard, too, but with a gallon of water, a claw hammer, and a vent pipe for air.

Kotchman always told them, "And another of his disciples said unto him, 'Lord, suffer me first to go and bury my father' " — a quote from the book of Matthew, possibly somewhat misinterpreted by the killer.

Convicted of four counts of murder and one count each of kidnapping and attempted murder, Kotchman, sixty now, was serving a life sentence in a California prison.

Morgan kept digging into Kotchman's background (much as the FBI had earlier dug into his backyard), studying the address of Kotchman's home, the dates of his kills — anything that might give them a leg up on locating a potential victim who had presumably been buried and was possibly still alive. He was still doing that when Reid came in with a copy of Max Ryan's book.

Morgan asked, "How long will it take you to reread that?"

Reid sat at the conference table, smiled just a little. "I read it on the ride back from the bookstore."

He'd been driven to and from the bookstore by local agent Kohler, who'd been doing odds and ends for the team.

Morgan asked, "And?"

Reid shrugged. "The book didn't tell me anything we didn't already know, per se."

"Per se?"

"Well, it did get me thinking. What would you need to re-create one of Kotchman's

289

crimes?"

Morgan shrugged. "Not much — a shovel, some plywood, some PVC pipe for the vent."

"And where would you get these things?"

"I can think of quite a few places," Morgan said. "But I know just who can narrow the search for us." He tapped some keys on his laptop and Garcia's face appeared on his screen.

"What's up?" she asked.

"We're looking for someone who might have gone shopping — he could have gone any number of places, but he'd have a very distinct list. He would've bought maybe three ten-foot sheets of plywood, ten feet of PVC, and probably a shovel. Can you do your magic and see how many times that's happened in the Chicago area in the last say . . . three weeks?"

"I'm on it."

"Be sure to include that Fix-it Mate where Bobby Edels worked. In Mundelein."

"Will do. When I know something, you will."

And, like any good genie, she was gone, just minus the puff of smoke.

They went back to studying other aspects of the crime and, although waiting was a large part of any law enforcement job, Morgan felt about to jump out of his skin. He was about to say to hell with it, long enough to grab some lunch anyway, when Jareau entered the conference room carrying a large manila envelope.

"Got it," she said, presenting the envelope to Hotchner.

"Got what?" the team leader asked.

"The forensic artist's suspect drawing. Minchell says this is the guy that hired him to procure the two gay men."

Hotchner was already studying the sketch.

"This is our suspect," Hotchner said, handing the drawing to Prentiss, who looked at it for perhaps ten seconds, nodded, then passed it along to Reid.

The younger agent studied it and, shaking his head, said, "Doesn't remind *me* of Detective Denson."

Reid handed the sheet to Morgan, who needed only a moment to recognize the face. "*This* is the guy?"

"According to your broken-nosed friend in the hospital bed, yes," Jareau said cheerfully. "Evidently, Minchell told the artist that the drawing was spot on — Minchell says that's absolutely the guy."

Morgan shook his head. "Son of a *bitch* . . ."

Frowning, Hotchner asked, "You know him?"

"Saw him — just once, but this is the guy . . . a police photographer. Daniel Dryden."

Hotchner sat up, his eyes sharp. "Where did you see him?"

"The Gacy house," Morgan said. He gave them a smile that had little to do with the usual reasons for smiling. "He was very helpful."

Reid's eyebrows were up. "We called it — a police buff, or even PD employee, injecting himself into the investigation."

"We've been getting crime scene photos from a crime scene photographer," Prentiss said, and rolled her eyes. "How old is he?"

Shrugging, Morgan said, "Fortysomething. Closer to forty than fifty."

Jareau said, "That fits the profile, too."

"Prentiss," Hotchner said, with coiled urgency, "get with Garcia — we need an address for Dryden. JJ, let the police in all the jurisdictions know we're looking to talk to this guy, but make sure the PDs know we don't want *Dryden* to know; and get a photo of Dryden over to that hospital and have Minchell confirm that the sketch and Dryden are one in the same. Morgan, Reid, get ready — soon as we have an address, we're going to call on Mr. Dryden."

Within several minutes, Prentiss had the info from Garcia, and soon the four profilers loaded into an FBI Tahoe and, with Morgan driving, made their way to Oak Park, a suburb that included the Frank Lloyd Wright historical district. They were on Oak Park Avenue, heading slowly north in heavy traffic.

Reid asked, "Are you going to call Rossi and the detectives?"

"Yeah, but only to tell them that we've tentatively identified the UnSub. I still think they should go to the Speck scene, as a precaution if nothing else. After all, he used the Gacy house."

Morgan turned right on Iowa, went two blocks, then turned back north. The Dryden home, a handsome brick structure vaguely in the Prairie style, sat on the east side of the 700 block of Linden Avenue, the only one-story on a block of two-stories.

As Morgan parked the SUV in front, Prentiss's cell phone chirped.

She answered, listened for a long moment, then said, "Thanks, Garcia," and clicked off.

"What is it?" Hotchner asked.

"Dryden's lived here for the last fifteen years. He's a former fashion photographer, briefly pretty successful, including some gallery shows of his more artistic efforts. But he was a flash in the pan and wound up working for the PD shooting crime scenes. He's got a wife, Connie — one of his former models — and two boys. Dryden has no criminal record."

Morgan said, "I wonder if his family is in danger."

Prentiss shrugged. "Well, he's a sociopath, so in a way that goes without saying. But do you mean something more specific?"

Reid was squinting at the house. "His list of mass murderers is finite — rather small, actually. He's accelerating in one sense, but winding down in another."

Prentiss was squinting, too, but at Reid. "What's your point?"

Reid shrugged. "He's in mass murderer mode now. Many mass murderers go on sprees, taking out their entire families and ending with their own suicides. His final photo, his last crime, could be a family portrait."

They got out of the vehicle and stood on the sidewalk for a moment. Once again, summer's heat gripped the city with fingers of high humidity that seemed to squeeze the very breath out of the city, leaving only car exhaust. The sun did its best to penetrate the dense foliage of the tall trees that sheltered the block, their shade the only hope of a break from the strangling heat.

Morgan asked, "Which serial killer, or rather mass murderer, would he be doing, killing his family and himself?"

Reid met Morgan's eyes with an atypically hard stare. "Daniel Dryden."

Prentiss's eyes widened as she got it. "Adding himself to the list . . ."

"And maybe a revised edition of the book he's following — coming right before Speck, maybe. Alphabetical order?"

The house sat sideways on the lot, driveway leading up to the front of the home, a separate two-story garage on the left side, front door facing the driveway on the north side. The west side faced the street with a large picture window, curtains open onto a long, wide great room.

Hotchner answered his cell. He said, "Yes . . . yes . . . Good."

He clicked off and the other profilers just looked at him. "JJ says Minchell has seen Dryden's picture and confirms his identity as the man he set up with the Hot Rods victims."

They went up the driveway, Hotchner first, Morgan second, hand casually on his

hip-holstered gun, Reid and Prentiss behind.

As they neared the door, Hotchner said,
"Prentiss, you and Reid go around back.
Make sure no one gets by you."

They nodded and trotted off.

Morgan and Hotchner gave them thirty
seconds, then went to the front door and
Hotchner rang the bell.

They waited quietly for an endless
moment before the door swung open
and they were greeted by a strikingly pretty
woman of thirty-five or so. Her eyes were
bright blue, her smile wide and friendly,
her cheekbones high, her nose straight.
Her blonde-highlighted brown hair curled
softly onto the shoulders of her a sleeveless
blue blouse; she also wore jeans and open-
toed sandals, and was both slender and
shapely.

Former model is right, Morgan thought.

"May I help you?" she asked.

Hotchner displayed his credentials. "Mrs.
Dryden?"

"Yes," she said, her voice rather musical.

"I'm Special Agent In Charge Hotchner,
and this is Supervisory Special Agent Morgan."

"With the FBI, yes," she said, the smile
fading. "You must want Daniel. Something

to do with his work? But I'm afraid he's not here."

Hotchner said, "Would you know where he is?"

"I'm sorry, no, not exactly where. He's on the job."

The team leader nodded. "May we come in?"

Her head tilted to one side, giving Hotchner an odd look; but nonetheless she said, "Of course," and stepped aside to allow them in.

Morgan followed Hotch.

The entryway was Spanish tile but the carpeting began almost immediately, the great room stretching out to the right, the kitchen straight ahead, the dining room just to the left.

"I'm sorry," Morgan said. "May I use your bathroom?" The request was one he assumed the middle-class housewife could not refuse.

"Why, of course," she said. "Down the hall, first door on the right."

He made the trip quickly, doing his best to see into the other rooms and listening intently for any sound that indicated they were not alone. He ducked into the bathroom, counted to twenty and flushed the toilet. He washed his hands quickly so she could hear the sink running, then rejoined her and Hotchner near the door.

He flashed his patented smile. "Thank you."

Mrs. Dryden gave him a half smile, a quick nod, and waved a hand for them to enter the great room.

The picture window dominated the west wall, and an entertainment center complete with a plasma TV engulfed the north wall. Along the south wall was a long beige sofa with two brown swivel rockers set out on either end as if standing guard, a small coffee table in front.

Hotchner got out his radio and instructed Prentiss and Reid to join them.

While they waited for the other agents, Hotchner asked, "Mrs. Dryden, are your boys at home?"

"No," she said, puzzled. "They're at the mall with friends — why do you ask?"

"Actually, I'm relieved. We need to talk to you about some things, and it's better done with your boys not around."

Reid and Prentiss came in and Hotchner made brief introductions. Morgan and Reid stood while the others sat, Mrs. Dryden and Prentiss on the sofa, Hotchner in one of the swivel chairs.

"I must say you're . . . frightening me,"

Mrs. Dryden said. "Is it something about Danny?"

"Yes, ma'am, I'm afraid so."

"Oh my God, is he all right?"

"As far as we know, he's fine physically."

"Far as you know . . . ? Fine *physically* . . . ? What —"

"Mrs. Dryden, I'm afraid your husband is a person of interest in an ongoing FBI investigation."

"My husband?" Her smile was half-amused, half-horrified. "*What* kind of person? Is this some kind of joke — you work with Danny, right?"

"You're aware of these murders the media's been covering lately? Really they've been taking place since spring."

Mrs. Dryden nodded. "The copycat killings. Danny's mentioned them in passing."

"Would you happen to know if he's worked all the crime scenes?"

"I have no idea," she said. She was frowning. "Why aren't you asking *him* these questions?"

"We will be," Hotchner said, "when we locate him. Mrs. Dryden, I hate to have tell you this, but he may prove to be more than just a person of interest. Right now, he's our chief suspect."

Mrs. Dryden's eyes were wide though the

skin around them was tight. "What? No . . . no, that's not *possible.*"

Hotchner said, "He's been identified by an eye witness."

"The witness is *mistaken.*"

"Perhaps you can help us clear up our thinking, then," Prentiss said quietly. "You see, in addition to this witness, Mr. Dryden strongly fits the profile we've developed."

"*What* profile?"

"We're part of the FBI's Behavioral Analysis Unit," Hotchner said. "And we've developed a profile of this suspect. Your husband fits it."

"You're *wrong!*" She was on her feet.

Prentiss stood, touched the woman's shoulder, but their reluctant hostess lurched away and held up her index finger like it was a knife she could use to defend herself.

"Stay away from me!" she said.

"Mrs. Dryden," Hotchner said, his voice calm. "I know none of this seems to make sense, but please listen to us."

"No," the woman said, backing away. "I . . . I don't want to. . . ."

Hotchner asked, "Does your husband leave at all hours?"

Reid asked, "Is he secretive about his work?"

Prentiss asked, "Has he had problems with

depression?"

The woman continued to back slowly away from them, her finger wilting now, tears starting to overflow.

Morgan asked, "Does he have a place he won't let you go, no matter what? A . . . fiercely private place?"

Mrs. Dryden was at the front door now. She said nothing, but her eyes cut toward that door . . . or something beyond it.

"He does," Morgan pressed, "doesn't he?"

Her voice was a sort of wail: "The . . . *garage* . . ."

Prentiss enfolded the woman in her arms and held her while Mrs. Dryden wept. Finally gaining a small measure of composure, the woman said, "His . . . his darkroom. It's just his darkroom — upstairs, garage."

Hotchner asked, "May we have a look?"

She frowned; for the first time, something like fear could be seen there. "Danny . . . he never lets *anyone* in his darkroom. But there's a, you know, practical reason — you could ruin something he's working on. Screw up a crime scene photo, you can screw up a case."

The words were clearly an echo of what her husband had said to her.

Hotchner said, "We can get a warrant,

Mrs. Dryden. But the faster we move, the sooner this will be cleared up. And if we're wrong about your husband, all of us want to know, sooner than later. Wouldn't you agree?"

Her face was frozen in confusion. The world had just opened up beneath her feet and she was having trouble not getting swallowed up.

Morgan said, "People will be looking to arrest your husband, Mrs. Dryden. And something could go wrong, and someone might get hurt. If there's nothing up there to tie him to the crimes, we may be able to eliminate him as a suspect. Wouldn't you want to help him if you could?"

She considered that for a long moment. What she decided here could be vital — one way or another, they would be getting into that garage today, yes. But getting that warrant could give Dryden just enough time to practice his deadly performance art once again. . . .

"If it might help clear him," she said, as if talking to herself, "I suppose I should do it." She gazed at Hotchner, her face streaked with tears. "But be very careful, won't you? Danny wouldn't want any of his work spoiled."

I'm sure he wouldn't, Morgan thought.

"We will," Hotchner said. "May we have the key?"

She went to a side table near the door, picked up her purse and withdrew a ring with half a dozen keys. She singled one out and handed the key on the ring to Hotchner, who passed it on to Morgan.

"That's to the garage," she said. "I'm afraid I don't have a key for the upstairs. Danny has the only one. . . ."

"If we have to force a door, we will," Hotchner said. "You do understand that?"

She swallowed and nodded.

"Thank you." He nodded to Morgan, who went outside, Reid trailing behind him. While they went through the garage, Hotchner and Prentiss would stay with Mrs. Dryden in the house.

Once outside, depending on Hotch and Prentiss to keep Mrs. Dryden away from the windows, Morgan drew his pistol, and moved forward cautiously. He was still on alert, even though he felt certain the woman wasn't lying, the possibility remained that the suspect was in that darkroom right now. On this job, one careless entry could be your last. Reid, behind Morgan with his own pistol in hand, had learned that lesson the hard way, when an UnSub had taken the young agent hostage.

The garage sat at an angle to the long driveway with two separate doors instead of one large one, a walk-in door on the south side, closest to the house. Morgan unlocked the door and stepped into shadowy darkness. Having just come in from the bright sunlight, his eyes took a few agonizing seconds adjusting themselves to the dimness.

Morgan strained to hear, but was greeted only by silence. His fingers found a wall switch and flipped it. Two ceiling-mounted bulbs came on to cast a pale glow. In the nearer of the two stalls sat a Ford Windstar van. The space beyond was empty and past that a workbench stood against the north wall, tools hanging on a pegboard. To his right, a flight of stairs led up to a windowless door guarded by a hasp and padlock. Above the door, a red lightbulb (not turned on) stuck out like a big blister.

Morgan holstered his weapon and moved toward the workbench, finally allowing Reid access into the garage. Shooting that lock off was not an option Morgan relished — that kind of stuff worked better in the movies. He had hoped for bolt cutters, but none presented themselves; he was granted his second wish, though: a crowbar leaning against the wall in the corner.

Morgan climbed the stairs with his new tool, and jammed the bar behind the hasp from underneath, braced himself and pulled up.

The hasp groaned but did not give.

He pulled harder, it groaned louder, but still did not give. Muscles burning, he pulled up on the bar and, finally, the hasp squealed and gave with such force, Morgan damn near went ass-over-elbows back down the stairs.

After barely maintaining his balance, he crouched and waited, to see if anyone was within the sealed-off room who had an opinion to express about his intrusion — for instance, bullets flying through the closed door . . .

Nothing.

Morgan opened the loft door. To his right, his hand found a switch and flipped it. The room remained dark, but Reid called from downstairs: "That red light just came on!"

Morgan turned it off and found another switch next to it. When he flipped that, two ceiling fluorescents flickered to life.

The long, wide room ran the entire length and width of the garage. The space was surprisingly cool for this hot, humid August day — *air-conditioning,* Morgan realized. Pretty pricey extra for a spare room above a garage, photo lab or not.

A long table along the back wall was home to a large laser printer, a flat-panel monitor, a mouse, and a keyboard. A two-foot computer tower squatted beneath the table.

Floor-to-ceiling bookshelves consumed the west wall. Shorter shelves on the north wall, below a window, held leather-bound, numbered journals. On two long, end-to-end tables midroom, where the chemicals and baths and pictures hanging to dry should have been, no sign of any photography darkroom equipment was to be seen. Instead, the tables were covered with maps, photos, and a few books.

Coming in, Reid said, "I figured as much. All digital."

Morgan jerked a thumb toward the computer tower. "You think you could get into that?"

Shaking his head, Reid said, "I wouldn't even try. Too much chance of losing evidence. We'll get the local computer forensics crew in."

At the tables, Morgan looked down at maps with had spots circled on them — *each one a crime scene.*

And the photos, grisly photos, were shots from every crime scene, as well.

"They could just be from the job," Reid

said, with a reasonable lilt in his voice. "His job is, after all, to go to crime scenes and take photos. He could explain all this stuff away as circumstantial."

Morgan pointed to one of the books, *Serial Killers and Mass Murderers: Profiling Why They Kill* by Max Ryan.

"Circumstantial," Reid said.

Then Morgan saw it.

From under the book where it had peeked out at him, Morgan pulled out a photo — Addie Andrews and Benny Mendoza . . . *before the shooting.*

The couple walked along obviously unaware their picture was being taken, coming down the sidewalk from Addie's house, probably shot from the park across the way.

Morgan held it up for Reid to see.

"That," Reid said, "will be harder for him to explain."

"Go get Hotch and tell him we're going to need a search warrant before we go any further . . . but there's not much doubt we've found our man."

"Well, his *lair,* anyway," Reid said, then, holding up a photo of a two-story brick townhouse with a flat roof. "This is interesting. And worrisome."

"Why?" Morgan asked. "What's that?"

"That is 2319 East One-Hundredth Street

— where Richard Speck murdered eight nurses. The crime that's going to be copied next, if we're right. And where Rossi and those two Chicago detectives were headed, when we saw them last."

CHAPTER ELEVEN: AUGUST 7 CHICAGO, ILLINOIS

Generally, Supervisory Special Agent David Rossi was fairly laid-back; right now he was on edge.

Hotchner had phoned twice, over the last two hours — once with the name of their suspect, crime scene photographer Daniel Dryden, and again to alert him that Dryden was still unaccounted for and might well be headed Rossi's way, if the picture Reid had found in the garage loft was any indication.

Rossi and the two detectives, Lorenzon and Tovar, sat in a black SUV, air conditioner doing overtime. The two cops were in front, the FBI agent in back.

Across the street, in the late afternoon heat, two African-American women sat on the front stoop of 2319, the first-floor windows and the inside front door open. A small window air conditioner chugged in a second-floor window. The women, both in shorts and tank tops, were watching three young children playing in a minuscule front yard, two boys and a girl, none older than five, taking turns chasing a plastic ball, kicking it, catching it, then kicking it again, each squealing with delight, oblivious to the humid heat.

Rossi explained the Dryden situation to the two detectives.

"Daniel fuckin' *Dryden?*" Lorenzon said with a head shake. "Him I would've never guessed. How would a zero like Dryden have the balls for something like this?"

Rossi said, "That opinion's part of what motivates him."

Lorenzon looked puzzled. "My opinion?"

"Not yours in particular, but that sort of mind-set. Dryden had some early success, and now he thinks he's a loser — and that's the feeling people get being around him. He's smart. No question, we've seen that. Yet in his day-to-day life, he doesn't have any self-confidence. He feels he doesn't have control. These killings, this is how he gets back some control."

Lorenzon was frowning. "Control of what?"

"The victim, for starters. You remember what we said about manipulation, control, and domination?"

"Yeah, sure."

"This is where that comes into play. Dryden manipulates, controls, and dominates his prey. For once, he's not on the receiving end of such things."

"How can he compare being snubbed to killing people?"

"We're not talking about reality, Tate — we're talking about the killer's perception."

Lorenzon nodded, but was still frowning in thought.

"Take a hypothetical," Rossi said. "Suppose you're driving in Chicago traffic, and get cut off."

"I don't have to suppose very hard."

"Then it happens again! Are you pissed?"

"Depends on how close the guy came, but, yeah, maybe a little."

Nodding, Rossi said, "Pretty normal response. Our killer would go straight to anger after the first time . . . and furious enough to kill after the second."

Tovar said, "That's screwy."

"Careful," Rossi said with a little smile. "You're getting into highly technical profiling terms now. Meanwhile, back in Chicago traffic, it would never occur to the killer that two separate people simply didn't see him or weren't paying attention. For him, this is all part of a conspiracy on the part of society to stifle him, to not recognize his talent, his brilliance. As far as he's concerned, cops like us are out to get him, not for his crimes, rather as part of a society that's *always* been out to get him."

Tovar said, "But this guy's been a functioning member of society for years. . . ."

"Sure," Rossi said. "Being a cold-blooded killer doesn't rule that out."

The two detectives gave him a look.

Rossi shrugged. "Sue me. It's true."

Across the street, the kids kept playing.

"You know," Rossi said, with a nod toward the children, "we need to get them out of here — no point in handing him victims."

Tovar said, "I thought he was after nurses."

"He's devolved to a 'close enough' state — maybe not nurses, maybe just wiping out everybody at that address."

Traffic on One-Hundredth Street was steady but everybody knew this was a residential neighborhood and held their speed down accordingly. The profiler and the two detectives climbed down from the SUV, then strolled across the street.

They were halfway when an eastbound gray Ford Crown Victoria, an older model, slowed as it approached. They were almost across when the car picked up speed.

As the car shot by, even though its windows were tinted, Rossi recognized the driver at once. Or was he just projecting his anxieties?

Before Rossi said anything, though, Tovar nodded and pointed. "Was that fuckin' *Dryden?*"

This confirmation was all Rossi needed.

He watched as the vintage Crown Vic took a right at the next corner. Sprinting toward the building, jerking his credentials from his pocket, Rossi yelled, "FBI — get these kids inside, now!"

The two women jumped up and ran to their kids, the children mesmerized by the screaming white man.

The two women were also yelling at the children, the caregivers apparently alarmed by Rossi charging at them, with Tovar and Lorenzon in his wake.

That suited Rossi just fine. Anything that got the women and children locked indoors was a good thing.

He yanked his pistol from its holster and one woman shrieked as she dashed into the house with a boy in her arms. Her friend, with two wriggling children to corral, having trouble keeping up, watched helplessly as the door shut in her face. Rossi was close enough now to hear the dead bolt slam home.

The woman outside pounded on the door. "Damn you, Laticia!"

Rossi touched the woman's arm and she spun on him, teeth bared, eyes wide with fear, her right index finger coming around and scolding him.

"Don't you *ever* touch me!"

Holding up his credentials, Rossi said, "I *am* with the FBI. It's all right, we're here to help."

"Help what? We haven't done a damn thing!"

The corner of the curtains of the town house fluttered and Rossi could see the other woman looking out.

He displayed his credentials. "FBI, open the door and let this woman in."

Laticia shook her head.

Rossi frowned. *"Now!"*

The woman disappeared from the window. Whether it was to open up or go hide, Rossi could not tell. He waited and, seconds later, he heard the dead bolt slide. The door opened and the woman on the stoop went inside with her two children.

From the doorway, Laticia stared at Rossi, who said, "Shut and lock this door, then call 911 — tell them the FBI said you need special protection."

Eyes wide with terror, the woman shut

the door and the dead bolt snapped into place.

Turning to his colleagues, Rossi saw they both had their weapons drawn, Tovar slowly scanning the neighborhood, Lorenzon talking into his walkie-talkie.

Lorenzon was shouting into the radio: "Well, fucking *find* him!"

"What?" Rossi asked.

Lorenzon shook his head and said, "While you got the families inside, I called for a patrol car to pull the prick over. Now, they can't find him *or* the car."

"Not a lot of Crown Vics in this neighborhood, except maybe for police cars. And it was pristine for its age."

Ninety percent of the cars on the street were what street cops commonly referred to as a Dodge POS or a Chevy POS or a Ford POS — piece of shit.

"Gave 'em the damn plate number," Lorenzon said, shaking his head again. "The only good news is that the computer IDed the car as Dryden's. Christ, he's owned it since his fashion mag days."

Tovar's face was red. "Where the hell *is* he then?"

Lorenzon said, "Maybe we scared him off."

"But where to?"

Before any guess could be offered, Lorenzon's walkie-talkie squawked to life.

"Shots fired," the cool voice of the dispatcher said. "State University. Science building, first floor. All available officers, 9501 South King Drive, Williams Science Building."

Rossi asked, "How far away is that?"

Lorenzon said, "Ten blocks maybe?"

"Shit!" Rossi grimaced. "Went straight to the source — nursing students."

"Goddamnit!" Tovar said.

The three men sprinted to the SUV and climbed in, Lorenzon getting behind the wheel. The African-American detective gunned the engine to life, hit the siren and flashing lights, then — as he dropped the SUV into gear — mashed the gas pedal.

They practically leapt to the corner, turned right, and were halfway up the next block when Rossi yelled, "Stop!"

Lorenzon slammed on the brakes. "What the hell?"

Rossi opened the door and jumped out.

"What are you *doing?*" Lorenzon asked.

"I know how this bastard thinks," Rossi said. "He wants to copy Speck. I think this is a diversion."

"Three nurses shot is a diversion?"

"I think so."

Tovar's eyes were huge. "What if you're wrong?"

"Then you two will nail him at the university."

Rossi slammed the door and headed back at a trot as Lorenzon sped off toward the university.

When he got to the corner, Rossi hoped to see a squad car out front, officers at the door listening to Laticia's tale of the three crazy men, waving guns, who had run at her, her friend, and their kids.

Unfortunately, he knew better.

The dispatcher's call for every available officer would drop the priority of Laticia's call to rock bottom. He made a quick 911 call himself, gave his name, FBI status and the address.

"That's the Richard Speck murder house," Rossi said, "and the copycat we're all looking for may be in there."

"Sir?"

"Just give the word."

Rossi clicked off.

He'd be happier if he could get inside that town house, but given his last visit, that was probably impossible. Problem was, he couldn't watch the front and back of the place from here, or anywhere else for that matter. The building was set up like a row house, eight two-story. If he went around back and Dryden came to the front, Rossi would never get inside before the killing started. The same was true if Rossi stayed in front and then Dryden came in the back. . . .

He had told Lorenzon he knew how the killer thought — well, now was the time to prove it. If he was wrong, more innocent people would die.

Think, Rossi told himself.

Dryden was normally organized, highly so. He had deviated from his plan when he'd seen Rossi and the detectives. The thing was, Dryden was devolving so fast, he couldn't bring himself to cancel his performance. Dryden had, instead, decided to open fire on nursing students at the university.

But that didn't mean the killer wouldn't still come back to his original destination.

Speck had strong-armed his way in through the front door, hadn't he? So Rossi took a calculated risk. The killer wanted to copy the murders at this address; therefore, Dryden would want to go in the front way. . . .

After ducking into a doorway across the street opposite 2319, Rossi got out his weapon, checked to make sure a round was in the chamber, then lowered it along his leg, barrel down.

His cell phone chirped and he responded. "Rossi."

"It's Lorenzon. SOB's in the wind. One student dead, two wounded."

"Damnit."

Ten minutes later, the sun setting, his patience wearing thin as he started to wonder if he was wrong about Dryden, Rossi was just about to holster his weapon and step out of the shadowy doorway when he saw something move across the street.

A vehicle crossed his line of vision, and Rossi wondered if his eyes were playing tricks on him.

Then, from behind a car parked two doors down from 2319, Dryden — all Johnny Cash in black T-shirt, black jeans and black running shoes — crept out, crossed the yard slowly, his head on a swivel, looking for cops. A bulge in his pocket might be a small camera, and Rossi was almost sure a black knife sheath was on his left hip and a black holster on his right.

Rossi slipped back into the doorway, counted to five, then peered out again. Dryden was mere yards from the front door now. Stepping forward, Rossi could see a bus coming eastward; the agent used the bus for cover to get to the middle of the street, then took three quick steps and ducked down on the driver's side of a parked car Dryden had just passed.

Rising slightly, the FBI agent looked through the driver's-side window toward 2319 . . .

. . . and saw the back of Dryden. The killer was only two or three steps from the front door now.

Rossi moved forward, using the car as cover, then popped up over the hood and yelled, *"Daniel Dryden, freeze! FBI!"*

Eyes wide, Dryden spun, a little revolver in his right hand, a hunting knife coming up from his side, in his left hand. He fired two quick rounds at Rossi, missing him, but Rossi did not return fire. The FBI man was a good shot, damn good, but didn't relish firing when the only backstop behind Dryden was a houseful of children.

Ducking back behind the car, Rossi hoped to draw Dryden into attacking him instead of the house. Two more rounds slammed into the vehicle, making it obvious Dryden was a lot less concerned about what lay beyond his target than Rossi.

Sliding his head up a little, Rossi peeked through the driver's side window and saw Dryden sprinting toward the car. Another round spiderwebbed the windshield and Rossi dropped and edged to the rear of the vehicle.

As Dryden crept around the car, Rossi slipped behind the back bumper. Dryden rose to see where Rossi had gone, and the FBI agent popped up, too, his pistol centered on the perp's forehead.

No kids to worry about behind the target now. . . .

"Drop them or die," Rossi said matter-of-fact. "Your choice."

Dryden thought for a long moment, but his weapons remained at the ready.

Rossi had the bastard cold. And the agent already knew the serial killer to be a coward — although Dryden had killed or wounded nearly a dozen people, all his victims had been innocents, caught unaware, and unprepared to defend themselves.

"You don't get a count of three, Dryden. Drop them now, or die right here, right now."

Dryden swallowed thickly.

And the weapons clattered to the street.

"Assume the position," Rossi said. "Against the car, feet back and spread 'em."

The black SUV roared up and the two detectives piled out of the vehicle just in time to see Rossi handcuff the suspect.

Lorenzon read Dryden his rights.

Tovar asked, "How did you know he'd come back to the house?"

Rossi turned his gaze on Dryden, who stared back with small, cold, dead eyes.

"He had no choice," the FBI agent said. "Not with *his* ego. You just had to prove you were smarter than us, Danny, didn't you? Only, turns out you aren't."

"I *am* smarter than you," Dryden said. He was trembling but his manner remained smug.

Rossi got a half smile going. "Really? Then why were we here when you got here?"

Dryden glared at him.

"*Both* times," Rossi said, twisting the knife.

"Go to hell," Dryden said.

Lorenzon gave a quick jerk on the handcuffs. "You first, asshole."

Rossi said, "Take Danny in. He and I need to have a little talk."

Two hours later, Daniel Dryden sat cuffed to a table in a brightly illuminated interrogation room at the Cook County jail. In an adjacent, dimly lit viewing room, Rossi stood with Hotchner, Prentiss, Morgan, and Reid.

Hotchner said, "Nothing of note found in his car."

The gray Crown Vic had been parked on the street a block from the Speck house.

"His revolver was a .22," Morgan said, "consistent with Richard Speck's weapon of choice."

Rossi nodded. "You have the pictures from the darkroom?"

The team leader nodded.

Reid said, "And I Photoshopped that other one — they're all in here."

Reid handed Rossi a manila folder.

"Should you be the one to interview him?" Hotchner asked. "You captured him — and antagonized him. You really think he'll talk to you?"

Rossi shrugged. "You can overrule me, obviously, Aaron. But when I got him pissed off, he didn't clam up — he went back and forth with me. I think I can get him to do it again. And at length."

Hotchner's eyes locked with Rossi's.

Then the team leader said, "We're only going to get one run at this — the clock is ticking and it's not a happy sound. Somewhere out there a man in a grave may still be alive."

"I know," Rossi said calmly. "Trust me, Aaron. I got this."

Hotchner considered that, for just a moment; then nodded.

Rossi entered the interrogation room, glanced at the reflective glass behind which observers lurked, then sat down opposite the dressed-in-black suspect, Rossi's back to the watchers. He set the folder on the table between them.

Dryden's blandly handsome face wore a faint smug smile. "Who the hell thought that I'd ever talk to you?"

Rossi smiled. "I did."

One eyebrow rose. "Are you the Special Agent In Charge?"

"No."

Dryden shook his head. "I only talk to the SAIC."

"I'm the special agent in charge of you."

The suspect grunted a laugh. "What's your name, anyway?"

"David Rossi."

Dryden's eyes, beady and a little small for his face, stared at Rossi for perhaps fifteen seconds. Then he said, "David Rossi the author?"

Shrugging, Rossi said, "I've been published."

"False modesty," Dryden said with a weird sideways grin. "Doesn't suit you."

Rossi gestured with open hands. "You're right. I've written best sellers. I've been on talk shows. I've done the lecture circuit. I won't fall back on false modesty."

Dryden's smile straightened out. "I won't, either."

"You won't?"

"No?"

"Why, have you accomplished something? I've accomplished some things, yes . . . but you? You're just another copycat. Files are full of them."

"I'm no copycat," Dryden said, and pounded the table as best he could, his cuffs wound through a metal ring on the table. "You wait. Before this is over, you'll be a footnote in *my* story."

Rossi laughed. "Oh? What story is that?"

"How I killed twelve people. You're just a glorified secretary, writing books about 'monsters' like me."

Rossi gave him a look. "You're kidding, right? I write about originals — Gacy, Speck, Bundy, Kotchman — true innovators in their chosen field. No writer, no reader, is interested in just another copycat."

Dryden lurched forward. "I am not a copycat! I *am* a true original!"

Leaning back in his chair, Rossi said, "Hey, I don't want to make you feel bad. Take some pride if you want to. But don't kid a kidder — Danny boy, you didn't even make double figures."

"*Twelve!* A goddamn dozen!" The little eyes had grown big. "Count 'em! Two in Chicago Heights, two in Wauconda, one each in Chinatown, one in Des Plaines, one in Aurora, three at the university, and the Kotchman kill who should be dead" — he checked the clock on the wall — "any time now."

That only added up to eleven, but Rossi didn't have the luxury of going down that road — he had a missing man to find.

"Yeah," Rossi said, "he probably *would* have been dead pretty soon . . . if we hadn't found him already. And two of the nursing students you just wounded. Gonna be fine."

Dryden eyes grew tiny again. "You didn't find him."

"What?"

"You couldn't have found him. I was too careful. Always a step ahead of you chumps."

"Right, right," Rossi said, picking up the folder. "Like you were so far ahead of us at the Speck house. That's why you're here *now,* because you were always one up on a chump like me."

Dryden's mouth opened but no words came out.

Rossi got up, stepped back from the table, allowing the folder to slip from his grasp, as if accidentally, the pictures sliding out of the folder and onto the table. The fake one Reid had devised, at Rossi's direction, was a blurry shot that showed a middle-aged man who looked vaguely like Herman Kotchman's abusive stepfather. This man was strapped to a gurney, covered in blankets, his head just barely visible as he was loaded into an ambulance.

"Excuse," Rossi said, gathering up the photos and stuffing them back into the folder.

He had given Dryden only a second or two to glimpse the picture, but Rossi knew that was enough. The killer's fallen face said they'd made a sale: Dryden seemed convinced they'd rescued his premature burial victim.

"How the hell . . ." Dryden began. The little eyes burned in their sockets. "It took me fucking *weeks* to find just the right farm!"

"Either we're not as dumb as you think we are," Rossi said. "Or you're not as smart . . ."

Forehead clenched, Dryden sat forward. "Let me see the photo again."

Rossi hesitated.

"Ha! I knew it — you dummied the thing, didn't you? Photoshop bullshit!"

Rossi took the photo from the folder and handed it to Dryden, who studied it. The photographer only needed a moment.

"I was right," Dryden said, and laughed. "You didn't even get the goddamn state right on the ambulance's license plate, let alone the town."

"Good to know," Rossi said. "In fact, you've just told me everything I need to find the guy."

"Yeah, right."

Rossi leaned in. "If you'll pardon me, Danny, I'm going to go help my team prove whether the chump here is me . . . or you."

"If you *do* find him?" Dryden said with a sneer. "He'll be dead."

"I don't think so," Rossi said. "And after we save him, you'll get to see him again, alive and well and on the witness stand."

Dryden had nothing to say to that.

Rossi went out and met the rest of the team in the corridor.

Hotchner asked, "What just happened?"

Rossi half smiled. "We got the answer."

Hands on hips, frowning, Morgan asked, "How do you figure that?"

"Victim's in Indiana."

Hotchner squinted at Rossi, as if trying to bring him into focus. "And how do you arrive at that?"

328

But it was Reid who answered: "Because the ambulance had Illinois plates."

Morgan's eyes widened. "You figure because the ambulance had Illinois plates, and this whack job said that was the wrong state, the vic is in Indiana?"

"Yeah," Rossi said with a shrug. "Don't you?"

Shrugging back, Morgan said, "How the hell should I know?"

"You really should know," Rossi said, "because you interviewed his wife. Has her husband been gone overnight?"

"No," Prentiss said. "She said he worked all night once back in April — and that was the night he killed Andrews and Mendoza."

Rossi asked, "What was the latest he got home?"

Hotchner thought for just a moment. "In the last few weeks," he said, "the latest Dryden got in was about two thirty a.m., according to his wife."

"All right," Rossi said. "Now, has Garcia looked into missing middle-aged men in the area?"

Hotchner nodded. "Three disappearances reported in the last two weeks. One's turned up already, and another is a husband who apparently left his wife for his secretary."

Prentiss said, "The third one was a businessman, Grant Shuler, in from Atlanta. Associates he was calling on reported him missing on July twenty-ninth. They say they dropped him off at his motel the night before, just after ten p.m., and haven't seen him since."

"All right," Rossi said. "Our time span is between ten p.m. and two thirty a.m. Our search grid will be an area that Dryden could drive to and back from in the allotted time."

"He's on to something," Hotchner said. "Let's get back to the office."

Forty minutes later, in the field office's conference room, they huddled over a map of the area.

Rossi said, "Even if Dryden had everything ready at the site — plywood coffin waiting in its hole — and with no traffic at all, it's over an hour to get to Indiana from Shuler's motel, and the better part of another to get home from the border. If we figure a minimum of a half hour at the grave site, that only leaves him an hour each way into the state. How far is that?"

Reid drew a circle that included an area bordered by extreme southern Michigan on the north, South Bend on the east, south to Fair Oaks, and Illinois on the west.

Morgan's eyebrows were up. "That's still

a lot of ground."

"Don't forget," Hotchner said, "he's imitating Kotchman."

"Get Garcia," Rossi said, nodding. "We need a little magic."

Prentiss made a video connection via her laptop.

"Garcia," Rossi said. "Match anything you can between Indiana and Modesto, California. Highways, town names, county names, anything that might resonate."

Garcia asked, "How soon do you need it?"

"Yesterday."

"No problem."

On the little flat screen, she turned away and fingers danced gracefully over the keys of her keyboard. She was back in less than five minutes, but looking glum.

"Nothing," she said.

"Anything even close?" Rossi asked, determined to keep any desperation out of his voice. *Had he gotten too cocky and cost Grant Shuler his life?*

"There's a Highway 120 near Modesto," Garcia said, "and a Highway 20 in the area of Indiana you're looking at. Best I can come up with."

"Good job," Rossi told her, happy to have a straw to grasp at.

The genie on the screen asked, "What now?"

"We're looking for vacant farms for sale along Highway 20."

Prentiss asked, "Why farms along Highway 20?"

"Kotchman lived on a farm," Reid said. "Dryden has been trying to re-create the crimes in as much detail as possible."

Rossi said, "He'll have found a vacant farm. Shuler will be in the backyard."

"I wish we had more," Hotchner said.

"It's what we've got."

Reid seemed more confident: "No, it all makes sense — let's go with it."

That was when Garcia piped in to say, "There's three vacant farms on Highway 20 within your search grid."

Hotchner leaned in. "Give us addresses and directions."

Prentiss went with Hotchner in a Tahoe, Reid with the two detectives in an unmarked, while Morgan and Rossi in another SUV went to the third farm. Using their cell phones, they stayed in constant communication. Morgan and Rossi had the farm farthest away.

Hotchner had summoned a medivac chopper to be in the area. If they found Shuler alive, the man would need immediate medi-

332

cal attention.

Lights flashing, sirens wailing, they sped through the muggy night into Indiana. They crossed the border, still flying, getting off the expressway and hurtling down Highway 20. Hotchner and Prentiss were the first to peel off, then twenty miles later, Reid and the detectives went their way.

As they rode, Morgan behind the wheel, the cloudless night bright with stars and a nearly full moon, Rossi could only hope they weren't too late.

Morgan said, "You know, you alter that timeline by as little as an hour, and we could still be in the wrong state. The victim could just as easily be buried in Wisconsin — that's only a little over an hour away from that motel, too."

"If the timeline is wrong," Rossi said. "But it isn't."

"Sound pretty sure of yourself."

"When I joined this team, the knock on me was that I was too much of a loner, too used to doing things my own way. Now, that we've solved something as a team, you're second-guessing my role? I been doing this a long time, Morgan, and here's a tip you didn't ask for but are going to get: you have to learn to trust your talent."

"I do trust it."

"You think you do, but you really need to *believe* that you're right."

"And you," Morgan said, "need to learn to trust the team."

"I'm working on that," Rossi said, nothing negative in his voice.

Morgan slowed as they approached a driveway on the left roadside. "I think this is it. . . ."

As if to confirm his belief, a FOR SALE sign came into view beyond a small hill. Morgan turned in and followed the gravel road toward a dilapidated white house and faded red barn that stood at the top of a hill.

Rossi's cell phone chirped. He pulled it off his belt and answered.

"Hotchner. We got nothing at our site, and Reid just called to say they struck out too. How are you two doing?"

"Just pulling in," Rossi said. "Let you know." He clicked off, then said to Morgan, "Down to us now."

Obviously vacant, the house was a tall, two-story box that looked hadn't seen a coat of paint since the sixties. The barn looked little better. Off to the left of the house, across a side yard, a path worn through it between the buildings, one door hung slightly open.

"Let's check there first," Morgan said.

Rossi nodded.

They got out of the SUV, crossed the yard and stood on either side of the open door, their guns drawn. The suspect was in custody, but an unknown accomplice was always a possibility. They nodded to each other, then went in low and fast, each fanning their guns around looking for a threat.

When each was sure his side was clean, he said, "Clear."

The only thing left in the barn was a navy blue Ford Bronco, locked up tight. They checked in the windows and saw nothing.

Rossi asked, "Where the hell did this vehicle come from?"

Morgan checked the plate. "Illinois. I can get Garcia to run it."

"Do it."

Morgan made the call, short and sweet.

They moved behind the house and, using their Maglites in the darkness, quickly found the PVC pipe sticking up out of the dirt.

"Bingo!" Morgan said.

Rossi's eyes flared. "We might have thought to bring a goddamn shovel. . . ."

But Morgan spotted the handle sticking out from behind a bush and then they did have a shovel, Dryden's shovel most likely.

Without a word, Morgan grabbed it and started digging near the pipe. The night was hot and it didn't take long until his face and bare arms glistened with sweat. He threw dirt over his shoulder, Rossi watching. When Morgan was down a couple of feet, they changed places and Rossi took over, his pace slower but more steady.

The sun was coming up now, the shadow of the house still making it hard for them to see.

Before long, the shovel touched something harder than dirt, but considerably less sturdy than plywood.

"Something," Rossi said.

They used their hands now, pushing dirt out of the way until they uncovered a shoe with a foot in it connecting to a still mostly buried leg.

"Hell!" Morgan said. "Son of a bitch didn't even use a box!"

Rossi said, "Wait a minute. The shoe is a Rocky. *Cop* shoe. This isn't the victim. . . ."

They dug faster now, uncovering the rest of the body until they were looking down at a man dressed in jeans and a T-shirt, his head shaved clean, exit wound in his back.

"Denson," Morgan said.

Rossi grunted. "Poor bastard *did* find the killer before we did. . . ."

And now Dryden's math made more sense: this was his twelfth victim.

Morgan's cell phone rang and both profilers jumped a little.

"Yeah," Morgan said into it. ". . . thanks." He clicked off. "Garcia says the Bronco belongs to a Jacob Denson."

Any sense that this was a crime scene was obviously secondary, since saving a life took precedence over preserving evidence. With care and something near reverence, they lifted the deceased detective's body out of the grave and laid him carefully on the ground. Morgan did the digging as they went back to work. He had gone another half foot down when he hit something that *clunked.*

The box.

They dug even more quickly, Rossi pitching in with his hands as they uncovered the top of the box. When its lid was fairly well cleared, Morgan used the shovel to pry a corner loose and — with all the strength of both men — tore the nailed lid off.

Inside lay a figure curled in a fetal position, clad only in white boxers and a sleeveless white undershirt.

"Mr. Shuler," Rossi said. "Mr. Shuler!"

The figure did not move.

Morgan gingerly lifted the man out of the

box, handing him up to Rossi, who lay him out on the ground and checked for a pulse.

"Faint," Rossi said, "but it's there. . . ."

Morgan whipped out his cell phone.

"Hotch! We've got him, but we need the medivac *now!*"

Half an hour later, with Shuler stabilized but in serious condition, the chopper took off for the nearest hospital. The rest of the team had caught up with them. They all stood over the body of Jake Denson, waiting for the coroner's wagon that would haul the detective to the morgue.

Rossi said, "He couldn't let go of the case."

Hotchner gave him a look. "Could you have?"

"Probably not."

Prentiss asked, "How did he end up out here?"

Hotchner said, "Most likely he held back some information from us."

Reid said, "Something convinced him Dryden was the killer — must have followed him out here somehow."

Morgan gave Rossi a grim smile. "See what happens to loners, Dave?"

Rossi said, "I see what happens when a decent detective lets emotion take over. If Denson had come to us with whatever he had, other people would still be alive."

"Including," Hotchner said, "Denson."

"Take hope from the heart of man,"
the novelist Ouida wrote,
"and you make him a beast of prey."

Epilogue:
August 8
Learjet

The plane banked to the east to glide through the night, the lights of Chicago receding. They'd bid Lorenzon and Tovar quick good-byes at the airport and felt the bittersweet pang of leaving behind others who'd fought with them in the trenches. Now they were all whipped, the cabin silent, everyone asleep except Rossi and Reid. The young man played chess, spinning the small board on the table in front of him after every move.

Rossi rose and hovered over the table. Reid seemed to not notice his presence.

The older man asked, "Who's winning?"

Ignoring the question Reid said, "Gideon and I used to play after a case, sometimes."

"Ah," Rossi said.

"You play?"

"A little."

Reid waved for him to sit and Rossi accepted. The young man reset the board and said, "Black or white?"

"You choose."

"You can go first," Reid said, spinning the board so the white pieces faced Rossi.

Rossi eased a pawn forward.

Reid countered.

Rossi asked, "You're not tired?"

"Sure. I don't sleep much."

"Don't need it?"

"I can get by on just a few hours."

"Ever have nightmares?"

"It's been scientifically proven that we all dream every night."

Rossi made a move. "Don't let it eat at you," he said.

". . . I try not to."

"Because, brother, does this job have a way of eating at you."

Reid moved a piece. "Gideon told me that, too, in so many words."

"That's because it's true. That's part of why he's not here now."

The young man frowned. "Are you saying Gideon was weak?"

"No," Rossi said, moving a bishop. "Gideon is one of the strongest people I know, but he lets things get in . . . well, it's hard *not* to let things get in. Let's say, Jason can let things get too far *inside*."

"You *are* saying he was weak," Reid said.

"No," Rossi said, calmly. "I'm also not referring to him in the past tense. He's not dead, Spencer, he's just not here right now."

Reid thought about that. "It's hard to keep someone in the present tense when they've entered the past tense of your life."

"I know. But he's got his own path. For a long time, Jason took this path, and took it for a lot longer than most; and now he's on a new one."

"You've lasted just as long. Longer."

Rossi considered that. "No. I was off the path a while. But this is what I'm supposed to be doing now."

Reid seemed to be considering his next move. Then he looked up and asked, "How do you keep things from getting too far inside?"

Rossi shrugged. "The wreckage we see, victims and killers, the lives destroyed, other lives scarred . . . you can't wade as deeply into it as we do and not have some of it seep in. I'm just saying, you can't let it consume you."

The game forgotten now, Reid asked, "How do you keep that from happening?"

"Think of it this way. We're doctors — hell, you even have the word in front of your name. But our patients aren't the victims — we diagnose the disease afflicting not the innocent but the guilty. We have to understand the sickness that has turned these human beings into monsters. We can't cure their disease, but we can sure as hell quarantine them."

"Okay. I get that. But that doesn't address how to keep the horror from consuming us."

"Reid, I see you do it all the time. You keep a distance, maintain an intellectual perimeter. Doctors have to stay objective . . . and they can't take their work home with them."

They were silent for a long time, then Reid said, "Sometimes it all just seems . . . not pointless, no, I understand that we accomplish something. But . . . hopeless. There's no *end* to this disease."

Rossi locked eyes with the young man. "Daniel Dryden would have kept killing if we hadn't stopped him, right?"

"He wasn't going to stop, unless it was with a grand flourish — killing his wife, his sons, himself."

Rossi nodded curtly. "But he didn't. Mrs. Dryden and her boys, no matter how scarred this will leave them . . . and it *will* . . . are alive. They are survivors. So — how many people did we save?"

Reid shrugged facially. "It's impossible to say."

"Right. But you agree, we did save some?"

Reid nodded. "But we'll never know those people."

"Now you're getting it. *That* is my hope."

"What is?"

"That I never have to meet any of those people. For now, they're safe . . . and that's enough for me until the next time."

"I can see that," Reid said. "And we can always hope that there *isn't* a next time."

Rossi gently pushed the chessboard away and got up into the aisle. "Afraid that's more hope than I can muster, Spencer. I'm pretty damn sure there's going to be a next time. So, for right now, let's get some sleep."

Until the next nightmare comes along.

PROFILE IN THANKS

My assistant, Matthew Clemens, helped me develop the plot of *Killer Profile,* and worked up a lengthy story treatment (which included all of his considerable forensics research and on-site location scouting) from which I could work.

Profiler Steven R. Conlon, Assistant Director, Division of Criminal Investigation for the State of Iowa Department of Public Safety, generously provided a great deal of help and useful information.

Lt. Chris Kauffman (retired), Bettendorf (Iowa) Police Department, and Lt. Paul Van Steenhuyse (retired), Scott County Sheriff's Office, again provided professional insights and expertise.

Also helpful were Matthew T. Schwarz, CLPE, Identification Bureau Manager, Davenport (Iowa) Police Department, and Sheila Rogeness, IAI Certified CSI, Lead Crime Scene Tech, Davenport (Iowa) Police

Department.

The following books were consulted: *The Encyclopedia of Serial Killers* (2000), Michael Newton; *Mindhunter* (1995), John Douglas and Mark Olshaker; and *My Life Among the Serial Killers* (2004), Helen Morrison with Harold Goldberg; and *Profile of a Criminal Mind* (2003), Brian Innes. Information was also gleaned from Court TV's CrimeLibrary.com.

Special thanks go to Executive Producer Edward Allen Bernero of *Criminal Minds;* editor Kristen Weber of Penguin Group (USA) Inc.; and Maryann C. Martin of CBS Consumer Products. Without them, this novel series would not have happened.

Thanks also go to agent Dominick Abel; Matthew's wife, Pam Clemens, a knowledgeable *Criminal Minds* fan who again aided the effort; and the author's frequent accomplice, Barbara Collins.

ABOUT THE AUTHOR

Max Allan Collins was hailed in 2004 by *Publishers Weekly* as "a new breed of writer." A frequent Mystery Writers of America "Edgar" nominee, he has earned an unprecedented fourteen Private Eye Writers of America "Shamus" nominations for his historical thrillers, winning for his Nathan Heller novels, *True Detective* (1983) and *Stolen Away* (1991).

His graphic novel *Road to Perdition* is the basis of the Academy Award–winning film starring Tom Hanks, directed by Sam Mendes. His many comics credits include the syndicated strip "Dick Tracy"; his own "Ms. Tree"; "Batman"; and "CSI: Crime Scene Investigation," based on the hit TV series for which he has also written video games, jigsaw puzzles, and a *USA Today* bestselling series of novels.

An independent filmmaker in the Midwest, he wrote and directed the Lifetime movie *Mommy* (1996) and a 1997 sequel, *Mommy's Day.* He wrote *The Expert,* a 1995 HBO World Premiere, and wrote and directed the innovative made-for-DVD feature, *Real Time: Siege at Lucas Street Market* (2000). *Shades of Noir* (2004), an anthology of his short films, includes his award-winning documentary, *Mike Hammer's Mickey Spillane,* featured in a DVD collection of his films, *Black Box.* His most recent feature, *Eliot Ness: An Untouchable Life* (2006), based on his Edgar-nominated play, is now available on DVD.

His other credits include film criticism, short fiction, songwriting, trading-card sets, and movie/TV tie-in novels, including the *New York Times* bestsellers *Saving Private Ryan* and *American Gangster.*

Collins lives in Muscatine, Iowa, with his wife, writer Barbara Collins; they write the Trash 'n' Treasures mystery series together as Barbara Allan. Their son Nathan, a University of Iowa graduate, has completed a year of post-grad studies in Japan, and spent much of 2007 working for the Barack Obama presidential campaign.